Changeling Press, LLC

ChangelingPress.com

Venus/Mama & Pops Duet
A Bones MC Romance
Marteeka Karland

Venus/Mama & Pops Duet
A Bones MC Romance
Marteeka Karland

ISBN: 978-1-60521-944-8

Publisher:
Changeling Press LLC
315 N. Centre St.
Martinsburg, WV 25404
ChangelingPress.com

Printed in the U.S.A.

Editor: Jean Cooper
Cover Artist: Marteeka Karland

The individual stories in this anthology have been previously released in E-Book format.

Table of Contents

Venus (Iron Tzars MC 13)
A Bones MC Romance
Marteeka Karland

Venus: I come from world filled with violence, death, and impossible choices. I've only backed down from fight once, and that left me with pain and regret. But now, I have chance to balance scales. I'm known as most dangerous member of Salvation's Bane MC. But truth is, beneath tough exterior, I'm still a scared young woman running from monsters, trying to protect those I love. That fear ends today. Only problem? Biker named Piston. Doesn't know meaning of personal space. He's always there, watching me, protecting me, and even though I'd never admit it, his presence brings strange sense of peace. He makes me want things I can never have.

Piston: For more than a decade, I've been Venus's silent protector. In the shadows, I've watched her, stalking her every move. When she settled in Palm Beach with Salvation's Bane, I made sure to be close by. I keep an eye on her, guarding her, even if she doesn't realize it. But when an enemy from her past threatens her, I step out of the shadows. Venus is on the hunt, and the monster she's chasing has awakened the beast in me. I protect what's mine. And Venus? She's mine.

Note from Venus: Thing you do in English -- unnecessary words in sentence? Do not exist in Russian language. Want to argue with way I talk? Name time and place.

Chapter One

Venus
Shortly After Lemon's Kidnapping...

"Are you sure you know where you're going?" Piston, annoying bastard, was like gnat buzzing around my head. I could bat him away, but he kept coming back for more. So I chose to ignore him.

It was dead of night with waning crescent moon. Cloud cover made even that light minimal. Ripper and Wylde, with Salvation's Bane MC and Iron Tzars MC, had been working on finding Victor Zaitsev ever since Victor's men nabbed Lemon thinking she was me. But I'd been searching for that motherfucker long before Lemon's abduction. Twenty years longer. Since before my sister, Millie, met and attached herself to Shadow from Bones MC. Before me, Millie, and Shadow made it back from Poland with our little sister, Katya. Why? Because he is bastard who needs to die.

Victor forced me into a splinter of FSB. Which is basically same as KGB. Just different letters. And not as open about their heavy handedness. His intention was to have someone on inside to keep him out of trouble. Once in the FSB, though, they made me into something... more. One of many killers, but even more than that. I was their secret asset. The assassin to send when all others failed. Training was brutal. Work, even more so. I became very good at what they tasked me with. Too good.

"If you're not sure, I can always call in backup."

Fucking Piston. He knew very well I didn't need backup. He wanted me to engage with him and I refused. Instead of taking hint, Piston kept coming back for more. Like gnat I thought of before.

"Too many people here as it is," I muttered,

never taking my eyes off my target. We were in middle of nowhere, Western Montana. It was privately owned stretch of forest land over thousand square miles. Small cabin sat in middle of woods as out of place as hunting cabin in middle of suburbia. While able to fall off grid, whoever built it would still have comforts of good old U. S. of A. Roughing it, this place was not. More like rich man's idea of roughing it. There were even solar panels set up outside cabin along with gas tank.

Piston said nothing. Just put his field glasses to his face and surveyed area in direction I was looking. "Never met a woman as prickly as you."

"Never met man who can't take hint like you. If you can't see target, stay out of my way. Last thing I need is to have to tell Rocket I killed you because you were stupid."

That shut him up. Of course, Piston was just as likely to be smirking at me as he was to be angry with me for my outburst. I could have glanced at him to find out, but I could just make out silhouette of man in open window of cabin.

I dressed head to toe in pink. Every day. Hair, nails, clothing, even my bike was pink. It had been my pink Harley that had made Victor's men believe Lemon was me. But reason I did was because I had to wear pink contacts. I had to wear pink contacts because contacts themselves were sophisticated surveillance equipment that enhanced my vision in both bright and dark conditions. Is long explanation, but basically, I could see like spy camera. I could zoom in or pan out as long as something was in my field of vision. Came in handy in combat. And spying. Only problem was they tinted my eyes bright pink. So, all the unnecessary pink was to conceal the necessary pink.

And no. The FSB didn't have such things. I got them from man who helped me once. I helped him back until the balance tipped in my favor. Now, he is one of very few people outside of motorcycle clubs I've worked with I can call friend. No, it was more than that. All those men and women were *sem'ya*. Family. Giovanni Romano was too. Not that'd I'd ever tell him that. Man was too arrogant as it was.

"Oh, I can see it fine. I'm just hopin' and prayin' to the sweet baby Jesus in the manger you don't honestly believe it's gonna be this easy to catch this fucker."

I didn't acknowledge Piston, but I had same concern he did. I could see Victor in that house. Just by small window in front. This situation was most definitely a set up. From this angle I couldn't see anything obvious, so I'd have to prepare for the *un*obvious.

"Stay out of my way, Piston." I put as much command and venom in my voice as I could, hoping stubborn bastard would understand I meant business. "No one asked you to come along. I've been doing this by myself for very long time."

"Surprised you lasted a week without a keeper." I could hear amusement in his voice and wanted to scratch his eyeballs out. Something else about me to stick out. My fingernails were filed into nearly razor-sharp two-inch-long daggers. Pink, of course. I used them like weapons they were. Just as I was trained.

Which brought me back to Victor. He wasn't nearly as smart as he thought he was. I gave myself about a thirty percent chance of killing him tonight, but I also thought it very likely I'd shake his confidence enough for him to rush to put distance between me and him. Victor would make mistake, and Wylde or

Ripper would have him. Assuming I was right and he knew I was after him. If he did, he'd be ready to get away. Of course, if Piston hadn't been on my ass, I'd have put my chances at fifty-fifty.

"Cost me this kill and you won't last another hour, let alone week."

Without acknowledging him further, I moved from my scouting position and toward cabin. I didn't have to look at him to hear his amused chuckle. I decided then that, no matter what, once I finished here, I was going to kill Piston.

The darkness was full of night noises. Bugs, frogs, and occasional cry of owl or small animal punctuated darkness. That was good because it meant everyone here was in house and not disturbing nature. It didn't miss my notice that, even though Piston often annoyed me, he'd managed to not announce his presence to wildlife around us. I didn't want to admire him for that, but it had been my experience that not many warriors could lie in wait long periods without disturbing creatures around him. Piston could. Even when he interacted with me, he managed to keep his energy low or something. It was almost like he was part of nature itself and I was the intruder.

Once closer to cabin, I circled around back. There wasn't window or back door, but was easier to slide underneath. Building was set on slope, so one side was about three feet above the ground, held by posts at corners.

I rolled under crawlspace. As I suspected, even though this place was built with comfort in mind, there was still rustic, authentic feel about the place. As such, wood board floor had gaps and made it easier to see who was inside and where they were.

Victor!

He *was* here. Figure in window was, indeed, Victor. So many lives he'd ruined. He'd terrorized Katya. Millie, too. I certainly hadn't been his only victim. Even now, he managed to control my life. He'd sent his men to get me. They took my young friend, Lemon, instead. It made me want to put distance between me, Salvation's Bane, and Grim Road. Which just pissed me off even more. Because, while I loved all old ladies of every club I'd spent time in, Lemon was one woman who truly got me. Even more than my own sister. I'd never told her about my life before and she'd never asked, but Lemon just *knew*. She was more intuitive than any woman her age had right to be and it made me want to make sure she was always this confident. I felt almost… motherly toward younger woman. It brought out in me Russian mother bear.

I rolled out from under cabin and to my feet. Darting around building, I took step forward, getting ready to kick in door when solid body shoved me to the side and I fell. Piston rolled to his feet, putting himself between me and threat I hadn't seen.

The fight was immediate and intense. Both men threw series of complicated punches and kicks. Like style of fighting Millie used. There were no rules to this fight other than to stay alive.

For some reason, I hesitated. I glanced at Piston who was holding his own. Though the two men seemed to be equal in skill, Piston was by far stronger physically. He was also vicious like I'd never realized. That brief moment cost me.

Victor saw me and drew his weapon. I sprinted few feet separating us and kicked out just before gun went off. I hit his hand so his aim went to the left, the gun flying across the yard. There was muffled grunt and I froze split second before whipping around to see if he'd hit Piston. Moment I did, Victor shoved past me, pushing me hard enough to make me stumble forward two steps. And he was gone.

Rage washed over me, through me. He'd been *right here*! Piston dropped body of man he'd fought and stalked toward me. I was so angry I wanted to lash out, to kill everyone in my way. It was past time Victor died and I'd been so fucking close!

But thing that overpowered all my anger, was fear. Fear knowing Victor had hit Piston. That Piston could have been seriously hurt or dead. Fucking man had gotten under my skin but good. So much so that thought of him in danger overrode all the instincts I had telling me to hunt and kill Victor. I'd literally spent lifetime hunting this guy down. Since I was barely out of my teens when he'd sold me to FSB in exchange for whatever favors he'd wanted. Even when I'd lived in his house with my mother and sisters, I'd known I'd have to kill him some day. This had been closest I'd been to him in at least decade. Who knew when I'd ever have this chance again? Fear of waiting another ten years for the opportunity to kill Victor fed my anger, but gave the emotion different target.

"Are you hit?" I snapped out the question.

Piston brought his hand to his shoulder and it came back sticky with blood. He shrugged. "Just a scratch. He grazed me but blew the head off the other guy."

I raised my gun and aimed at Piston's face, cocking weapon. "You cost me important kill! Give me one good reason why I shouldn't blow your fucking head off right now!" Piston merely raised an eyebrow but said nothing. I was vibrating with rage. Never in my life had I been in this kind of situation and knew I wasn't going to pull the trigger. I never pulled my gun unless I intended to use it, but I knew as sure as I knew my own name I could never kill Piston.

With what I hoped was vicious snarl, I holstered my weapon. Just because I couldn't kill him didn't mean I couldn't kick him in the balls. Piston must have sensed what I was going to do because he took step back, angling his hips away from my dominant leg. Did my heart good.

"Fucking stubborn man!" I was over Piston following me, sticking his nose in my business. "I fucking had him!"

"You were gonna get yourself killed." Fucking man sounded all reasonable and shit when he was missing entire picture. He'd ripped off strip of cloth from hem of his T-shirt and wrapped it around wound on his shoulder. Wasn't great, but stemmed flow of blood.

"I wasn't in danger, *ublyudok*! Do you not understand killing is what I do?"

"Completely." Did nothing faze the man? He stood squarely in front of me like fucking oak tree. Completely immovable. "Still don't mean I'm gonna stand by while someone comes up on your six with a fuckin' knife in hand ready to stab you in the kidney." Piston didn't raise his voice above low rumble. His tone of voice is one of many reasons Piston was so dangerous. One could never tell by sound of his voice or his expression exactly how upset he was.

"I knew he was there, *sukin syn*!" Sort of. But I wasn't letting up. "Him and another man in bushes! Same man who helped Victor escape!" I wanted to pull my hair out in frustration. I'd killed men for less, yet I hesitated with Piston? What was wrong with me? "I've been hunting Victor Zaitsev for half my life. I finally had him in my sights and you drew his attention. Do you even know how dangerous this man is? *Yebat!*"

"We can contain any damage he tries to do, Venus. Killing him is not worth you dying with him." How could man be so relaxed? Was like he could care less of work involved in getting this close to Victor.

"Do you not know who Zaitsev is? He has Salvation's Bane in his sights. My home! How long before he realizes his men had Lemon, your vice president, when they thought they'd captured me?"

"Not possible." Piston shrugged and shook his head. "We killed everyone involved in Lemon's kidnapping."

"Are you sure they didn't get *any* information out? Really fucking sure? Because if there was even picture of her to get through to Zaitsev, he will know about Grim Road and Iron Tzars and significance of both clubs." It was like man was daft or something.

He gave me an impatient look. "Of course, I know that. I also happen to believe there is safety in numbers. All three clubs are on alert after Lemon got kidnapped. Wylde got close to Zaitsev this time. He can do it again."

"Ugh!" I picked up brick laying on the porch and threw it at *zasranets*. "Go away! If I see you again, I kill you."

The fucking man just smirked at me. "You can try, baby girl."

I lunged for him. Which must have been exactly what he'd been going for because the second I was within striking distance, Piston grabbed one wrist and spun me around. He embraced me from behind, pinning my arms at my sides while his body surrounded mine. It was easy enough hold for me to get out of, but I couldn't seem to muster enough strength.

Anytime I'd found myself in this position with Piston, his wild, woodsy scent seemed to mesmerize me. All I wanted to do was to fall into him. Let him hold me in protective cocoon. Because with those big, brawny arms of his around me, I felt safer than I had in my entire life. It was like I'd finally found my true home. Even more so than with my sister, Millie or, more recently, Lemon. This man called to something primitive inside me that wanted his dominance. Just not at expense of my own.

I allowed contact far longer than I should have before stomping on his foot with my heeled boot. He grunted but didn't let go of me. Was still satisfying. Sort of.

"Not nice, Venus," Piston growled beside my ear. "I'll be punishin' you for that little stunt."

I gave him snort of derision. "You can try, *baby boy.*" I made sure to put as much of sneer into my voice as I could. I was highly skilled assassin. Sure, Piston was one hell of warrior, but he was no match for me. In few months he'd been glued to my side, I'd found he had many tells in battle. Killing him would be easy as taking candy from baby. And I would kill him. Soon. Any day now…

Chapter Two

Piston

Venus first turned up on my radar over a decade ago when she was in the FSB in Russia. The agency I worked for was very interested in her for some reason. I was never given the details, but I got the feeling they were interested in luring her away from Russia. Likely because they were afraid of her. I played my cards carefully regarding Venus. I told them the strict truth, but I left out a lot.

Like how I'd never seen her equal in a hunter. Or that that real shade of her hair was a very pale blonde. Or how young she looked when she let her guard down, which wasn't often. Or how beautiful she was. I kept that to myself because I didn't trust the CIA any further than I could piss. If they were interested in this woman, she was someone I needed to protect.

For years I kept to the shadows. When she joined Salvation's Bane MC, I found a home with Grim Road MC. They were completely off the radar and close enough for me to keep an eye on Venus.

I had to smile. If she knew the extent to which I've been on her six and for how long, she'd gut me like a fish.

But that's the thing about being in deep cover. You learn how to keep secrets, even from yourself. And Venus? She was one secret I'd vowed never to spill. Much to the dismay of my handlers. They knew there was more to her than I reported.

Tonight, as I held her pinned against me, feeling the rise and fall of her chest, the stakes felt higher than ever. Her anger and her fire were intoxicating, making every moment with her a volatile mix of danger and desire.

"Listen," I whispered into her ear, my voice low and steady against the chill night air. "I'm not your enemy, Venus. I think you know that."

"I know you are pompous ass." She hissed at me over her shoulder, but I wasn't fooled. If this woman wanted to be free, she'd be free. And I'd be lying in pool of my own blood.

Interesting.

"Glad to see my charm didn't go unnoticed."

She struggled in my hold a bit longer, then relaxed with a huff, her body still tense but no longer fighting. "You're infuriating, you know that, Piston?"

"That's part of my charm too," I replied, the corner of my mouth lifting slightly. I loosened my grip just enough to let her know she could break free if she wanted. It was a test as much as it was a truce.

Venus turned within my arms to face me, her gaze fierce and calculating. She wasn't afraid of me, she knew she could take me, but she wasn't ready to kill me yet. Made me wonder why. One thing I'd learned about Venus over the years was she never did anything without at least a frame up of a plan.

With slow deliberate movements, she backed up one step. Then another.

"Is this a truce then?" I kept my hands to my sides but was ready to defend myself if necessary.

"I'm not sure." She gave me a curious look, her gaze moving boldly over me. Then her brow furrowed. "I'm *really* not sure."

"Then let's call it a truce. We can always decide later to resume fighting."

Venus's lips twisted into a skeptical smile, but she nodded slowly. "Fine, truce for now. But don't think this means I trust you, Piston. We're not buddies."

"Wouldn't dream of it," I replied, my voice low and even. Her distrust was like a sharp blade held at my neck, yet there was something exhilarating about not knowing when she might decide to slash. It was all I could do to keep from smiling. My cock didn't care if she saw him or not and shot hard so fast I nearly winced. Thankfully, if she noticed, she didn't mention it.

We stood in silence for a moment, the tension between us palpable. The night air was warm against my skin, and somewhere nearby an owl hooted, a solitary sound that seemed to emphasize the isolation of our current circumstances.

Venus finally broke the silence. "So, what now, Piston? We just stand here in dark staring at each other until one of us breaks?" There was a hint of amusement in her voice, a playful challenge I hadn't heard before.

I shrugged nonchalantly. "We could do that, or we could put this temporary truce to better use."

"What do you propose?" Her voice was cautious yet intrigued, her eyes scanning my face for any hint of deceit.

"We work together," I said simply. "You have your skills and resources, I have mine. Together, we can find and kill the fuck outta Zaitsev."

"Why do you want to kill him?" She was genuinely curious, but I knew she was filing away all this information for inspection later. She'd remember everything about our conversation, my expressions, the inflection of my voice, and dissect it for every ounce of information. Just like she'd been trained to do. Same as me.

"Isn't it enough that his goons kidnapped my vice president?"

She nodded slowly. "Sure. But I don't think that's whole story with you."

Smart woman. "I'll tell you my secrets if you tell me yours."

"Right." She picked up the gun Zaitsev had shot me with, checking the weapon before tucking it against her back in the waistband of her pants. "I'm going back to Tzars. Lemon wanted me to check on Dani."

I raised an eyebrow. "Lemon. Wanted you to check on her sister." I spoke slowly, wanting to make sure I'd heard her right, because it sounded suspiciously like Venus, the badass assassin for the FSB, was... running. From me.

Two things were foremost in my mind. First, it didn't sit well that she wanted away from me. Granted, she didn't know me as well as I knew her, but I was becoming more and more protective of Venus. I wanted her close where she couldn't get into more trouble than she could get herself out of. Though I'd watched her from afar for years (stalker much?), I liked having her close. I blamed my vice president. Had it not been for Lemon getting kidnapped, I might never have gotten this close to Venus for this long. I damned sure wouldn't have gone with her to kill the man she'd been trying to take down for a decade.

The second thing, though...

Yeah. Having my arms around Venus -- even to keep her from eviscerating me with her dagger-like nails -- awoke something inside me I had thought was way the fuck dead. I was forty-seven years old, for crying out loud. While I had an active sex drive, I hadn't been this hard for this long in years. Hadn't had a need for it. If I had an itch, I scratched it with a club whore. No fuss. No muss. And no one expecting to be all up in my space.

Part of what I did at Grim Road was take care of… issues. Permanently. I'd love to say it was why I'd come with Venus on this errand, but I'd be lying. I'd claimed her in my mind the moment I'd seen her. Couldn't keep my mouth shut and made it official so I could get her into Grim Road where she could come and go as she pleased. Then I'd followed her back to Iron Tzars… where she'd promptly run back to Grim Road in the guise of making sure Lemon was settling in well. As if Lemon couldn't protect herself.

What I couldn't figure out was why she didn't just kill me. I'd been expecting it, yet she hadn't made a move on me until tonight when she'd pulled that gun in my face. Sure, I'd noticed the occasional glance at my crotch. On more than one occasion, I'd caught her staring at me with those freaky eyes of hers. I was quite possibly the only other person in the world, other than Giovanni Romano of Argent Tech and herself, who knew what her vision was capable of with those contacts. And I'd bet my balls she'd be furious if she knew I knew.

I followed her to where we'd left our bikes. She climbed on hers, tossing her hair over her shoulder before reaching down to turn the key. I had to admire her. She rode that pink monstrosity like a boss. I was surprised she hadn't already taken off, but she kept fiddling with her bike.

"Everything good?"

"No. Everything is not good." Her response was muttered, and she didn't start her bike.

"All right." I tossed a leg over my own bike in a slow, deliberate movement. "What can I do to help?"

She didn't look at me and for long moments I thought she wasn't going to answer me. Then she started her bike, revving it a couple times before putting it in gear. Then she met my gaze with that eerie pink stare. "I think it best you go back to Grim Road."

"I go where you go, Venus. Pretty sure I made that clear."

Then, her control snapped. I knew she had a fiery temper under there. I'd met her sister Millie once and she'd said as much, but I hadn't seen it. Until now.

"Why won't you just go away?" she yelled at me. The outburst of emotion was so unlike Venus, it gave me pause. I knew I was pushing her, but maybe it was time I backed off. "Go away and leave me alone!" Were her eyes glistening? Tears? Surely not. I was seeing things. Or the fumes from the bikes were irritating her eyes.

"Venus, talk to me." I yelled to be heard over her bike, but she just revved the engine a couple of times and took off like a bat outta hell. "Fuck."

With a sigh I took off after her. Like hell I was going back to Grim Road. With that pink Harley of hers and the way she liked to push the speed limit, shew was sure to hit a speed trap. There was no way she'd make it through North Carolina, where we'd tracked Victor Zaitsev. It wasn't like she was heading out of the woodlands. She took off in the direction I thought Zaitsev had run with whoever she'd suspected helped him out. If they were on foot, we'd catch them, but I didn't think they were. I'd heard a small engine start earlier when Venus had left her prey to check on me.

Speaking of which, my arm was starting to burn. Blood dripped steadily from my deltoid down to my elbow. I did my best to ignore it, needing to keep focused on Venus. The woman wanted to shake me too badly for me to let her go. Besides, I thought she protested too much.

I followed her through the woods. It wasn't long before she picked up the trail we'd been looking for. Unfortunately, there was no way to take our heavy bikes through the trail Zaitsev and his companion had taken.

"*Blyt!*" Venus had stopped her bike and turned it off. She sat there, staring longingly into the woods.

"We'll get him, Venus."

"I should already have him! Why are you even here? Why have you latched on to me like baby monkey?" There was a wild look in her eyes. This... didn't compute. I knew this was a critical moment. I just wasn't sure why.

I took my time fiddling with my bike, trying to figure out how best to form the answer to that question. "You interest me."

"Interest you?" She gave me an incredulous look. Which was odd in itself. Venus rarely gave anything away. But with me, she was becoming less and less guarded. "What does that even mean? 'Interest you'," she scoffed.

"You're a unique woman, Venus. A unique *person.*" It was true in the strictest sense of the word, but it was a tepid description of my reasons for sticking close to her. "I like being around you." Yeah. Lame. She wasn't ready to push my claim on her yet, at least not in a personal sense. Everyone in Grim Road knew she was mine. That information had trickled out to her own club. Iron Tzars was very aware I'd put a claim on Venus as well. Because Sting, the president of Iron Tzars MC, had been my official military contact on my last mission for the CIA.

"You don't claim woman you simply find interesting, Piston." She had me there.

"What do you want me to say, Venus? That I

want you?" I met her gaze without flinching, even when she looked like she was ready to kill me to death. "I do. More than I've ever wanted any woman in my life."

She snorted out a scoffing breath but didn't say anything more. She started her bike and backtracked out of the woods to the road. Then the highway. Finally, she made her way to the interstate. I followed, letting her take the lead, but putting myself on the inside of the lane she drove in with Venus slightly in front of me. I was sure I was in her periphery, but not so close I irritated her.

We drove for hours, only stopping for gas when we were running on fumes. My shoulder burned and ached where the bullet had kissed my arm, but I wasn't about to let Venus see that as a weakness. So, I simply ignored it. I'd clean and dress it properly later.

True to her word, Venus headed straight to Iron Tzars. She probably thought Sting would put me out on my ear, assuming he didn't just shoot me and be done with it. Unfortunately for her, Sting and I had been tight after the mission where we'd met. We'd only worked together that one time, but the man had earned my respect. I thought I had earned his too. I supposed we were getting ready to find out. Another eight hours of hard riding would tell the tale.

Assuming Venus didn't say to hell with it and eviscerate me by the side of the interstate. I had to grin. That scenario was more likely than me making it to Evansville on her six. Then again, I thought she might be growing to at least tolerate me. After all, I was still breathing. Right?

Chapter Three
Venus

"What do you mean you're not kicking him out?" Even though I tried to keep my voice neutral, I knew I sounded on edge of losing my mind. I never thought Piston would make it past front gate at Iron Tzars compound. Not only had he followed me straight to main clubhouse, but Sting had welcomed him like long lost relative. Male bonding moment of huge slaps on back made me want to puke. I tried to keep my mask of indifference. I really did.

"Piston's a good guy, Venus. He's always gonna be welcomed in my club." Sting still had grin on his face. Either he was oblivious to tension between me and Piston or he didn't care. He'd called Eagle, medic in Iron Tzars, and other man had cleaned and dressed Piston's wound. Eagle said Piston had let it go too long to put in stitches, but one more scar wasn't going to matter much. Again, they'd slapped each other on back and this time I had to stifle urge to gag.

Breath in. Breath out. Don't go on killing spree.

"Piston!" Older teenager called out just as younger girl ran at full speed straight to Piston and jumped, throwing herself at him and wrapping her arms and legs around him.

Piston chuckled. "Hey there, little Clover Bee. How's my girl?"

Clover didn't speak, but peppered Piston's face with kisses. She had huge smile on her face and obviously loved Piston. She had been non-verbal since being put into group home for wards of state. I wanted to stay angry, but seeing how much Clover was at ease with the big, gruff biker softened something inside me I'd have rather stayed hard.

"She ran all the way from the family side." Daisy, the older girl with Clover smiled affectionately at the little girl in Piston's arms.

"Because she knows she's my favorite." Piston gave Clover raspberry kiss to her neck. The little girl sucked in a surprised gasp, but her lips were firmly shut even though she was smiling. With one last kiss to Piston's cheek, Clover scrambled down and ran back the way she'd come. Daisy waved and chased after the little girl.

"She's still not talking." Piston sounded like he knew he was stating obvious and didn't phrase it as a question, but expected Sting to answer.

"No. She doesn't say anything. This was the first time she's gone anywhere without someone holding her hand since the last time you visited."

"I'm glad I can provide a distraction for her." It struck me then that I hadn't seen Piston smile like he was now. There was affection as he continued to look after the retreating child.

Another pang hit my chest. I'd been having those lately which wasn't something I was used to having to deal with. Only emotion I ever showed was anger or displeasure. And only to get reaction I wanted from someone.

"Yet another reason Victor will die."

Sting raised an eyebrow. "You think he's responsible for what happened to the girls? El Diablo seemed to think they got everyone involved."

"He did. In that cell. El Diablo cleaned his city but did not shut everything down. Was just one cell Victor controls."

"Is it like El Diablo to leave even one leg of a trafficking ring open?" Sting looked appropriately incredulous, but I knew the truth.

"El Diablo took out what he could reasonably enforce." Piston glanced over at me as he spoke. Checking with me? Why would he do that? "His city, and everyone knows he considers Palm Beach his as well. He knows shutting it all down is impossible, but he can make it more difficult for anyone to do business in his territory."

I gave Piston side-eye. I wasn't in mood to agree with him, but I could find no fault with his logic. Fact was, I was thinking same thing. "I agree. While El Diablo protects his territory fiercely, he knows how much control he can reasonably expect."

"Why was Victor after you, Venus?" Sting gave me quizzical look, and I could tell the answer mattered to him.

"If you're worried about me bringing trouble to your club, Sting, don't. I would never bring danger to your door and risk children and your women."

Sting gave me an impatient look. "Venus, the club can protect our own. If you need us, you get word to us or just get your ass here as fast as you can."

"I promise you, I am more capable of taking care of myself than you are of protecting everyone in compound."

"Venus." Sting scowled at me, looking from me to Piston and back. Younger man raised an eyebrow at Piston. They seemed to be communicating silently, and it grated on my nerves. I also knew I was being bitch.

"I don't know why I'm included in this conversation. Two of you seem to have everything figured out anyway."

Sting gave Piston a grin. "Bit prickly, ain't she?"

"Only when around this ape." I bared my teeth at Piston. "He brings out *suka* in me."

"How about a visit with Iris and the other

women?"

Again, I felt that pang in my chest. Spending time with the old ladies of Iron Tzars, even though all of them were at least a decade younger than me, was one of my favorite things to do. I considered all old ladies of Salvation's Bane to be my family and the women of Black Reign were just as close. Women of Bones were all like sisters, especially since my own sister, Millie, was there. But women of Iron Tzars were... more. There was something about all of them that soothed me. I had found home in Grim Road, too, but Grim was Piston's home. And I wasn't sure I wanted to be in such close proximity to him.

"Is my usual room in clubhouse open?"

"It is. Danica will want word from Lemon. They Facetime every day, but I think she would feel better to hear how Lemon's doing from someone other than Lemon. Apple misses her sister, too."

I couldn't help but smile. Lemon was hell on wheels, but she was still teenager. It was easy to forget. "Tell her I'll meet her for dinner in common room. I have many stories to tell to lift her spirits."

"Don't we all." I glanced over to find Piston grinning while he toed gravel at his foot. Obviously, there was some memory he was reliving that amused him. Out of nowhere, surge of something that felt suspiciously like jealousy slammed into me. It was on the tip of my tongue to remind big baboon Lemon was taken, but I managed to keep retort to myself.

"Right." Sting had wary look on his face as he glanced from me to Piston and back. "Well, you both know where to go. Make yourselves at home."

I didn't wait around, instead securing my bike before slinging my backpack -- pink, of course -- over my shoulder and heading inside. I needed hour of peace and quiet. To decompress and get my thoughts under control.

Piston was thorn in my side. I hated him. I was also more attracted to him than any person I'd ever met. Man or woman. There were reasons I never had relationships. First and foremost was the fact that, being in relationship meant you had to care about someone. Caring about someone meant you had to protect them. Protecting them meant you put yourself between them and danger. I'd found out hard way, when I'd left for my training in FSB, best way to protect people you cared about was to stay away. Or not care in first place. Through years since leaving Russia, this was rule I'd broken. Not intentionally, but by becoming part of Salvation's Bane, I'd put club directly in path of my enemies. Something I hadn't seriously considered until Victor had abducted Lemon. So, Piston needed to get lost. Which meant I needed to push him away harder.

Room I used at Tzars was barren of furnishings save single-size bed, small table doubling as desk, and storage cabinet. I rarely needed it, but Sting's woman, Iris, had insisted I have more than simple bed. I was surprised she hadn't insisted on more furniture, but she'd respected my boundaries and refrained.

There was knock at my door. I had to grin, wondering if Daisy and Clover had let the other kids know I was here. They liked pink. Especially my eyes. I opened the door, not to the gaggle of kids I expected, but to big baboon I'd been trying to get away from.

I scowled. "I'm busy." I tried to shut door, but Piston stuck his heavily booted foot in way preventing satisfying slam I wanted.

"Calm down, Shortcake. You're not so busy we can't have a little chat." The look on his face was positively carnivorous.

"Shortcake?" I frowned up at him.

Smile split his face, but it wasn't happy look. Was more like he was mocking me, or maybe there was hint of challenge there too. "Yeah. Shortcake. Because you're sweet when you wanna be." His grin got wider. "And you remind me of that little doll back in the eighties. My little sister had several of them." Then he chuckled. "Strawberry Shortcake and Lemon Meringue. Gonna have me some fun when we get back to Grim Road."

It took me moment for what he'd said to register. "Strawberry Shortcake. And... Lemon Meringue?"

"Yeah. Little dolls. One dresses in pink with strawberries over her dress. The other in yellow. One smells like strawberries, the other..." He let obvious linger, not finishing his sentence.

"Are you... calling me... some kind of... *doll*?" That couldn't be right. "Because if you are, you know you die now. Right?"

The very last thing I expected was for Piston to bark out genuine laugh. This kind of displeasure usually had my prey quaking in fear. But not this man. Of course, not this man. Because, for some reason, he *saw* me, yet still wanted to be near me.

I rolled my eyes, trying to brush off his amusement as well as unwelcome warmth flooding me. "What do you want, Piston?"

He leaned in, his bulk feeling like wall even with door somewhat between us. "Let me in. We need to talk." His words were serious, but he still had amused expression on his face I didn't like. Not since Victor had sent me off to start my training had anyone been amused by me. When I stared at someone like I was looking at Piston now, only feelings they had were fear. Terror even. Not Piston. He looked like he knew exactly what he was in for and relished the challenge.

With exasperated sigh, I stepped back to let him in. Partly because I knew he wouldn't leave until he'd said his piece, and partly because I was secretly relieved to delay the solitude that would force me to confront my conflicted feelings about him. And the pressing need to find Victor again.

Room felt smaller with Piston inside. His presence was too large, too intense. He looked around, probably noting Spartan furnishings with raised eyebrow, but said nothing about it. Instead, he crossed his arms and leaned one shoulder against closed door casually. When he said nothing, only stared at me, I had to stifle urge to squirm under his gaze.

"Well?" I frowned, trying to read him. Might as well have tried to decipher hieroglyphics for all good it did me. There was amusement on his face but also that hungry look in his eyes. How long had it been since man had looked at me in sexual way? Had anyone ever? I was adept at reading people. Came with territory. Intent was everything in my world. If I didn't read someone's underlying intent, it could get me killed. With Piston, all I saw was hard lust. Like he wanted nothing more than to strip me bare and lick my body from head to toe.

"Well, indeed," he muttered, wiping his hand over his mouth.

"*Byad*!" I took in deep breath, looking to heavens for patience. If I believed in God, I'd definitely pray for the stuff. In abundance. Or just the will to actually kill big fucker. "I don't need this." I had to turn away from him, which normally I'd never do. If I hadn't, he'd have seen how much that fucking look affected me. Because it had. More than any sexual encounter in my life, this man affected me. With only a look.

I chanced glance in his direction in time to see him move from door and cross scant distance between us. He took my arm and turned me back to face him. His grip was firm but not harsh. Once I faced him, he did the same with my other shoulder. My leather vest was sleeveless so his warm, calloused hands on my bare skin was unexpected thrill. There was no way to stop soft gasp from escaping my lips.

For long moments we stood like that. Piston stared down into my upturned face. His jaw worked, bunching at the sides like he was angry. At me? Not that I cared. Or maybe, he was just as turned-on as I was getting and fighting it just as hard as I was.

The next thing I realized, my hands were on his chest, my fingers curling against his T-shirt-covered skin. Muscles played, giving me delicious hint at what lay under the thin cotton, and I wanted to dig in and hold him to me. My nails, which I kept razor-sharp, had to be poking against his skin. Wouldn't surprise me if I'd left little pricks of blood in my wake.

"Fuck," he muttered. Then he was kissing me.

I stiffened, unsure if I wanted intimate contact or not. I should push him away. Should drive my nails into his belly and eviscerate him. As soon as I got my fill of his delicious kiss…

His lips, warm and insistent, melted resolve I had thought fortified by steel and shadow. I kissed him back with ferocity that surprised even me, my hands moving from his chest up to tangle in his hair. If I scratched him accidentally, he didn't seem to notice. Every fiber of my being screamed that this was wrong, yet it felt terrifyingly right.

Piston's hands moved with possessive urgency, tracing line of my spine before pulling me closer. His touch sparked wildfire threatening to consume everything I'd built around myself. My defenses, my missions, my very identity negated relationships. Yet hadn't I just been thinking how I'd managed to build relationships with people over years?

Yes. I should kill him. And I would. Just as soon as this unbearable tension eased. Just as soon as I figured out how to breathe again without his scent filling my lungs.

And that kiss, it wasn't gentle or tentative. It was all-encompassing, fervent, as if he was trying to meld our souls into one. His lips moved against mine with desperate intensity that left no room for doubt. This wasn't just lust. It was something fiercer, something that didn't care about deadly secrets we both carried or the scars we'd hidden under our clothes and bravado. And I knew Piston had as many secrets as I did.

As his tongue sought entrance, my initial resistance melted like ice on hot blade. Against such incomprehensible lust, I had no defense. I should have. My training had been intense in not only combat and killing, but seduction as well as how to control myself and not get caught up in moment. But I now knew something I doubt anyone of those sadistic bastards who trained me knew. There was no way to combat feelings this intense, because they couldn't be inspired by just anyone. And, oh, how they'd tried...

What I was experiencing currently, though, seemed to shove past back where it belonged, weaving through layers of my guarded self, unraveling years of solitude and survival instincts in moments both fleeting and eternal. Piston moved a hand to nape of my neck. It anchored me to present, to him. His fingers threaded through my hair, pulling slightly, sending shivers down my spine that were both pleasure and dire warning.

Suddenly he pulled back, his breath ragged, his eyes searching mine in dim light. There was vulnerability there I hadn't expected to see -- mirror to my own raw exposure. We were warriors, killers, not meant to find anything but death in our futures. Right? That mantra had been drilled into me from beginning of my training.

His gray eyes, dark and stormy, seared into mine with intensity that both frightened and excited me. "You should've killed me when you had the chance," Piston whispered, his voice rough with emotion.

The truth of his words stung like slap. I should have. Yet, here I was, drowning in depths of his gaze instead of plotting my next move. "Maybe I still will," I managed to say, though threat lacked conviction now tangled up in heat between us.

Piston's half-grin was edged with dangerous knowledge. "Maybe you will," he conceded, the low rumble of his voice challenge and promise rolled into one. The edge in his voice could have cut glass, and it ignited something defiant within me. "But not tonight."

Charged silence stretched between us, thick with words unspoken and moves unplayed. All those lethal skills we both had, our secrets and lies, none of it seemed to matter in that moment. I wanted to take this where we both obviously wanted, but, for the first time in my life, was utterly terrified. I'd rather be in plane crash again than open myself up to the pleasure I might find in this man's arms.

His hands traveled back down my back with ghostly touch I felt through my leather vest -- the vest that proclaimed me part of Salvation's Bane MC -- felt like both caress and dare. I knew in that instant we were trapped in web of our own making, each push driving us deeper into chaos.

He leaned in again, his lips brushing mine with gentleness that belied his strength and the earlier aggressive kiss. This time I didn't stiffen. I opened my mouth and thrust my tongue between his lips at same time he licked at mine.

This dual exploration became another kind of battle, not one of strength or skill, but of vulnerability and surrender. As his taste mingled with mine, a mix of danger, desperation, and underlying hint of something like hope blossomed in my chest. I could feel layers of calculated defenses crumble within me. I had time to wonder if this was all some kind of cruel test, but simply couldn't hold on to anything other than man with his arms around me and his tongue lapping at mine.

Our kiss intensified, no longer just a clash of lips and tongues but something more… connected? His mouth on mine felt just as desperate as I did. He was right. I should have killed him, but I knew I couldn't. Knew I *wouldn't*. That was problem. Because, for the first time since I was teenager, I had someone I knew I couldn't kill. Sure, men and women in Bones, Salvation's Bane, Grim Road, Iron Tzars, and even Black Reign were people I respected and maybe even cared for, but if I had to, I could kill every single one of them. I'd hurt afterward, but I could do it. Maybe. But Piston? Yeah. I wasn't sure I could kill him, and had no idea why.

I tried to pull myself back, to reassess this whole situation. Except my stupid mouth wouldn't be parted from the pleasure of his. My pulse hammered against his touch as if trying to beat out rhythm for new kind of existence, one where fear and pain weren't foundation or even factor.

Finally, I managed to push against his chest and duck my head. I had no doubt there would be smirking grin on his face if I looked up and wasn't sure I was prepared to deal with any emotions resulting from that embarrassment. Heavy groan seemed to be ripped from his chest as he pulled me closer, resting his chin on my head.

"Shortcake." There was wealth of need and affection in that single word. It also was like needle scratch back to reality.

"Don't call me that," I muttered, familiar defensiveness rebuilding its walls around my heart. Shadows deepening in the fading light seemed to grow denser, as if they too sensed the gravity of what was unfolding.

Piston's chuckle was low and somewhat pained. "Why not?" he asked, his voice teasing yet edged with something like sincerity. "It suits you."

"I refuse to believe I resemble smelly doll in any way." My chin went up and I gave him full force glare that should have shriveled his dick on spot. Instead, I felt it pulse between us. Yeah. I'd missed that before. How, I have no idea because it seemed Piston was big. All over.

Chapter Four

Piston

A couple of things went through my mind as I looked down into the upturned face of a woman who could be the deadliest female in the world. First was the fact that she hadn't already cut off my dick for kissing her. Some might scoff, but, personally, I called it progress. Second, she actually did look like an angry little Strawberry Shortcake.

Her expression was as disgruntled as it got, but I absolutely could not stop my lips from twitching. When that expression abruptly changed to something altogether lethal, my cock got impossibly harder. Instead of grabbing her hands to keep her from stabbing me with those dagger-like nails of hers, or shoving away from her, or any number of safe, sane, and cunningly clever things, I simply gripped her hips and pulled her more firmly against me. Let her feel exactly what she did to me. If she still wanted to disembowel me, I'd take it like a man.

"If that name repeated outside this room, I'll know where it came from."

"It's only for the two of us." I grinned down at her. "Shortcake." To my surprise, Venus gave me an annoyed look, but her lips turned up just the same. It was only a half smile, but it melted my heart. I'd known she was a remarkable woman all those years ago, but never truly appreciated her worth until I got close to her. "You're still irritated, but I'll take it."

"More than irritated." She chuckled, but the initial mirth was wearing off and her anger was poking through the surface. She muttered, "Cannot afford this."

"Can't afford what?"

"Nothing." She stepped away from me slowly, as if waiting for me to pounce on her. "You should leave. I'm tired."

I raised an eyebrow but gave her a slow nod. Then I narrowed my gaze on hers. "If you try to leave without me, I'll know it."

"No doubt you have spies all over compound."

I didn't even bother to deny it. "Yep. Keep that in mind when you're sneakin' out."

"You might think you know me, Piston. You do not."

"Oh, I know more about you than you might think. You and I aren't so different."

"El Diablo said much the same thing," she muttered. "Look. If you want to scratch itch, I suggest you find club whore. I've got too much on plate as is to fuck with you, Piston."

"If you're tryin' to piss me off so I'll leave, you're goin' about it the wrong way." I gave her a steady look, doing my best to keep a rein on my temper. She was trying to get to me. Even though it was working, I didn't want her to realize it. She'd push until something snapped.

Venus sighed, running a hand through her hair, clearly frustrated yet battling some inner turmoil that kept her rooted in place instead of throwing me out. The shadows played across her face, highlighting the sharp contours.

"Too damn stubborn for your own good."

She turned away, her shoulders rigid. The taut line of her back spoke of battles fought and scars hidden beneath layers of both leather and spirit. "And what would be right way?" she asked, her voice cold as the steel of the knives she favored. "You know. To piss you off."

I studied her for a moment longer, understanding that every word, every breath between us was a step on a minefield that could either blow us apart or bind us closer. "Do you really want to piss me off bad enough for me to leave you? Be honest. If not with me, at least be honest with yourself."

She scoffed, turning to look over her shoulder with a glare that should have killed me. Just made my cock all the harder. "I have no idea what you are talking about," she snapped. "I don't particularly care if you're pissed off or not. You go your way. I go mine. Problem solved."

"Like bloody hell," I muttered under my breath. "Like it or not, Venus, you're stuck with me. You can leave. You can go whatever way you want. But I'll always be close." With that, I made a strategic retreat, leaving her to her thoughts.

She'd run. Likely tonight, if the children didn't delay her. I knew enough to know if they waylaid her, she'd never disappoint them by taking off immediately unless it was an emergency. I wasn't worried, though. She could disappear when she wanted, but I'd been following her for most of her life. Watching over her. Protecting her.

Falling in love with her.

I took a deep breath in and held it. Letting it out slowly, I did my best to center myself. Venus was the only person in my life who could shake my control. I'd die for my brothers in Grim, but I was always in control. The mere thought of Venus in danger or even remotely at risk was enough to send me into a killing rage. Always had been from the moment I saw her. I tried to keep my distance, to do what I'd been ordered and nothing more, but I couldn't. Not then and certainly not now.

I headed back to the common room and down the hall to Sting's office. I needed some time with him and Wylde. Zaitsev was not getting away. If Venus wanted him to die, he was already dead. He just didn't know it yet.

"Any luck?" I queried as I stepped into Sting's office. The other man sat with his booted feet propped on the desk with his fingers laced together over his stomach.

"Wylde's been at it since he realized Zaitsev was on the move again. Said he's got a decent idea where he's headed but needs a few more hours to be certain."

"Will it be somewhere he stays put? I don't want to go on a wild goose chase."

"Yeah. That's why Wylde wants more time. He says he and your guys at Grim Road think they've found all his safe houses. Once they're sure, Wylde said they could force him to one of them and lock him down. Then you and Venus can take out the trash."

I liked this plan.

"You know, she's just as likely to kill you as she is to let you help her kill Victor Zaitsev."

I grinned at the thought. "Oh, yeah. She's gonna fight me, but honestly, Sting, that's half the fun."

Sting chuckled. "You're one sick bastard."

I shrugged. "Can't deny that. Guess I like the adrenaline rush."

"Yeah? Let me know how you like it when that rush gets you killed." It was more an amused comment than anything else. Sting knew me well enough to know that, if I'd decided I wanted Venus, I'd never give her up. She might not accept me now, but we were further along than I expected at this stage. Granted, I had moved at a glacier's speed up until now, so even though it probably seemed fast for her, for me it had been literally a decade in the making. Something I needed to remember as I navigated the minefield that was Venus's heart.

Sting's gaze shifted slightly, the levity fading from his eyes, the gravity of our situation not lost on either of us. "Be careful, man. This isn't just about whatever game you're playing with Venus. Zaitsev is dangerous, and not just to her. He's a threat to everything she holds dear. Wylde found out that much about him. Seemed it was very difficult to get what he did. At first, anyway. He said he thought there might have been some kind of outside interference helping him find information about the guy, but he wouldn't say who or what he suspected."

I nodded, the weight of responsibility settling on my shoulders. "I'm not underestimating Zaitsev. I know what he's capable of. I watched him sell Venus to the state when she was a girl so he could have some pull inside. He didn't know it at the time, but the FSB knew exactly what he wanted to do. It was a major reason her handlers in the FSB sent her for the kind of training they put her through. Not only did they see her potential, but it made Zaitsev easier to control. All they had to do was make him think Venus was feeding him whatever intel he wanted. Then they controlled the narrative."

"I take it the man has enough money and/or power to make him a threat to the state?"

I shrugged. "Hard to say. I think he's simply an oligarch with more political sway than someone was comfortable with. Likely because of how he makes his money."

"Selling skin." Sting stroked his beard a couple of times.

"Yep. Could be they wanted to make sure he

kept his business dealings private, if you know what I mean."

Sting nodded. "Someone wanted a warning in case he decided to name names. That way, they had time to kill him before he embarrassed anyone enough to make waves."

"Most likely. Though I suspect it had more to do with people outside of the country. People whose political and social standing in Europe and America could affect how the rest of the world treated their country's leaders."

"Yeah. I could see how that could be a problem. And why some might want rid of him."

"Can't get rid of him. Not if they want to keep the money and the goods rolling in. Zaitsev is complete scum, but he has several powerful men protecting him for various reasons. None of them good." I stood and groaned as I straightened.

"Gettin' stiff, old man?" Sting smirked at me, and I scowled.

"Ain't too old to beat your ass for the young whippersnapper you are."

Sting burst out laughing and I chuckled with him. "Stay here as long as you like, Piston. We'll protect you and Venus if necessary. She might as well be one of mine. Lord knows if she asked to patch in, I'd never tell her no. Tzars don't usually patch women, but for Venus, I'd make an exception and dare anyone to go against me."

"I'll remember that. Might take you up on it."

"Do me a favor, will you?" Sting stood then, moving around his desk.

"Name it."

"When you find him next time, kill the bastard. Fuckers like him don't deserve to live."

"We'll get him, and we'll make sure it's permanent."

With those words hanging between us, I left Sting's office for my own room in the compound, located conveniently next to Venus's. Something Sting said during our conversation was bugging me and I needed to put it to rest. Wylde told him Sting he thought there had been someone helping him get what he needed on Zaitsev. I had the feeling I knew who that help was.

Taking out a satellite phone, I sent a message to the only contact in the phone.

Me: *Victor Zaitsev. You helping with the intel*?

It was a couple minutes before there was a reply.

Giovanni Romano: *Yes. Venus*?

Me: *With me at Tzars.*

Giovanni Romano: *She's a big girl.*

Me: *You're a big ass.*

Giovanni, the bastard, got a kick out of knowing Venus was the woman I'd chosen for myself. He said my infatuation with her was the reason he decided he never wanted a woman of his own. He said he was content watching Alexi and Azriel dance around their women and to load up their kids with pixie sticks before sending them home. I didn't point out Alexi and Azriel's kids were adults now. Mainly because that would have reminded the other man how they'd nearly lost Alexi and Merrily's daughter, Bellarose a year ago. Had lost the child she'd been carrying.

Bellarose, more than anyone, seemed to be a beacon for Venus, since the attack on the Tzars compound by a man named Milo Hutch. That man was long dead, but I think what happened to Rose and to Eagle's woman, Nyla, was so similar to Venus' situation she would keep being drawn to Iron Tzars.

She had a connection with the women in this club she didn't have anywhere else. Hutch had used Nyla much the same way Victor used girls. Hutch was just more of a pimp than Victor. Both evil, but Victor Zaitsev was on a whole other level.

Time to get a couple hours sleep. I needed to reset my brain and body. And God knew I'd need strength of mind and body to deal with Venus when she decided she was going back on the hunt. Whenever that happened to be, I intended to be with her every step of the way.

Chapter Five

Venus

It took five days for Wylde to be satisfied he had everything in place to keep Victor holed up in quaint little house in Belle Meade, just outside of Nashville, Tennessee. By "quaint", I mean estate in elite neighborhood. But it was enclosed with locked gate that made it convenient for bastard to lie low for as long as he wanted. He had all creature comforts he needed to not have to leave and not have to think about fact he was being hunted. Call it luxurious prison.

I'd thought about blazing, leaving Piston at Iron Tzars, but he would have followed me. Better to know where he was than have him interrupt something important.

It took me and Piston roughly six hours to get from Evansville, Indiana and Iron Tzars to Nashville. We stopped on outskirts to find place to park vehicle where we could make quick getaway and still be hidden. When I was satisfied I was ready to go, we made our way to the estate to stake out place and get feel for general routine of occupants.

"I don't like this." As usual, Piston was being buzz kill.

"No one said you had to be here. Besides, your own tech guys said this was best place and best time." We didn't look at each other. He had field glasses to his face, likely going over our entry and exit routes. I was accessing new thermal imaging update Giovanni wanted me to try. My brain wasn't used to processing it all yet, so I had dull ache behind my eyes and knew I was going to have to give my vision a break soon.

Everyday use as simple colored contacts was no

problem, but activating enhancements could send me into migraine if I wasn't careful. Testing update had seemed like good idea given we had short amount of time to find Victor and be off property, but I might have underestimated how badly new spectrum would affect my vision. Probably difficult for my brain to process the drastic change.

"Nope," was his only reply.

I sighed, rubbing my temples to ease ache building in my head. "Listen, Piston, I'm not thrilled about setup either, but it's our best shot. Victor's not going to stay put forever."

Piston grunted, lowering his binoculars momentarily to look at the property as whole before putting them back. "Yep."

I used my phone's app and adjusted the intensity of the thermal imaging interface, squinting as I tried to sort through the haze of heat signatures. "*Blyat,*" I swore softly.

"If you have to adjust that thing so much, perhaps you should turn it off." Piston had gone back to studying the grounds with his binoculars, not looking at me at all.

"Mind your business. I'll mind mine."

He didn't move. "Just sayin'. This isn't the environment to test new technology."

I froze. "What are you talking about?"

He gave a derisive snort. "Nothin' at all. Just stating an opinion."

"There are supposed to be four guards plus Victor." I tried to turn the conversation back to the situation at hand. Mainly because there was too much to unpack, and so many implications I wasn't sure I could wrap my head around them all.

"There are."

He didn't continue. I didn't want to give up my secrets any more than he wanted to give up his. As unbelievable as it sounded, though, I thought our intel was bad. Or, at least, not accurate. I'd blown Piston off earlier, but I had same bad feeling he did.

I huffed out a breath. "Opinion would be nice, Piston."

"Already told you my opinion."

"All you said was you didn't like me trying new tech in field."

"Did not. Said this wasn't the best environment. Gotta check new tech in the field sometime. Just probably not this particular field." Still, he kept those stupid field glasses to his face, not looking at me.

"That was it! Only opinion you offered!" Hard to believe I was reduced to whisper-yelling, but there it was. I was exhausted, playing this game with Piston took far more energy than I had at moment because my head was beginning to seriously hurt.

"What exactly do you want to know, Venus?" There was no inflection in his voice. Just man carrying on conversation.

"I can only find two places in house with warm bodies."

"Oh? I take it your new tech didn't work out so well."

"If you want me to kill you, all you have to do is ask. Would rather end you without getting blood pressure up," I snapped. "I can only find two out of five people who are supposed to be in house! Perhaps they are merely in two groups in separate rooms, perhaps not."

Piston did turn to me then. "You sayin' you can't deal with five people in this house if they're ready for you?"

"I can deal with anything Victor throws at me. But, no. I'm not keen to head into ambush."

Piston lowered his binoculars, finally giving me his full attention, the lines around his eyes tightening. "Fine. Let's assume your tech's right, and we're dealing with fewer opponents than expected. Maybe it's an advantage. Fewer to take out, fewer complications."

"Or it's trap," I countered, feeling the migraine pulse behind my eyes. "Victor's not complete idiot. He's likely baiting us."

He nodded slowly, considering this. "True. Victor knows we're after him. Could've sent some of his guys out as a distraction or to prepare for something bigger. But do you honestly think Crush, Byte, and Wylde got it wrong?"

"Not likely," I muttered.

"Not likely." Piston repeated my words, but not like confident statement. More like he didn't believe statement any more than I did.

"We've got less than hour before we're supposed to be gone."

Raising an eyebrow, Piston gave his ultimatum. "Shit or get off the pot, woman."

I bared my teeth at him. "*Zasranets.*" He was right though. Either I took risk, or backed off and hoped we could find bastard again.

Pulling out my phone again, I switched off the vision enhancements and shook my head slightly. Yeah. I had to get this done fast because I was definitely headed toward a migraine. Hopefully without the app running, it would ease the eye strain and the pain. It was time to get to work. I wanted Victor dead tonight.

I slipped my phone back into my pocket and

drew my weapon, checking the chamber silently. Piston mirrored my actions, his movements swift and practiced.

As I moved toward the shadowed side of the house the moon played hide and seek behind thin clouds, casting an eerie glow on the property. Despite the lack of concrete evidence, every instinct screamed that danger lurked inside.

As we approached rear entrance, I tested handle cautiously. It turned with soft click. Unlocked. Just like Wylde said it would be. I paused, frown creasing my forehead. This was too easy. There should be some resistance. Anything. Sure, Crush assured us he'd taken care of security system, but it wasn't like Victor to leave any entrance to his lair unguarded when he was being hunted.

"What's your game, *svoloch*?"

"I want to try another entrance before we fully commit." Piston's voice was barely above a whisper.

"Will it change the outcome?" I met his gaze with a raised eyebrow.

"No. But it might give us more of an advantage if this is a trap."

I gestured with my hand. "Lead way."

Moving with practiced stealth, we retreated and approached property again from west side, where shadows lay thickest. The grass was wet with dew, muffling our footsteps as we crept closer to the large back windows that gave us a partial view inside. My heart thudded in my chest, each beat a loud drum against the silence around us.

Once we reached house again, we paused, crouching low against wall. Piston peered through window. The soft glow of television flickered inside, casting shadows that danced across the back wall.

Three figures could be seen lounging lazily on vast sectional sofa, seemingly engrossed in whatever drama unfolded on screen.

"Three inside," Piston murmured, his voice low and controlled. "Looks like they're not expecting company."

"Perhaps I'm paranoid."

I glanced inside the window, needing to get look inside for myself. It wasn't that I didn't trust Piston. Man might be my nemesis, but he was damned good in battle. I simply wanted to see if I could find something he missed. As he said, three men were in the room. One spoke as he stood, pouring a couple fingers of whisky for each of them. The appeared to chat lightly, one of them grinning as he spoke, waving his hand to make some point. The others laughed before each of them drank.

"Victor isn't there."

"Which other part of the house did we need to check?"

I frowned. He obviously knew more than he was letting on about my vision. No one knew, yet somehow, he did. "Center of house. I can't tell which room, only that it's in center of second level."

He thought for a moment before speaking. "We take out these three, then make our way from here." When I nodded, he ducked under the eave to the other corner of the window. Wylde said we had until exactly two-thirteen before security system was automatically switched back on. That gave us thirty minutes. If Victor was in this house with no extra guards, it wouldn't take us that long. If we ran into resistance, there would be bit of time crunch.

Piston met my gaze and held it. I nodded once, then we both raised silenced weapons and fired twice at glass pane. It didn't shatter. Instead, four blossoms appeared as our shots disintegrated against the bulletproof glass. All three men turned to the window, pulling weapons. One spoke into his phone just before floodlights illuminated every square inch of property from this side.

"Bloody hell." Piston lunged for me, pulling me after him. That was all it took before we both sprinted around corner to a shadowed depression against side of house.

"I'm not leaving until I know Victor's not here." I checked my weapon, scanning our surroundings for the enemies I knew were close by.

"Now's not the time to argue, Venus." Piston reloaded his gun with a fresh clip, even though he'd only used two rounds. Obviously, he was expecting to have to fight our way out. Which was problem because, even though there was plenty of land with this place, we were still in residential area. It was why we went in with suppressors on our weapons. Last thing we needed was to have law enforcement involved. "Move!"

He shot twice at figure moving among trees scattered over this side of grounds. Second shot had man spinning around before he landed face down on the ground. Another man met similar fate, this time from my weapon.

We both darted from our cover, headed back to edge of property and tree line used for privacy. Way we'd come in. Several bullets kicked up earth where they landed near our feet or just in front of us.

Piston hung back, covering my back as we ran. I heard him fire several times as I kept running, sprinting for cover and not looking back. I wasn't used to watching out for someone else in battle because I always went in alone. Now, not only did I feel responsible for Piston, there was heaviness in my chest that had nothing to do with running as hard as I could over rough terrain, and everything to do with worry Piston would be shot. Or worse.

The second we reached street, Piston moved up beside me and urged me forward even faster. Sirens wailed in the distance, and I wanted to pull my hair out.

"I can't fucking believe this. What happened?"

"We'll figure it out later. Let's just make a clean getaway and regroup." Piston grabbed my arm when I slowed slightly and urged me on, not letting me lag behind. "Just a little farther."

"I know where truck is," I snapped. "I'm not idiot." He shot me look but said nothing else.

We'd left truck several blocks over, but hidden in small park. Once we reached truck, we both climbed in and he started the engine. Or tried to. He turned key but nothing happened.

"You've got to be fuckin' kiddin' me." He tried several times, but nothing happened. Finally, he popped the hood of the truck and we both got out. The second he raised the hood, I knew we were fucked.

"Where's fucking battery?" It was only thing that would come out of my mouth.

"Good Goddamned question," he muttered. Piston pulled his weapon again, even as he put a sat phone to his ear. "Wylde, you better fuckin' know what the fuck's goin' on, man."

Piston listened in silence, closing hood of truck before he motioned me to follow him. There nothing in truck to lead back to any of our clubs. License plate had been removed and the VIN number removed, and Piston and I had worn gloves so we didn't leave prints on inside of the house or truck for this very reason. Vehicle was as clean as if it has been recently detailed.

We hurried through sparse trees and across several roads around affluent neighborhoods and fucking golf course. My mind raced through countless scenarios as we tried to stay out of sight. Had someone tipped off Victor, or was it just our bad luck there was more security than our best tech guys could dig up? And the bulletproof glass? That certainly wasn't in the briefing we'd received from Wylde before leaving Evansville for Nashville. Was it a setup from the start? Or were we just that unlucky? And how far-reaching were the consequences going to be now that things had gone south?

We reached another street, quieter and darker than the ones before. "We need new plan," I said, catching my breath. Sirens had faded the farther away from Belle Meade we ran, but my heart continued to pound furiously against my rib cage.

Piston was on the phone again. We both crouched behind large shrub as he listened intently. "Yeah, got it," he finally said and disconnected the call. Turning to me, his expression was grim. "We need to make our way to the Kiss of Death MC compound."

"Kiss of Death?" I spat the name. "They're all dead. We cleaned house when their president tried to move his club to Palm Beach. Opened a BDSM club called The Dark as front for his trafficking ring. We killed every one of that lot and burned club to ground."

"Yep. But Bohannon and Torpedo came here, to this club, to stabilize the region after Kiss of Death was no longer a player in the area. They decided that, since Bane had wiped them out, no one would protest if they kept the name." He shrugged. "Having a recognizable name, even if it's under new management, so to speak, sparked less resistance. With a little TLC, I think they've managed to hold things together."

"I assume by TLC you mean some kind of tough love?"

Piston smiled. "Yeah. Something like that."

It took another couple of hours before we finally stumbled to the gates of the MC in question. Bohannon and Torpedo met us at the gate, along with several other members of his club. It was almost anticlimactic. Sure, we'd been shot at and killed more than couple of people, but we hadn't directly engaged anyone, including the police. Which was a miracle in itself given the neighborhood.

Bohannon stepped forward and reached out a hand for me. "Venus. I didn't think I'd see you in our new digs."

I grinned as I took his hand. "Wasn't aware you had new digs. Kiss of Death MC? Really?"

He shrugged. "No reason to reinvent the wheel. Locals are used to the name. While we'll eventually give the club a better public reputation, for now it suits us to have everyone think we're a true outlaw club."

"This is Piston. He follows me around like puppy." I gave a dismissive wave to my companion. Choke on that, *svoloch*.

"I know Piston," Torpedo said as he stepped forward and took Piston's hand. "By reputation anyway."

Piston just grinned. "Whatever you heard, it's all true."

Torpedo chuckled. "Figured as much. Data got word to us through your man, Wylde. I've got the boys goin' after your vehicle. We'll have everything taken care of by morning. It's late. I'm bettin' you'd like to get some rest."

"He's not my man." I shook my head.

"He's Iron Tzars. Right?"

"Yep. I'm not Tzars."

Torpedo gave me an odd look. "Sting insinuated you were." Odd, but Sting was kind of into head games at times.

I started to say that no, in fact, I wanted to figure out how that bastard Victor got around us, but Piston cut me off. "Yeah. A room with a bed and a shower would be great. We'll be out of your hair tomorrow."

"No problem." Bohannon jerked his chin toward the clubhouse. "Got you all set up."

What Bohannon failed to mention and what I was too tired and frustrated to realize until it was too late, was that the bastard had given us one room. With one bed.

"*Blyat*," I bit out. When I chanced a look at Piston, he didn't even try to hide his grin.

"One bed. No other furniture. Seems like we might be getting cozy." I just stared from bed to Piston and back, unable to form words. "No problems? Good."

"I'm not sleeping with you, Piston. Not happening."

Slow grin spread his lips. "Who said anything about sleep?"

Chapter Six

Piston

The expression on Venus's face was one I wanted to remember for the rest of my life. In fact, it was a look I'd be telling children in the clubs about for years. When we were old and I was gray and Venus finally got tired of all the pink and was gray with me, I'd be tellin' everyone about how the most feared woman I'd ever met turned a very unflattering shade of red at the mention of doing something in a bed other than sleep.

Her fists clenched at her sides, and for a moment I thought she might actually take a swing at me. But instead, Venus let out a long, slow breath and shook her head. "You are impossible," she muttered, though a slight twitch of her lips suggested she was fighting back a reluctant smile.

At that moment, though, both humor and desire swirled in the tension-filled room like a tangible force. I knew Venus well enough to understand her boundaries and her triggers. She was as fierce in her personal space as she was in a brawl, and crossing that line without an explicit invitation was something I would never do. Didn't mean I wouldn't push her. Just a little.

"Not impossible." I took a slow step toward her. "But I'm bettin' you're not nearly as opposed to sleepin' with me as you're lettin' on."

"Sleep, Piston. Sleep is operative word." She gave me a stern look. It was kind of cute, really. I mean, once you got past the daggers she had for nails and knowing that one swipe across a man's privates could very well emasculate him.

"Sure. Sleep can come. You know. *After.*"

Her eyes got wide and she actually took a

defensive step backward before stopping herself. Her head went up and her eyes flashed with defiance. "Not happening."

"Oh? Tell me you didn't like it when I kissed you. Tell me that and make me believe it." I crossed my arms over my chest and looked down my nose at her.

She opened her mouth, probably to tell me she hadn't liked me kissing her, but nothing came out. She tried again. Still nothing.

"*Blyat!*"

The next thing I knew, Venus took the two steps separating us. Her hand went to my beard, and she pulled me down to her and fused her mouth to mine.

The kiss was fierce, almost punishing, as if she was trying to prove a point with her lips and teeth but ended up proving something else entirely. Her fingernails dug into the skin of my face as she pulled me closer, and I could feel the fire that always simmered just beneath her surface when we were together flare up like a torch thrown into dry straw.

Venus was the first to pull away, breathing hard. Her eyes were bright with something that wasn't anger. There was heat there, undeniable and raw, and it burned all the more brightly framed by the flush on her cheeks.

"I hate you," she whispered, her voice husky.

I chuckled low in my throat, though laughing was the last thing I felt like doing. I was just as affected as she was and didn't care who knew it. "I know, Shortcake."

Venus's chest heaved as she glared at me, her fury mingling with the unmistakable glow of desire. "This changes nothing." I thought she was trying to sound angry and perhaps she did. Her voice, though, betrayed the conflict swirling within her. "You're still bastard and I still hate you."

Her breath was hot on my face, her anger palpable, yet so was the pull between us, like opposing magnets being forced together.

"You might hate me," I said, my voice low and steady as her stormy gaze locked onto mine. This was a pivotal moment. I knew it as well as I knew my own name. I wanted to push her, but I knew better. Yeah. I was probably gonna fuck her tonight, but it wouldn't change much. At least, not on the surface. "But you can't deny there's something here. Something that ain't just gonna disappear because you want it to."

Venus snorted, a sound that would've been dismissive if her eyes hadn't been scanning my face like she was trying to read a complicated map. "You think you know everything, Piston."

"I don't," I admitted without hesitation, I had my hands resting on her hips, but not holding her back. I had to. Otherwise, I'd have them fisted in her hair as I fucked her mouth with my tongue. "I don't know near everything. If I did, you'd have been in my bed a very, *very* long time ago."

I saw the exact moment my words registered. Her eyes widened, then narrowed. I timed my movement perfectly and covered her lips with mine the second she opened her mouth, likely to give me a piece of her mind.

If it was possible, this kiss was even more fiery than the last. There was a struggle for dominance and, I gotta tell ya, I have no idea how I managed to win that initial battle. Probably because it was a sneak attack.

You know what? No. It wasn't a sneak attack. *She* kissed *me* first, Goddamnit! She started this. It was only fair I finish it. True or not, the thought gave me the strength I needed to power through the intoxicating taste of her sweet lips and tongue and prove to her I could handle her. I could command her when necessary. It wasn't something she necessarily wanted, but she needed it. No matter what she wanted, no matter how much she might be attracted to me, Venus -- Ulyana Volkov -- would never permanently attach herself to a mate she thought of as weaker than she was.

This was the moment I'd trained for my entire life. Nothing had ever been as important to me as this woman. Nothing ever would. I had no children. Had no prospect for having children. Even if I knew for sure she could have children, the woman would never put herself in a situation where she couldn't control what was happening to her body. For Venus, it was all about control. It had been drummed into her from the day Victor had shipped her off to what amounted to assassin school.

Now, adopting little girls? Absolutely. She'd gather them in droves and make them just as outrageous and deadly as she was. Little boys were out of the question because she'd make them into men who were capable and willing to take over the world. Then she'd cheer them on from the sidelines with a pink concoction that looked like some fruity little drink with no bite, of which one sip would knock you on your ass. No. Being pregnant was an obvious vulnerability and that was something Venus would never allow herself. She'd been trained to view children the same way. As a something to be used against her. Over the years, however, I saw how she passively watched over every child in any club she visited. Like she'd already adopted the lot and hadn't bothered to tell anyone.

With a grunt, I lifted her up without breaking our contact. She wrapped her legs around my waist as I pressed her against the nearest wall. I pressed as much of my body against hers as I could so there was no way she could miss the way my cock stood hard and proud for her.

Venus gasped into my mouth and I took her breath into my lungs, breathing in as she breathed out. She shuddered, but one hand landed on my shoulder and she clutched me to her, those nails of hers once again digging into my skin. Which made me even harder for her. I wanted to feel those wicked things digging furrows down my back. If she drew blood, I'd wear the scratches like badges of fucking honor.

She slid her other hand around my neck and grabbed the hair at my nape, pulling hard enough to send a jolt of pleasure-pain shooting straight to my dick. I growled against her lips, my grip on her hips tightening in response. The wall was unyielding behind her, but I doubt either of us cared. I knew I was a writhing mass of need and fucking lust by this point. I knew I couldn't give in to those desires though. Not this time. Later. After she fully trusted me. Or, rather, once she realized she fully trusted me. If she didn't already, I'd have been dead the first week we spent together hunting that motherfucker, Victor.

I shoved a hand up the bottom of her leather vest. Fuck, it wasn't easy. I was certain I scratched or pinched her skin more than once. If I did, Venus didn't care. If anything, it spurred her on.

Next thing I knew, she had my vest and shirt off, and the front zipper of her vest undone. Her breasts mashed against my chest and she rubbed herself over me like a cat marking its territory. Her nipples grazed over my chest hair and she gasped, looking into my eyes with that eerie pink gaze of hers.

She bared her teeth at me. "This doesn't mean anything," she said, her voice thick with lust and something else I was too chicken shit to try to decipher. Mainly because I needed every single ounce of control I had to make it through this encounter on top. If she got the best of me, if I lost myself in her body the way I wanted to, I'd never get another chance with her. I absolutely had to prove to her I could handle anything she threw at me and come out on top.

I held her gaze, even though I knew the reason she was looking at me now was her go-to effort to throw someone off. And, let's face it, those pink eyes would normally do the trick. They weren't just strangely colored contacts, they were bright fuckin' pink. It wouldn't surprise me if they fucking glowed in the dark. I didn't flinch. I held her gaze with what I hoped was a steady one of my own.

"Tell yourself that, baby. But it means *everything.*"

Her lips twitched in a semblance of a smile, though it was as dangerous as it was inviting. I knew she'd been a trained and very skilled seductress. I'd seen her smile exactly like this many times before she pounced.

Venus pushed back slightly to study me, her expression unreadable. "You think you're ready for this? For me?" she challenged, her voice laced with both skepticism and intrigue.

"Oh, I'm very ready, Venus. The question is, are you?" Did I have doubts? Yep. I had many. Not doubts that we belonged together -- I was already hers and had been since the moment I claimed her, when I'd gone to help get Lemon back. Venus needed to realize she was mine as well. She wasn't there yet. My doubts centered on myself and if I could be what Venus needed. I was a strong, dominant man, but Venus was unlike any other woman I'd ever encountered.

"You think so?" She tilted her head and, for the first time, I thought I might have penetrated that shield she kept around her all the time. She tried to look amused, but there was something in her eyes that told me she was now wary. She sensed the predator, but couldn't find him.

"I'm not just ready, baby. I'm here to prove I'm exactly what you need. And I will be everything you could ever imagine in a partner." I replied, tightening my grip on her hips and pressing my cock harder against her. I thrust my hips between her thighs so the hard ridge of my cock rubbed over her clit. I knew I got it right when she shivered in my arms. Her gaze skittered from mine and she grunted, almost in pain.

When sweat erupted over her skin and beaded on her forehead and upper lip, I couldn't help the smirk I knew painted my lips.

Our breaths mingled, those fierce eyes of hers imploring me to challenge her, to prove my resolve. "Everything," she repeated, her voice now a whisper caught between defiance and a plea. It was clear Venus was wrestling with her own desires and the harsh rules set for her long before she was capable of defying them. From there they'd been drilled into her until each of those rules became part of her psyche. The weight of that stare felt like a challenge carved in stone, daring me to carve my name alongside hers.

Suddenly, her hands moved with purpose, tracing the contours of my face before pulling me closer. Her lips sought mine again with an urgency, like her actions were almost a plea for me to make good on my promise. Our kiss deepened, tongues clashing in an erotic dance.

As her lips moved against mine with an almost ferocious need, I could feel the barriers she built around herself beginning to crumble. The intensity of her kiss conveyed more than words ever could; it was her response to my challenge, daring me to keep up with the storm that was Venus.

With every touch, every clash of our tongues, I felt more of her walls fall away. Oh, she fought to hold them up. Probably thought that, if she could wrest control from me, I'd give in and fuck her already. Then she could use my inability to resist the call of her body as evidence I wasn't strong enough to handle her. She could bend me to her will and Venus would never belong to a man she could control.

She reached between us to unfasten my jeans. My cock sprang free and I nearly groaned at the instant relief. Sure, I still throbbed and ached like a motherfucker -- especially when she reached between us to stroke my cock -- but I felt like I had some room to breathe. Which is what I needed to keep control of this situation.

I gripped her hips, shoving her off me so that she was on her feet. Venus was a tall woman. Unlike her sister, Millie, who was short and slight, Venus was five-ten with some bulk to her. She definitely had the look of a woman who was physically fit. I might be a decade older than her, I was six-five and very heavily muscled. As intimidating as she could be to most men, I wasn't most men. And I knew by the looks the woman gave me when she thought I wasn't looking, Venus liked what she saw.

I spun her around, mashing her against the wall. My cock wanted to nestle between her cheeks, but was prevented by all that Godforsaken pink. Which kinda made me smile too. I knew why she wore pink. I also happened to know she hated every second of it, but had embraced the woman she'd become when she landed with Argent Tech and the Shadow Demons.

"Did I say you could touch?" I growled the words beside her ear, needing to instill a bit of unease in her.

"Fuck you, Piston," she spat back over her shoulder.

I gave her an evil chuckle. "Oh yeah. You're gonna fuck me all right."

She gave a screech of anger, trying to swipe back at me with her nails. I was ready for her and caught her wrists in my hands, bringing them over her head and holding them there. She managed to get my leg through my jeans, though. Probably brought blood too. If this situation had been less dire, I'd have smiled. Which would likely have set her off, and not in a good way.

The weight and strength of my body pinned her solidly against the wall. I gripped both her wrists in one hand for the few seconds it took me to undo and jerk off my belt. I got it looped around her wrists, held by the buckle and my hand on the end of the leather. I pulled her wrists so her arms bent at the elbow, putting her hands behind her neck. I caught her chin in the crook of my elbow, gripping my belt strap in the same hand, effectively restraining her hands and restricting her head movement at the same time.

"Now," I rasped next to her ear. "What were you saying about fucking me?"

"You know what I meant!" Venus yelled at me as she kicked, scraping her heavy motorcycle boot down my shin. I felt it, but the move wasn't as painful as it could have been had my jeans not had the front reinforced with leather.

I wrapped my other arm around her waist and lifted, mashing her harder against the wall. Her feet flailed, landing blows to my thighs and shins a couple of times. Once she got my knee, but not enough to do real damage. Which told me I was doing exactly the right thing. Had Venus truly wanted free, she'd be free. And I'd be dead.

"And you know what I meant." When she stilled, I continued. "Now. You wanted my cock? Maybe I should give it to you."

A fine tremor took her body again and her skin erupted in gooseflesh. She shuddered, then Venus actually whimpered. God, I was so close to getting what I'd wanted for a fucking decade! Yet, all of this, everything I'd dreamed about having in my life, could crumble at the first sign I couldn't handle Venus enough to control myself. She needed a man stronger than her, and I was determined I'd be that man. No matter what it took.

When she shivered again, sweat erupting over her skin this time, I set her on the floor. I found the button to her pants and unfastened it, then undid her zipper. When she only whimpered again, I worked them over her hips until the pink leather was halfway down her thighs.

Again, I wrapped my arm around her waist. I'd loosened my grip on the belt letting her have some movement in her arms. If Venus felt threatened, there was no doubt she could be free any time she wanted. My job, as I saw it, was to make it so she forgot about wanting to get away from me. If I could override that instinct and help her embrace her own pleasure, maybe, *maybe*, I could win her heart.

My dick bobbed between her legs. When it

bumped against her upper thigh, Venus's knees gave out and she sagged against me, her breath coming in ragged pants. I paused, holding her still, but giving her a moment to fight me if she wanted free. She didn't. Instead, she bared more of her neck to me, a sign of surrender.

"Do you want my cock?" I growled as I rubbed my length along the seam of her pussy. Her wetness coated my dick with silky cream, letting me know how much she needed to fuck. Needed to come. The trick would be to get her to beg me for it. She had to acknowledge it was my cock she was begging for. Me who she wanted to fuck.

"I… I…" She panted, her body limp against me. The only reason she was still on her feet was because I held her up.

"It's not a difficult question, Venus. Do you want my cock buried balls deep inside you or not?"

"Piston!" My name was a strangled cry on her lips. It was my answer, but I needed more.

"That's my name, baby. Now tell me what you want me to do." I ran my lips up and down her neck, grazing my teeth against her and tickling her delicate skin with my beard. "Do you want me to fuck you? To put my dick in that sweet, wet pussy?" She moaned, a desperate sound. "The noises you're making tell me you need to come. Perhaps I'm wrong? I should let you go. Leave you alone and never fuckin' touch you again." I made my words harsh. Angry. I had to push her as hard as I could while still staying in control.

"NO!" She practically screamed the word. "I need to come!"

"Ah, now we're getting somewhere." I praised her by moving my dick more firmly against her pussy. I slid through her lips in s sensual glide, rubbing over her clit, just not as much as she needed. I was sure she was getting just enough stimulation to keep her on edge but not push her over. "Tell me, Ulyana. Tell me what you want me to do. All you have to do is tell me. You don't have to beg. You don't even have to ask. Just tell me what you want me to do and it's yours."

Chapter Seven

Venus

I had no idea which way was up or was down. Somewhere in back of my mind, I thought I should be concerned he knew my real name. No one knew it but Millie and Shadow. Millie's lips were sealed. If Piston knew Shadow, the other man might have helped brother out and given up information about me. But right now, I couldn't process complex things. No man had ever taken such complete control over me before. Was muddling my brain. Sex wasn't new to me. I'd done just about everything one could imagine in that area. But nothing I'd ever experienced could have prepared me for what I was currently experiencing with Piston.

When he'd caught my hands, then tied them with his belt, my first instinct had been to fight, but I just couldn't make my body resist him. His big, brawny arm around my throat, him holding leather belt binding my wrists were show of raw strength on his part. There might have been a small window where I wasn't completely sure I could break his hold if I'd wanted, but strangely, helplessness only turned me on even more.

I'd thought I'd been in love once. Guard in Victor's home had caught my eye. At one of hardest times in my life, Mikhail was there. Until I thought my sister was making play for him. I lost my mind and almost got us all killed. It was when I first realized hard lesson FSB had tried to teach me. Caring about someone makes you vulnerable. That was first time I thought understood why I needed to never let my guard down. Even my sisters -- especially my sisters -- could be used against me.

Now, I understood why they'd taught me to seduce. Because I was currently one being seduced. Thing was, I was hundred percent certain Piston was much better at seduction than me because I'd never inspired the kind of madness Piston was currently bringing me to.

Had he made me beg, I might have resisted. I might have been able to pull myself out of haze of lust and need he'd so expertly built within me. But no. He gave me a choice. Let him give me pleasure I craved. Or tell him to go fuck himself. I needed to do latter. But I was *going* to do former.

"I want you to fuck me," I whimpered. I was sure I'd be mortified later by how easily I caved, but right now, I needed to come like I needed to breathe.

"You sure? If I do this, I'm takin' you bare. I'm gonna plant my cum in your pussy and keep my dick inside you all fuckin' night."

"This is supposed to change my mind?" I was on the verge of hysteria.

His dark chuckle made me shiver. "Not at all. It's supposed to warn you. I fuck you now, I'll fuck you whenever I like from this point forward. I'll be puttin' my cum in your pussy at every opportunity, and you won't stop me."

"*Blyat! Blyat! Chto eto za bezumiye?*"

"Not madness, baby. This is your reality. I will give you pleasure you've never even dreamed of. But in return, you're gonna belong to me. You'll be mine from now on. Where you go, I go."

"I can't promise you happy ever after, Piston. My life is --"

"Complicated? You think I don't know?"

"Do we have to talk about this now?" I practically sobbed out question. Serious turn of subject should have dampened this need inside me, but it didn't. It only made me impatient to see if Piston could make good on his promises. Surprisingly, I found I loved idea of everything he described. I just wasn't sure I could give him that much of myself.

"You need to know everything before I do this, Venus. But I'm not going to make it easy for you. You're not easy. You wouldn't trust easy. But you trust me. Don't you." It wasn't a question.

"You're imagining things." Why did my voice sound breathy and weak?

"This wet pussy against my dick says otherwise." As he spoke, he moved in slow, easy strokes. Every brush against my clit threatened to send me over edge whether I was ready or not.

Then he stopped, the head of his cock at my entrance. He didn't press forward and actually breach my entrance, but stayed as still as statue. I think him stopping stimulation was actually worse than teasing he'd been doing.

"Why did you stop?" I practically sobbed out the words.

"Because you won't tell me what you want me to do. You're in complete control here. All you have to do is tell me what you want."

"Fine! Just fucking fuck me! I want you to fuck me!" I yelled at him, all my anger and helplessness and loneliness and longing came rushing inside me, just like thrust of his cock.

Without another word, Piston gave me what I asked for. He took my breath as he pounded inside me. At some point he let my hands go, but all I could do was brace myself against the wall. I tried to push back, to fuck him like he fucked me, but he had me pinned between the hard wall and his equally hard body.

He worked my body with brutal finesse, knowing exactly how to play me to keep me on edge, never falling over. His grip on my hips was just shy of painful, but I reveled in it. I found I wanted that helpless feeling I had when he'd manhandled me. Thought of him tying me to his bed for him to do whatever he wanted with me played in my mind on repeat even as it gave me a taste of what that scenario would entail. He'd said he would put his cum in me whenever he wanted. Did I really want that?

"*Blyad*!"

"That's right, baby. I'm fuckin' you. I'm gonna fuck you all fuckin' night. Then, when we catch that son of a bitch, Victor, I'm gonna bring you home and fuck you some more."

"*Da! Da!*"

With a yell, Piston shoved away from me only to spin me around again. He lifted me into his arms. I found myself being carried to the bed across the room. My pants and boots were still around my thighs so I couldn't wrap my legs around him. He set me on my feet long enough to shove my pants all the way down my legs. My boots were harder to get off, but somehow we both managed. By the time we did, though, both of us were breathing heavily. More than a few grunts and moans filled the room as I became more and more frustrated. This whole situation was pure madness!

Before he put us on bed, Piston lifted my naked body into his arms, those strong arms iron bands around my torso. He shoved his cock inside me again, and I screamed Piston's name.

He lay on top of me -- his jeans still around his hips -- wrapping his arms around me tightly. He began to fuck me in hard, sure, fast strokes. I screamed over and over again, still riding that edge of orgasm but unable to fall. Piston's harsh grunts were heavy in my ears and made my inability to come all the more frustrating. If that bastard came before me, I really would kill him.

"That's it, baby. You're right there, aren't you? So close you can taste it." His words were nothing but pure sin. I should be burning in hell for all dirty images his gruff voice brought to me.

Sweat dampened my skin. I couldn't breathe. All I could do was dig my nails into Piston's back and do whatever he said moment he said to do it. I probably brought blood, but damned if I cared.

I was getting ready to slice into his jugular vein when Piston shifted his body just slightly. He must have known exactly what he was doing because his arms tightened around me just as my body fragmented, exploding with force of nuclear bomb. I swear I saw stars and possibly passed out for few seconds.

I couldn't see, my ears rang with my own screams, then my hips thrashed, convulsing as second wave swept me away. This time, my body went rigid right before I screamed, digging my nails into Piston's back and shoulders. Need to hold him to me was primal, something I was helpless to resist.

At some point, I relaxed under Piston. His heavy weight on me was more comforting than I ever thought possible. I'd always insisted being on top during sex. With Piston, the urge to roll us so he was underneath me never occurred. He dominated me and I craved more.

When he finally rolled off me, I whimpered with loss. He didn't go far, though. He held me against his chest, one arm around my shoulders, the other palming the back of my head.

"That's it, Venus. My warrior woman." He crooned to me like he might a child. Could be because I was trembling and... were my eyes damp? "My woman. Just relax. Let it all out. I'll always be here to catch you."

Fuck. My eyes were wet. My breath was coming in little hitches and I couldn't seem to stop it.

Finally, I gave up and just went limp against him. He wanted control? Well, he had it. I was too exhausted to care.

With one final deep breath, I closed my eyes and let sleep have me. I'd trust Piston to keep me safe. Besides, if I was killed before I woke, I'd die happy.

Chapter Eight

Piston

I woke with a sharp pain in my shoulder. My eyes snapped open and my first thought was, *I've been stabbed.* I looked down to find a mass of hot pink hair laying silkily against my chest while the little daggers Venus called nails were dug into the flesh just below my shoulder. She'd broken the skin. I'd be upset except for two things.

First, Venus was sound a-fuckin'-sleep. In my arms. In my bed. That thought put a grin on my face. Second, she'd basically stabbed me because she was clinging to me, holding me close so I couldn't get away from her. That thought not only put a smile on my face but settled something inside me I hadn't realized was so tense. She might not realize it yet, but she'd claimed me as hers the same way I'd claimed her. Except her claim was in the form of scratch marks and stab wounds. Kind of like sleeping with a cat.

Oh. And I wasn't dead.

I sifted my fingers through the bright pink strands of her hair. Her pale blond roots were beginning to shine through where she'd been too busy to touch it up since we took off after Victor the last time. Which brought an end to my contentment.

Victor had known we were coming for him. The trap he'd set was hasty and not very well thought out for someone like him, but we'd probably gotten too close too fast. He hadn't had time to do much while on the run either. I hadn't been thrilled with the choice of places for the tech guys to drive him to. The neighborhood he was in might be on the outskirts of Nashville, but there were houses that were very close together. I'd talked to Crush, and he'd said they tried pushing him in another direction, but the man had made a beeline for Nashville. Probably knew the surroundings would make it more difficult for someone to get to him than it would be for him to escape.

It was time to pull out the big guns. I was surprised Venus hadn't already. I reached for my phone and, never taking my fingers from Venus's silky hair, pulled up the contact information for Giovanni Romano at Argent Tech -- one third of the Shadow Demons -- to text him.

Me: *Victor Zaitsev.*

I put my phone down to wait. It was quite possible Giovanni wouldn't answer for a while. But he always answered. Also, I thought the name would get his attention enough for him to message me back.

My phone buzzed. That was fast. I picked up the phone again to read the text.

Romano: *Venus?*

I raised an eyebrow. Not only was his response fucking fast for him, but his first thought had been for Venus? Not to ask "what about him" or "yeah, he's a bastard" or any number of things. It made my hackles rise. Giovanni knew how I felt about Venus. If he thought he was making a play for her, he should have thought about it a long fucking time ago.

Me: *Mine.*

Romano: *Safe?*

Me: *With me.*

By definition, that meant she was safe. Fucking prick.

Romano: *Call me.*

Me: *Give me ten.*

Romano: *You have five.*

Motherfucker. If I didn't need his help on this, I'd

tell him I'd call him when Venus woke up, but, a) I did need his help, and b) I wanted to protect Venus's privacy. I had no idea how close she was to the bastard, but, as much as I wanted to video chat with Venus sleeping soundly against my chest, I couldn't do that. Not without her permission. Which made me grin. She'd totally give me permission.

I carefully extracted myself, taking care of her nails. Venus mumbled in her sleep, her brow furrowing. She bared her teeth and hissed. Sounded angry. I had to stifle a chuckle. My little shortcake was a tad grumpy if you disturbed her sleep.

Once out of bed, I pulled my pants over my hips and fastened them. The frenzy before had been fucking mind-altering. I hadn't even managed to get my damn boots off. I went to the bathroom and did my business before brushing my teeth. Took me ten minutes. Might have dragged it out a bit.

I opened the bathroom door slightly so I could keep an eye on Venus. Our relationship was still new. I had no doubt she'd try to make light of it later out of self-preservation. She'd likely try to bail on me at the first opportunity. I glanced in the mirror and a deep sense of satisfaction filled me. Venus had, indeed, dug her claws into me. I even turned around to admire the scabbed-over scratches on my back. Painful? Yep. Worth it? Also yep.

Before I could call Giovanni Romano back, my phone rang. Sometimes, it was fun to poke the bear.

"You're an impatient bastard, Giovanni."

"Where's Venus?" It was more of a demand than a question.

"Asleep."

"Hurt?"

"Nope."

"What about Victor Zaitsev?"

"We're hunting him. Shoulda had him, but he set a trap for us. He knew we were coming."

There was a silence. Then, "Why is Venus not answering her phone?"

"Told you. She's asleep. Been a long couple'a days."

"She always answers her phone." Giovanni almost sounded angry. He definitely wasn't happy.

"Not anymore. Not when she's sleeping." It was a bold claim, but one I would stand by. She was not going to be at Giovanni's beck and call, no matter what tech he supplied her with.

Again, there was a pause before Giovanni asked the question I'd been waiting for. "What's she to you, Piston?"

"Everything. She's mine."

"She know that?"

"She's not answering you, is she?"

"Christ, man. I hope you know what you're doing. Ulyana isn't a woman you want to fuck around with. If you're not serious, you're going to hurt her more than you can possibly imagine."

"Oh, I can imagine, Gio. I've known her as long as you have."

"What do you need?" So like Giovanni. There was never a transition with him. The conversation always went from one topic straight into another. He got the information he needed, then moved on.

"I need to know where Zaitsev is. The Tzars and Grim's tech guys had him pinned down, but he still managed to get around us."

"Victor Zaitsev is cunning and, more than that, he's paranoid. Too many years of drugs and booze. Unfortunately, Venus was under his control before his mind started going. She's his stepdaughter, the one he intended to be his ace in the hole."

"A plant inside the Federal Security Service."

"Yes. The FSB." I could hear keys clicking in the background as Giovanni did some shit with his computer.

"Zaitsev was content to leave Venus alone after she and Millie escaped. He figured it was better she was a continent away from him because once the woman sets her mind to something, there's no stopping her."

"That's not new information, Gio. Give me something I can work with."

"He's tracking Venus."

Everything inside me stilled. My gaze went to the sleeping woman in my bed. "What the fuck do you mean?" My voice was soft and low, but there was no doubt Giovanni heard the menace there.

"Just what I said. He put a tracker in her before he sent her off for training. It's old."

"Does Venus know?"

"No. At least, she probably didn't realize what it was at the time. Small dose of Propofol and she's out while they put a tiny tracking device in her deltoid."

"Why not take it out of her?"

"I wasn't sure at the time how dangerous it would be. I'm still not. Believe me when I tell you I'd prefer she not have it. That fuckin' tracker is the reason I sent her out into the field. I wanted her as far away from the estate as possible. I found it a couple months after she got here. She was the best at what she did already, so sending her out was the best option."

"For you?"

"For her, Piston. I sent her to one of Cain's partners in ExFil. She was there for a special mission.

It's how she met Thorn, which was a happy coincidence I can't take credit for. Worked out for the best, though. She and Thorn got along from the very beginning."

I was starting to see red. If Giovanni knew but Venus didn't, that meant he was using Venus for more than just testing new tech. I took a calming breath. "Why did you give Venus those contacts, Gio?"

"There is no one like Venus, Piston. She's the best at what she does. Even El Diablo thought twice about crossing her back in the day."

"You're just dropping all kinds of bombs, ain't 'cha." I still held the phone to my ear but had to lean against the bathroom vanity on my other arm. Otherwise, I'd probably throw the satphone through the fucking window and go after Giovanni and kill him to death.

"That ain't the half of it, but you're gonna have to get the other shit from Venus. As to why I gave her those contacts? They also allow me to not only keep an eye on her, but if I need to, I can access the chip in her contacts and see what she's seeing."

"You son of a bitch," I breathed. "Does she fuckin' know?"

"It didn't seem like something she'd approve of, so no. She doesn't. Besides, have you told her how long you've been following her?"

"Gio…" The threat in my voice was clear. Even for someone as dangerous and cunning as Giovanni.

"It was for her own good. All of it. I can send her help if she needs it, though admittedly she's never needed it. The woman is… special. She's built for killing."

"Tell me something I don't fuckin' know."

"How about this? You need to get away from

Kiss of Death. They're too secluded. Bohannon and Torpedo haven't gotten all the infrastructure set up to protect them from a threat like Zaitsev. They don't have backup from another club. My suggestion would be to get her back to Grim Road or Salvation's Bane. In fact, I'm letting Thorn know to expect you and to get the other two clubs ready for trouble."

"Other two? You really think we need to involve Black Reign? Bringing in El Diablo just opens up a whole other subset of problems."

"I do. Zaitsev is not like any threat you've been up against."

"I'm aware of how dangerous he is. I assume this is all about his daughter, Katya. Does Zaitsev not know where she is?"

"No. Millie got the trackers out of that girl when they first rescued her. Since she went to stay with Millie and Shadow at the Bones compound, Shadow has done his best to keep a low profile for all three of them. Occasionally Millie takes a job for Cain with ExFil, but they're careful not to put her on the radar. Until you kill Zaitsev, the safest place for Venus is anywhere Katya is not."

"If that bastard's able to keep tabs on Venus, why is he just now coming after her? It's been a couple of years since they rescued the girl." I was rapidly getting a headache. There was so much to do I didn't know where to start.

I heard Giovanni exhale a long breath before he said anything. "If I had to guess, I'd say he's found someone willing to train the girl."

When he didn't elaborate, I had to bite my tongue to keep from snapping out an order for him to spill it. "Gio, you're gonna have to give me some more information. I can't read minds and I don't like playing games. Train her for what?"

"Not now. Get Venus back to Salvation's Bane, and we'll talk. I'll meet you there." The line went dead.

I felt like I'd just been run over by a steamroller. There was so much to unpack in this conversation I didn't know where to start. A quick glance at Venus told me she was still asleep. My heart softened as I looked at her.

She'd drawn her knees up to her chest and tugged the comforter around her. All that pink hair fanned out around her like a punk halo. She even looked younger, relaxed in sleep. Sure, I'd seen her asleep many times over the years. But never like this. She was out cold. Made me puff out my chest just a little in pride. If she didn't trust me, there was no way she'd sleep so soundly. No matter how much I wore her out with sex. Yeah. I was fucking proud.

With a smile, I slipped back into bed, pulling Venus into my arms. More than anything I wanted to fuck her again. This time, I'd go slow. Appreciate her battle-hardened body. Taste her nipples and sweet pussy like I wanted to. *Feast on her…*

"Wass dat?" Her words were slurred and not very coherent, but I got the gist.

"Giovanni. He wants us to head back to Bane territory."

She was quiet for so long I thought she'd gone back to sleep. Then she grunted as she pushed herself up. Her hair was in her face, and she used her hand to brush it out of the way so she could see me. "Now… what?" She still sounded sleepy, but I could see the awareness in her eyes as she looked down into my face.

"We've got a lot to discuss, but he says Zaitsev is tracking you."

That got her full attention. Instantly, all appearance of sleep vanished. "Explain," she snapped.

"This isn't a quick conversation, Venus." I also wasn't sure how she was going to react to knowing Giovanni was aware all along. "We need to go back to Florida. Where we go is up to you, but Giovanni suggested Salvation's Bane."

She stared at me, searching my face for whatever she needed. The moment she found what she was looking for, her face hardened. "This is bad. *Da*?"

"It is."

That seemed to surprise her before she schooled her features once again. "Didn't expect you to admit that."

"I'll never lie to you, Venus. Have I kept secrets from you? Absolutely. You have your own secrets. That all ends now. *Right* now. From this point forward you and I are a team. So we need to start with the most important issues."

"What would those be?" She gave me a wary look as she got out of bed. She was still naked, but didn't bother to cover herself. Instead, she looked like she was readying herself for battle. Looking for threats around the room even as she kept her main focus on me.

I tilted my head slightly, studying her. "I'm not your enemy, Venus. I never will be. I'll always be on your side, no matter what."

"But you know something. Something I'm not going to like."

"I do." I stood and held out my hand to her. She shook her head, all that pink hair spilling over her shoulders to cover her breasts. "Venus, come to me." I made my tone unbendable. She would come to me or I'd force the issue, and I was pretty sure she knew it.

Finally, with a sigh and a slight shake of her head, she moved around the bed, snagging my shirt from the floor and putting it on. The action filled me both with regret and pride. Regret that I couldn't stare at her tits any longer, but pride that she was wearing my shirt. She noticed my expression and gave me an impatient look.

"I know I'm shorter than you, but my eyes are little bit higher." Her tone of voice was irritated, but I could also see the flush of pleasure she tried to hide.

"Yeah." I scrubbed my hand over the back of my neck. "I'd apologize, but I'm only sorry you put on the shirt. It is, however, my shirt, so I'll let it slide this once." I gave her a wink and the corner of my lips lifted in a smile.

"Piston." It was a clear warning, though I thought she was fighting her own grin, so I raised my hands in surrender.

"What? You're a beautiful woman. Besides, I like looking at what belongs to me." I took a cautious step toward her. When she didn't retreat, I took another step until I was standing inches from her. "I like knowing I'm the only man who'll ever see your beautiful body ever again."

She sucked in a breath, color sweeping from her face down her chest to disappear beneath my shirt. Then she cleared her throat, lifting her chin stubbornly. "I assume what you have to tell me has little to do with sex, so can we get to it?"

"Pity," I muttered before reaching for her. I pulled her into my arms, and though she was a little stiff, she soon relaxed a bit. "So," I started. "Giovanni wants us to go to Salvation's Bane. He wants to get all three clubs involved. He's actually going to meet us there."

She started, pulling back far enough to look up at me with raised pink eyebrows but not stepping out of my embrace completely. "Really?"

"That's what the man said."

"You said Victor is tracking me. Giovanni knows this how?"

"I'll get to that. First, though, I have some things to confess to you. You're going to listen to everything, then we're gonna discuss it. Then, we're gonna get our asses back to Grim Road."

"You said Gio told us to go to Bane."

"I did. But I'm not ready for that, and I want Crush and Byte involved in this."

"What about Wylde? He's just as good and has been helping us already so he knows what to look for."

"Giovanni thinks there's safety in numbers."

Her gaze slid away from me, her brow furrowing in concentration. "You said Victor is tracking me."

"According to Giovanni, yes."

"Again… Giovanni knows this how?" Yeah, this was gonna be bad. The expression on her face said she was angry, but not exactly surprised.

"Don't know how long he's known or how he knows, but that's what the man said, and he refused to elaborate. At least not over the phone."

"I have satphone. Should be secure since it's Gio's."

"Mine is too, baby. He still refused to tell me."

"So you know him too." It wasn't a question.

"I do. He hired me a long time ago. I wouldn't say we were friends, but we're more than acquaintances."

"Hired you to do what?"

"To keep an eye on you."

Chapter Nine

Venus

I felt blood drain from my face, then flush in absolute *fury*. "Keep eye on me."

"Yes."

"How long, Piston?" I clenched my hands into fists, my nails digging into my palms. The pain grounded me as points pierced my flesh.

"Since the day you first met Giovanni."

"*Blyad!*" I shoved away, needing to put space between us. I felt like when I had to get on airplane. Panic seized me, making it hard to breathe. Only this was much, much worse. "Was all this" -- I waved my hand back and forth between us -- "Just so you could stay in my life? Did you think I'd roll over, let you do whatever Giovanni told you to with me? Did you --" I had to gasp for breath and loathed myself for it. This was weakness I could not afford to show. "Was this all honey trap?"

Piston gave a humorless laugh. "Baby, the only person trapped in this relationship is me. I was trapped from the day I first laid eyes on you. Anything I did earlier was more for me than you because I've been in love with you for a fuckin' *decade*."

I gasped in another much-needed breath, not sure if I could believe him, but wanting to with all my heart. And that was a problem. My sisters were only people I could honestly say I loved. Everyone in MCs I worked with I considered mine to protect, but I wasn't certain I could honestly say I loved any of them. Maybe. If push came to shove, though, I could sacrifice them all. *Maybe*. But Piston? I'd gone from him being annoyance to getting used to him. Somewhere along way I'd grown to rely on him. He had my back even if

I felt need to push him away. I knew he wasn't going anywhere so I felt safe doing so. After what he'd done to me few hours before, I realized I might possibly feel more for him than I should. With my stomach rebelling now, I knew I was fucked.

I was in love with Piston. And everything I thought I knew about him was possibly lies.

"Ulyana…" Piston didn't move closer to me, but he was watching me like hawk. Probably afraid I was going to eviscerate him. Or run. While I wanted badly to do former, I was afraid I was going to do latter. And that just pissed me off.

"It was Giovanni, wasn't it? He told you my name." I remembered him using it before and knew something was off.

"He did."

"How much did he tell you about me?"

"He kept the personal stuff to a minimum. Honestly, I don't think he considers anything personal to be important unless it directly affects the situation at hand. If he knew a situation would have an adverse effect on you he wasn't certain you could power through, he'd tell me, but otherwise, the only thing personal I really know is that you had a rough plane ride escaping Victor with Millie and that you have issues flying now."

"So he didn't tell you the reason I ended up in Salvation's Bane."

He narrowed his eyes. "No," he said slowly. "I just assumed he sent you there."

"No." I frowned. "At least, I don't think so. Am starting to wonder." It didn't escape me I was talking through my doubts with Piston when he should be last person I trusted. Had he truly been in shadows all this time?

"OK. Why did you take up with Bane? You made a pretty good impression on Thorn or he wouldn't have patched you in. He's *the* fuckin' hardass in a room full of hardasses, so you have his respect."

"I helped him out of tight spot on ExFil mission. Together we saved his team even if mission got scrubbed."

"Must have been one hell of a save. He basically took you in the same day you came back."

"It was." I looked around, finding my pants and snagging them. "I need to leave."

"Venus, stop." That fucking gruff voice of his was my bane. It had been hard to resist him before, but after we'd had sex, after he'd completely blown my mind, I wanted to obey him. At least, my body did. My mind was screaming and railing at me to bust his balls and leave.

I took a breath. "I don't want to." *Blyat*! I sounded like petulant child.

"We're not done. No matter what you believe my motives are, you know I'll always protect you. You *know* it."

He was right. I did know, but I didn't want to give in too easily. "Just because you've been shadowing me for years doesn't mean I know you as well as you know me. And you've already been lying to me."

"I have never lied to you. I didn't tell you everything about me, but I've never lied to you." His face hardened as he spoke. Clearly, Piston didn't appreciate my accusations.

"So? Tell me now."

"Not a whole lot for me to tell. You came back to the US with your sister. The two of you split up. You ended up with Giovanni. When you did, he pulled me off a security detail he had me on with ExFil and put me on your six, permanently."

"Permanently?" What the hell? "Did he not trust me?"

"Was that when he started supplying you with tech?"

I didn't answer right away. Mainly because it was on tip of my tongue to spill everything, and I wasn't going to do that. Not right away. I tried to fool myself into thinking he could rot in hell before I told him anything, but the fact was, Piston had proven himself to me. I was stubborn, but not so much I wouldn't admit how much help he'd been. Even if I didn't want to admit it. Because I'd also been replaying scene in my head over and over when he'd shoved me aside night Victor had slipped through our fingers.

Victor got away because I'd hesitated to leave Piston in middle of deadly fight. Not because of anything Piston did. Had he not interfered, I might have been killed. Finally I sighed, sitting on edge of bed in nothing but his T-shirt. My pants were bunched in my hand, and I laid them beside me. There was plenty of time to get dressed later and I wasn't drawing more attention to my naked body than I already had.

"Thorn is… family." How to explain this?

"Family how? MC family?"

"No. Is my first cousin. His father's youngest brother is my father."

Piston's eyes narrowed as he put it all together. "Wait. Thorn. Why does this feel like it's more important than you simply being Thorn's cousin?"

I debated my next move. I didn't want to disclose what I'd learned because I didn't want to put any of the people involved on Victor's radar. That meant the fewer people who knew who Thorn was related to and how, the better. Not necessarily because Thorn needed protecting either. Because it meant every foundation of every club I was associated with would be in jeopardy. Especially Bones. If anyone knew secrets kept in that club, it could be used to take ExFil away from Cain and quite possibly land several of Bones in prison. For treason.

"I'm here to help *you*, Venus. Not Giovanni. Not Thorn. Not even myself. I'm the killer who has your back. There is no one I wouldn't destroy to protect you." I saw the truth in his eyes but wasn't ready to give in just yet.

"Why should I believe you?" My voice was barely above whisper.

He didn't hesitate with his answer. "Because you're a woman who trusts her instincts, and you haven't killed me yet."

When his words penetrated, something inside me gave way. Before I realized what I'd done, I threw myself at Piston, wrapping my arms around him and clinging so tightly he probably thought I was trying to kill him by strangulation. Dam I had guarding my emotions disintegrated into nothingness. Everything came rushing out. I sobbed into Piston's chest, clinging to him like I'd never held on to anyone in my life. I couldn't even remember going to my mother for any kind of emotional support. After my father died, I'd been too busy taking care of both Millie and my mother to indulge in grief.

"Shortcake." His soft murmur was right at my ear. He had his arms around me, holding me as tightly as I held him. One hand moved up and down my back before threading through my hair and holding my head against him. "It's all right. Everything's gonna be all right. I swear to you, I'll kill whoever you want me to, just… *please stop*."

Alarm in his voice made me laugh through my tears. Had I ever in my life cried more than few simple tears? "*The* badass in room full of badasses, huh?" I swiped my cheeks and offending moisture. "Yet few tears bother you?"

"With you? Yes. If something is bad enough to bring you to tears, I need to kill it."

I looked up at him and smiled. "Fine. How about you help me kill it? We can do it together."

"Wherever you go, Venus. I'm gonna be with you. Like I said. We're together now. You're my woman. I'm your man. You have my loyalty over anyone else."

Fresh wave of tears flooded my eyes, but I was strangely happy. "Sorry. Don't know what happened."

Piston gave me a strange look. "What happened?"

"The crying," I explained. "I don't cry."

"Ah." He brushed his thumb gently under my eye to catch a teardrop. "I see." He grinned. "You know what happened. I'm your safe place."

I wanted to scoff, to tell him to go fuck himself, but fact was, he was right. "Fine. Don't let it go to head."

Look on his face was positively wicked. "Oh, it'll go to my head all right, baby."

There was no help for it. I laughed and, again, it felt like something unfurled inside my chest. This whole situation was creepy as shit, but I couldn't deny the connection I had with Piston. If I was honest, he'd intrigued me from first moment I saw him. When I'd come to Lemon's aid. It should feel strange knowing he'd been in background of my life ever since I'd come to America, but it was kind of endearing.

"Why did you decide to stop being in shadows? To stay closer to me and even tell everyone you were claiming me?"

"Because the second I saw you with Lemon, watching with pride as she pulled out every single facial piercing of one of those fuckers who'd take her, I was done. I knew there was no way I could sit by and calmly watch while some other bastard in Grim claimed you. Besides, I thought ten years was enough self-torture. Not being near you while having to watch you from a distance, was too fuckin' long. So fuck Giovanni."

That got bark of laughter from me even as my heart swelled. This was what it was like to have companion. Someone to always be in your corner. I felt like I'd just staged successful coup.

"He is ass. Always has been."

"He gets too hard on us, I'll remind him how I was in the room the first time little Suzie hacked him. She'd just turned seventeen. I thought Giovanni was gonna blow a gasket."

Piston moved me so that I straddled him. His shirt rode up my thighs and I whimpered in need when my pussy came into contact with his hardening cock through his pants. He raised eyebrow and corner of his lips raised in cocky smirk.

I rested my hands on his shoulders. His bare chest beckoned me to touch and taste. I wanted to lick him from chest to dick and back. Then start all over.

Piston caught heated look in my eyes, his own gaze darkening with desire. "You keep looking at me like that, Shortcake, and we won't make it outta this compound before I have to fuck you again."

Raspy tone of his voice sent shivers down my

spine. Tension crackled between us, thick and urgent. I leaned closer, my breath hitching as I brushed my lips against his ear. "Who said we were going anywhere before you fucked me again?"

His hands tightened on my hips, pulling me even closer until there was no space left between us. His breath was hot on my neck as he trailed kisses down to my collarbone, each touch igniting sharp lust I knew better than to fight.

My heart raced as I leaned closer, our lips mere inches apart. I could feel heat radiating from his body, engulfing me in haze of warmth and want. It was overwhelming, intoxicating, and for this moment in time, world outside our little bubble ceased to exist.

"Venus," Piston whispered, his hands sliding up my back to draw me even closer. "You make me forget everything else in the world other than finding new and interesting ways of makin' you scream my name."

And then his lips were on mine, urgent and searching. His kiss was anything but gentle, but not the raging dominance I'd needed before. I was under no illusion Piston was making profound statement during our previous encounter. I needed that dominance then. I needed to know man I had allowed into my tight circle of family could handle what I threw at him and stand tall and in control. Well, Piston had done that in spades. Now, he was simply giving me what we both wanted.

His mouth moved with tender ferocity that made every nerve in my body sing. I found myself responding in kind, my hands threading through his hair, pulling him closer. As our kisses deepened, world around us dimmed, sounds and sensations blurring into haze of heated whispers and soft rustling of fabric.

Breaking away for air, Piston's eyes glowed with

raw intensity as he looked at me. "I mean it, Venus. You've turned my world upside down."

I smiled, brushing kiss on his jawline. "You're not standing still in mine either."

The laugh that escaped him was half-humor, half-pained groan as he reached between us to undo his jeans and free his cock. Hard, pulsing length of him sprang free, hitting my clit as it bobbed between us.

Our mouths moved together with ferocity born of raw desire and long-awaited release. Even though he'd taken me to heights I'd never imagined not that long ago, I was back up on edge again, wanting to do swan dive into the madness I knew would surely overtake me when he fucked me. My fingers tangled in his hair, pulling him closer as if I could merge our very souls with this kiss. The way he devoured me felt like vindication of every silent moment he'd spent yearning for me from afar. And yes. I believe everything he'd told me. I also believed he meant it when he'd said he was here for me. Not for Giovanni or anyone else. Piston was silent menace to my flamboyant viciousness.

Piston broke the kiss, his breath ragged as he looked down at me with eyes burning with the same fierce passion fueling my own. "You're mine," he growled, his voice thick with possession and an unspoken promise. "And I'm yours, Venus. No one and nothing else matters."

"I won't deny that. Not ever again."

"Good. Now. I'm not gonna fuck you before I taste what I'm sure will be a very sweet pussy."

His words hit me like electric charge, sending shudder through my body straight to my clit. The air around us thickened with anticipation as he shifted, his movements deliberate and filled with unspoken command I found impossibly arousing.

Gently, he pushed me until I was lying on back on his bed. Texture of sheets against my skin combined with rough, calloused touch of his hands only heightened all sensations already bombarding me. Every touch, every kiss that followed only amplified the lust he built with a simple look.

Piston's hands traced fiery path down my body, igniting sparks wherever they landed. He paused at my thighs, his fingers teasing sensitive skin there before shoving them apart. His nostrils flared as he lowered himself so his shoulders were between my legs.

His hot breath grazed over my sensitive flesh, making me shiver in anticipation. Piston's eyes locked with mine, intense and unyielding, as he watched my reactions closely. With slow, deliberate motions, he extended his tongue and traced the outer edge of my lips. The look in his eyes said he was savoring taste as he went. His movements were practiced and precise, calculated to drive me wild. At least, if they weren't they should have been. Because that's exactly what they did.

I gasped and sharp cry escaped my lips. I arched my back off the bed, urging him to do more. "My clit," I gasped.

"What about your clit, baby? It's wet and swollen." He winked at me as he licked my hot and aching pussy, sucking each lip lightly before taking long, slow lick from my opening to just below aching bud in question.

"Suck it," I hissed. "Lick it."

He complied with smirk, diving deeper, exploring me with fervor that bordered on reverence. The room spun as waves of pleasure cascaded through me, each swipe of his tongue making me whimper and moan in pleasure.

I rocked my hips, meeting his tongue as he lapped at my wet folds like he meant to eat me up. He sucked my clit between his lips, curling two fingers inside me, hitting spots deep within me I'd never known existed. The second he did, I exploded in blistering pleasure.

Piston's movements became frenzied as tremors racked my body, and my pussy clamped down around his fingers. His breathing was deep and even, and every sound I made was met with deep answering grunt from him. Hearing his own grunts and growls escalated my need. He continued his relentless assault, bringing me to brink again with expert flicks and swirls of his tongue coupled with rhythmic thrusting of his fingers.

Breathless and delirious from waves of ecstasy, I managed to pull him up to me, our lips crashing together in messy, desperate kiss. I could taste myself on him, and it only served to fuel fire burning within me. Every touch was electric, every glance between us laden with unspoken promises of more.

Piston reached between us and guided his cock inside my pussy. Then he started hard, driving rhythm I couldn't keep up with. All I could do was hold on. So I dug my nails into his ass and spurred him on best I could. "Fuck!" He threw his head back as I squeezed flesh of his butt. "Mother fuck!"

"Fuck me, Piston." I wanted words to come out as order, but was very afraid they were a plea.

"Ain't gonna last long. Too fuckin' good. Too motherfucking good!" His cock pulsed inside me and with one ferocious, brutal yell, Piston put his cum deep inside me.

Chapter Ten

Piston

I held Venus close. After we were both spent, and she lay with her head on my chest, I took up the earlier conversation.

"You good, baby?"

"Better than good." Her contented purr was music to my ears. I chuckled lightly as I sifted my fingers through her hair.

"That's what I want to hear." I kissed the top of her head. "Much as I hate to ruin the moment, we still have some things to discuss before we decide where we're going and what we're gonna do."

She took in a deep breath before letting it out slowly. "Giovanni hired me to work at Argent. Not in company itself, but off books kind of thing. I told him I needed to stay hidden, and he had no problem with that arrangement. I helped field test weapons for him. I did better than anyone else he had working for him, taking his weapons to very limit of what they could do without hesitation."

I had to bite back a growl at that. "Sounds dangerous."

She shrugged. "Was. I was there for only couple of months before he sent me off to test his latest gadget. But he wanted me to work with it in real world. Away from his testing ground. He'd already had it tested and adjusted and adjusted some more. Besides, it was really more of spy tool than weapon."

"Your eyes," I said. "The contacts."

She grinned up at me. "You knew about those?" Though she didn't seem surprised, I thought she might be.

"I know some. Not all. Have a feelin' you were

havin' trouble with them when we found Victor that first time."

"Contacts enhance my vision. Much like camera. I can zoom in or out. Isolate subject and zoom in. Some of it is through contacts themselves, some I have to do from app on my phone. Gio did update to add infrared vision. He had only uploaded new version with upgrades few days before. My eyes hadn't had time to adjust to new band of light I was seeing. Gave me headache. Had trouble getting my bearings. Kind of made me want to puke."

"Right. Also, about your contacts."

When I didn't continue immediately, she frowned. "What about them?"

"Giovanni can… well, see through your eyes, for lack of a better description."

She pushed up on one arm to look at me in confusion. "What do you mean?" She swallowed and I knew I was right. This wasn't going to go well.

"He can see what you see. I guess they're like little cameras. He can not only get a real-time feed any time you're wearing them, he can track you through them."

She gave an exasperated grunt before laying her head back on my chest and settling back down. "If that bastard was looking at me when I was naked and standing in front of mirror, I may kill him."

"You decide that's what you want to do, I'll go in first and clear the way for you to play as long as you like, baby." That got another chuckle from her before she got serious again.

"You said Victor has been tracking me and that Giovanni knows."

"Yes. He said there's a tracking device in your shoulder. I don't know which one."

"How long has he known this?"

"It's the reason he sent you to ExFil. Before you met Thorn."

"Fucking bastard," she muttered. "The mission with ExFil was where he sent me to test fucking contacts." She closed her eyes. Her nails dug into my side where she clung to me. In all fairness, I was holding her just as close. The claws coming out -- literally -- were a reflex. Yeah. Venus was good and pissed. Instead of expressing her anger, she changed the subject.

"My father was Thorn's oldest brother. I told you that. Thorn doesn't know."

"Yeah. I remember. It's got me thinking, though. There's more there I should know but can't put my finger on what it is."

"Thorn's uncle was Mama's oldest brother."

OK. That threw me. "Mama? From Bones MC? Mama and Pops?"

"Yes. I'm Mama's niece."

"Does she know?"

Venus shook her head. "Thought about trying to tell her. When she came to Salvation's Bane. She came to care for Thorn's woman, Mariana, after she'd been hurt. Father of her unborn child beat her nearly to death. He did kill baby she carried. Mama came to help her heal."

"Why didn't you?"

"Didn't seem like right time. Everyone, especially Mama, had so many things to take care of and my long-lost family didn't seem important in grand scheme of things. After that, decided it didn't matter. Bane was my home."

"Then why have you been wandering from club to club?"

"Wouldn't say wandering. I go where I'm needed. Millie belongs to Bones and I have to see my sister. I came to Grim because I saw Lemon get taken. Little spitfire reminded me so much of Millie I wanted to help guide her and help her reach her full potential. Because of my friendship with Lemon, I met Apple and Danica which led me to Iron Tzars. Now I have people there I want to watch out for. Never really thought of myself as having family other than Millie before Thorn let me into Bane. Now, they're all my family."

"What about Black Reign and El Diablo?"

She seemed to think about that one a moment. "I did something to Lyric I'll never be able to make up for." The softness in her voice, the way she had to clear her throat after she spoke, both told me something had happened that rattled her. Though I'd watched Venus closely once she settled into Salvation's Bane, I hadn't done more than watch from a distance for years. I didn't pry into club business because I didn't care. The only thing I did was shadow Venus.

"What happened, Venus? Whatever it is clearly upset you."

"When Lyric first came to Bane, she'd been held by a splinter of this very club. Kiss of Death was trying to set up business in Palm Beach and had opened up a club called The Dark. Bane burnt it to the ground, but president of Kiss of Death, wonderful person called Rat Man" -- Venus actually rolled her eyes --"had spies in Bane, planting bugs and gathering information. Lyric was one he sent to us. Was Rat Man's bad luck he sent her on day Rycks happened to be visiting us."

"I take it he knew her?"

"Had kid with her, though he didn't know it at time. We thought Lyric was spy Rat Man had sent to

Bane. He had, but she wasn't mole we were looking for. Process for finding out those things is never pleasant. You know this."

"Can't afford to have a nice little chat sometimes."

"*Da*. Anyway, with her being woman, task fell to me for interrogation."

"Ouch." 'Cause interrogation and nice never went together in the same sentence.

"*Da*. I hit her couple of times. Was ready to cut her." She held up a hand, displaying those fucking daggers she had for nails. "Rycks intervened, claimed her in front of club to prevent torture I was getting ready to dish out, and got everything out of her. What impressed me most about Lyric was how she responded to everything."

"Oh? What happened?"

"She took everything I dished out, was prepared to take even more, and she didn't protest or beg or even tell us about her child because she believed doing so would put little Bella's life in danger. She kept silent. I hit her face. Twice. And for first time in my life it felt like I was doing exact wrong thing. I didn't know it at time, but when I found out…"

"So you feel like you owe her."

"I do. I protected her afterward. When Rycks went to get Bella and bring her home. I protected them both. In process we found out real mole was one of Bane's club girls."

"Well, Lyric is Rycks' old lady now, so I'm assuming everything worked out."

"*Da*. Still didn't make me feel better. So I started looking out for both Lyric and Bella. Then I found out Celeste was granddaughter of Mama and Pops. Daughter of their only son. That made her my family too, so she and her daughter, Holly, had to be protected. Holly was vulnerable because she had a childhood cancer, but is in remission now. Her oncologist is Blade from Bane. So, you see? Domino effect, and now I have people I need to protect in more clubs than I can keep up with." She sounded disgruntled, but one look at her face showed the affection she felt for every person she'd mentioned. "Since I'm around everyone everywhere now, I have more people I care about than I ever have in my entire life. Exhausting, trying to do it all."

"But you do."

She shrugged. "As much as I can."

"Giovanni thinks he needs to call in all hands on this one. I think I said he's meeting us at Bane. He says he's calling in everyone else, even Black Reign."

"Which means, he suspects Victor is either in or around Palm Beach area."

"Likely."

"He tell you anything more?"

"Only for us to get there. No doubt he'll be there long before we will."

Venus snorted. "Right. Pesky helicopter."

"So the question we need to discuss is simple. Where do you want to go from here?"

"What do you mean?" She braced herself with her arms on my chest, looking up at me questioningly.

"Do you want to go to Bane like Giovanni told us? Or do you want to go someplace else? What do *you* want to do?"

She gave me a startled look. "I didn't realize that was option."

"'Course it is. I happen to think we need to play this according to your instincts. You know Victor better than anyone, even Giovanni. So what do you want to do?"

She looked down, resting her chin on her hands. "I don't know. Since I haven't been able to kill Victor in all these years, my judgment might not be best with regard to him."

"It is. How long have you actively been trying to find and kill him?"

She frowned. "Since we brought Katya to States."

"So a few years, but not the whole decade."

"At first, I was just glad to be away. I was more concerned with how I was going to get to Katya and bring her home than I was with killing Victor. He moved her around a lot before settling her back in his mansion. Probably because he knew I'd be looking for her. I'd never leave my sister behind if I could, but I had second sister to protect as well." She sniffled. "Should have listened to Millie back then. We should have gone back for her and Mama."

"I assume you're meaning your mother? Not Mama and Pops."

"*Da*. Everything went to shit when we escaped. Mama refused to leave and Katya was only five. Risk was too great to have more than Victor's goons after us because he would absolutely call it kidnapping and bring to bear full force of FSB. I was still young and not too ashamed to admit, now, I was terrified of them coming after us. I thought I knew best, you know, because I had all that training from FSB. Truth was, I knew if they came after us, Millie would die. Almost did anyway with only Victor's goons after us."

"But you didn't. Then you made it to America."

"FSB had plans for me to infiltrate Argent Tech. They wanted better weapons and thought I could get schematics for whatever they wanted. Since I was on my own, I thought perhaps Argent was good way to keep eye on FSB infiltration of company. I was straightforward with Alexi Petrov when I interviewed with him."

"Didn't realize one of the CEOs of the largest tech company in the world did interviews."

"Alexi did. I started off my interview with his HR department by telling them the Russian government was trying to steal their technology. Given who Alexi is -- and I'm not talking about being Argent's CEO -- he sat me down with Azriel and Giovanni for several hours and discussed everything."

"So that's when he found out you were with the FSB before you... defected, for lack of a better word."

"Exactly. Alexi gave me position in Experimental Tech and kept me on his private payroll."

"Which meant your name wasn't in the system. But Victor could still track you."

Venus's expression hardened. "That's something we need to fix before we leave this compound."

"What did you have in mind?" I knew where this was going, and I had to grin. My woman was something else. She was reclaiming her family on her own terms, and I couldn't wait to watch.

"I think is time I introduced myself to Mama as her niece."

Chapter Eleven

Venus

After briefing Bohannon on situation, Piston called Ice at Bones MC. Ice was Cain's son. He and his brother, Cyclone, had taken over the club when Cain had decided to concentrate on running ExFil. Ice had spoken with Mama, and she and Pops had agreed to come to Kiss of Death and take tracker out of my shoulder. Every tech guy in all five clubs was headed in our direction to study chip in every way they could before Mama took it out. We didn't tell Gio. Giovanni Romano could suck my dick.

I'd taken my contacts out with no intention of ever wearing them again. I'd get new ones of no-tech variety. For now, especially since I needed to throw everyone off, I decided to get rid of pink and adopt less noticeable look. And, *da*. It took day and a half to strip my hair of all dye. I finally gave up and matched my hair color as best I could with yet another product. Came close to shaving it all off, but Piston helped me after that. Apparently, man likes how my hair tickles his balls when I ride him. Who knew?

At end of second day, everyone was in place with proper equipment and stood around me with scanners and computers and other gizmos and gadgets. I might use some of Giovanni's tech, but tech savvy I was not. Not only had club officers showed up, but Suzie and Zora as well. Suzie's husband, Stunner, was Bones MC's new enforcer while Zora was Data's wife.

Of all people working on this, I thought I trusted Suzie most. Not because she was more trustworthy or anything -- she was only one, other than Alexi's wife, Merrily, who had ever bested Giovanni. Merrily had done it right under his nose, while bastard had been actively trying to keep her out.

Suzie had done it for fun.

"It looks pretty straightforward." Byte pushed his glasses up his nose as he stared at computer screen while Crush waved some kind of wand over my shoulder. "Kinda old and not terribly sophisticated. I'm not seeing anything dangerous." They'd quickly confirmed what I suspected and found the chip in my left arm. It was small and not very noticeable, but once I knew about tracker, I knew where it had to be. Just to be sure, they'd scanned my whole body, including CT imaging Mama had managed to have taken at a friend's clinic. I hadn't yet told her who I was, but once all pink was gone, it was painfully obvious we were related.

"I agree." Suzie had been pushed by Giovanni to do her graduate work at MIT. After a couple hitches involving a hit put on her and Stunner by a jealous crazy student, she'd graduated with honors and promptly went to work for Giovanni. Being Cain's daughter, she knew how to keep a secret, even from Giovanni Romano. She glanced up at Mama. "The battery in the chip should be about halfway through its lifespan or less, if you have the timeline right. Still shouldn't be hard to remove and dispose of however you see fit."

"Will it still work once it's out of her body?" Piston hadn't spoken much while I was poked and prodded, but he never once left my side. Now that they were close to making decision whether or not to go ahead with removal, he was hovering and asking questions.

"As long as it's not damaged, yes." Suzie gave me a small but friendly smile.

"Good," was all Piston offered.

After that, Mama took me to exam room. Bohannon's club doc had a small office set up for routine injuries, but Mama was going to remove tracker once tech guys gave go ahead. Now, I waited with Piston while Mama got prepped.

"I swear to God, Jo, it's like lookin' at you when we first met." Pops scrubbed a hand over his face, shaking his head slightly like he couldn't believe what he was seeing. He didn't even try to hide what he was thinking.

Mama was different. Mama had studied me covertly for the first day, staying in background while guys took all kinds of digital images. I had no idea exactly what they were talking about or meaning of all terms and phrases, because they weren't important to me. The only thing I wanted to know was how difficult would it be to remove and how much down time I would need.

"Who are you, girl?" Mama marched up to me, demanding an answer. "You're too old to be Kurt's child and all siblings are accounted for except Logan."

"My mother knew him as Demetri Volkov. But his real name was Logan Peyton." I watched Mama carefully, needing to know what the other woman was thinking. She was expert at hiding her emotions.

"Logan. Peyton. My brother, Logan." She tilted her head at me, taking a slow step toward me. I was about an inch taller than Mama was, but I wasn't fool enough to think I could take her easily in fight. Yes, I'd come out on top, but only if I respected her abilities enough to not think of her as a woman in her seventies, and look at her as deadly warrior she was. Not doing so would definitely get me killed.

"*Da*," I answered softly.

"How did you know?" This time, it was Pops who asked the question. "His real name. And how did you put him and Mama together?"

"Because Victor is one who blew his cover." I never imagined how hard it would be to acknowledge this out loud. "I... I was there when they killed him." Even after so many years, I could still feel the horror and terror and grief and loss of that day. I hadn't been a child, but I wasn't yet an adult either. "Victor gave his real name and told everyone he worked for United States and executed him on spot." Mama's expression didn't change.

I blinked rapidly to get emotions under control when I'd never had difficulty with not showing my feelings before. "Anyway, when Victor sent me off to FSB, I put what they taught me to good use. I looked into names of both Logan Peyton and Demetri Volkov. According to their records, Peyton was a double agent undercover as Demetri Volkov. When Victor made our mother his wife, he destroyed everything associated with Logan." I cleared my throat and, with shaking hands, pulled photo from my vest pocket and handed it to Mama. "That picture was taken two days before Victor killed my father." I pointed to photo Mama now held but hadn't looked at. "That is Demetri Volkov. The child is me."

Mama studied image. Holding it close to really look at it. When she met my gaze again, her expression gave nothing away. "What else?"

"I know you're Josephine Peyton. And you're supposed to be dead along with Michael Wilbanks. I also know CIA would lay waste to Bones if they knew you were still alive and Bones had been hiding you all this time."

"What do you want from this, Venus?" Mama

was as direct as I'd always known her to be.

"I want Godforsaken chip out of my fuckin' shoulder. After that, I want to kill Victor."

"And us?" She raised an eyebrow.

This was it. The moment Mama decided my worth. Never in my life had I expected someone's opinion of me would matter so much. Piston's opinion mattered, but I knew where I stood with him. He'd been the one to pursue me. Not the other way around like I was doing with Mama. I could have kept all this from her and remained in background, content to watch from afar. But that's not what I wanted.

"I want to claim my family."

Mama smiled then, the sight warm and welcoming. "My dear Venus, you have always been family." She stepped toward me and laid her palm on my cheek. "The only thing this changes now is you don't get to go your own way. Even though more than one of us has been concerned you're too much of a loner, we've all given you space because Thorn said that's what you preferred. Now you don't get that luxury. You tell us what you need. We make it happen."

"I swear to fucking God, if you make me cry, I'm disowning you." I muttered. "I haven't cried since I was child until couple of days ago. Now I can't seem to stop with that nonsense."

Mama smiled. "Doesn't matter if you do or not. I'm not disowning you. Ever. Now. Come here. Your Aunt Jo needs a hug from one of her two favorite nieces."

Yeah. I was going to have to eat my words, because I cried like little baby as I clung to Mama. I knew I needed to give Millie heads-up, but it would also be kind of fun to see what happened if I let Mama and Pops blindside her. Yeah. I was bitch. Didn't mean it wouldn't be fun to watch. Besides, Millie would get over it.

When Mama finally let me go, I was relieved when she had tears in her own eyes. I supposed if Mama could have moment, so could I. We both laughed.

"I always thought there was something familiar about you but could never put my finger on it." The older woman now had both my hands in hers, petting me like she might child. I thought she might be trying to reassure me, like she knew how uncomfortable the idea of permanent family had been to me. I had to smile because, for first time since I'd left Russia, I thought of family not with dread or even longing. There was only warmth and fullness in my heart I had no hope of describing or understanding. All I knew was I'd do anything to protect this family. I also realized that I'd had this same family for several years and hadn't acknowledged it.

"It was all the pink," I said with chuckle. "I told myself disguise was necessary, but I think it was excuse to hide."

"So? Pops and I have been hidden for decades. We do what we must to survive and to protect those we love." She finally let me go. "Now. Taking out his chip should be straightforward. It's not too deep under the skin. I'll give you a local. If I have to go deeper than it looks, we'll talk about something a little stronger."

"Sounds good."

Chapter Twelve

Piston

Mama had no trouble removing the tracking chip. The only question was what to do with it. Which, I had a thought.

"I don't want Giovanni involved in this," Venus said, pacing back and forth while I sat sprawled on the couch watching her.

She was dressed in jeans that molded her hips and thighs lovingly. Not pink. Just a standard blue denim. The top she wore was a camisole tank in black that showed tantalizing glimpses of her toned abdomen when she moved her arms. Pale blonde locks down to her waist replaced the pink, and her eyes were now a clear, pale blue like a summer sky. Yeah. I was one lucky bastard to have this woman in my bed. Even luckier for her to be mine and no one else's.

"So? Don't involve him. He's been blowing up my phone wondering why we haven't left, by the way."

"What did you tell him?"

"That we needed to rest after that last hunt before we made a thirteen-hour ride."

"He buy it?"

I shrugged. "Hard to say, but if I were guessing, I'd say no." It was hard to keep the grin off my face. "I didn't really try too hard to convince him. Bastard thinks he rules the world but I think he's gettin' the idea I simply don't give a fuck."

She stopped then, giving me a brilliant smile. "Good. I like that."

"What do you want to do?"

She moved to me, stripping off her shirt and tossing it to the couch. "There's loaded question if I ever heard one." Her jeans and panties followed her shirt before she straddled me, her knees on either side of my hips, naked as the day she was born.

I grinned up at her as she reached for my shirt, tugging it off me and tossing it next to us with her own clothing. "I suppose it is." I rested my hands on her silky thighs. The muscles playing beneath her skin was sexy as shit. All of Venus was sexy. Battle scars marred the perfection of her skin, but instead of making me furious like I thought it should, the reminder of her prowess in battle only filled me with pride.

She reached between us to unfasten my pants, and I shifted to allow her easier access. When my cock sprang free, I couldn't help but groan. As much as I'd been in control the first time I fucked her, she'd made up for it since. I didn't think she minded that I didn't try to dominate her again, though. Unless I was greatly mistaken, my little shortcake was having fun. I knew from watching her all these years that she rarely had sex with a partner. Anything she needed to take care of, she did herself. I thought maybe she was enjoying just being with me. It was telling that she'd never liked making herself findable enough to fuck someone before, yet with me she didn't even try to stop herself. That told me she really did trust me.

Venus leaned in close, her breath hot against my ear. "We have work to do, but it can wait," she whispered seductively. "At least, for little while."

I chuckled. "Baby, ain't nothin' little about me. Least of all anything to do with what we're about to do here."

Her lips traced a path along my jawline as I wrapped my arms around her, pulling her closer. "Now, there's something I'll never dispute, Piston."

She kissed me then, brushing her lips lightly

against mine in a tantalizing kiss that promised much more. The heat of her body pressed against mine sent shivers of anticipation racing through me. "I want you," she whispered against my lips. "Now that I've had you, I can't seem to get enough." She sounded almost helpless, like she might not be happy about admitting she what she wanted but was surrendering to it nonetheless.

Her hands roamed across my chest, fingers tracing the tattoos and muscles as if memorizing every detail. I nodded, lost for a moment in the depths of her eyes, so clear and intense. "Yeah," I managed to say. "I can't get enough of you either, and I'll be Goddamned if I'll apologize for it."

She grinned up at me. "At least I'm not only one."

"Oh no, baby. You definitely ain't the only one. I could spend every day for the rest of my life worshiping your beautiful body and it still wouldn't be enough."

Her expression softened, and she leaned forward to capture my lips, tangling her hands in my hair, pulling me closer. Venus deepened her kiss as our bare skin slid against each other, igniting a fire inside me I was sure could burn down worlds. Our breaths mingled, quick and ragged, as the room filled with the sounds of our urgent lust.

Breaking away from the kiss for a moment, Venus looked into my eyes with a fierce determination. "When we leave here, we're not coming home until Victor is dead," she said, her voice thick with emotion. "He absolutely will not touch my family." Her eyes glistened and I knew she was feeling the fear that Victor was ready to come after her family to retrieve his. He wanted Katya, and if he knew how deep Venus was in with all these clubs, he would be merciless in his attack.

I'd seen the warrior inside Venus on many occasions over the years. Sure, I had only recently been by her side, but this was Venus on a whole other level. Where before she'd killed because she thought it was the best or was the path of least resistance, now, it was personal. She wanted Victor to die by her hand. She would want to look into his eyes as he took his last breath and know with absolute certainty the son of a bitch was dead.

I should have made her take a step back. I should be trying to calm her down and make sure her head was in the right place before we went on this hunt, but I'd be Goddamned if this single-minded viciousness didn't turn me the fuck on.

"No. He won't. He's going to die like the fucking vermin he is."

Venus shifted her hips and the head of my cock kissed her entrance. I thrust up as she sat back, and I was inside her balls deep.

Our lovemaking was fierce. Venus rode me with wild abandon, throwing her head back and embracing the moment. Watching the ecstasy on her face was the most fascinating sight I'd ever enjoyed.

She moved up and down, bracing her hands on my shoulders as her hips snapped front to back in a splendid dance. I let myself be happily swept along.

With a cry, she arched her back, screaming as she orgasmed around my cock. I gasped, unable to hold back my own release. I gripped her hips and thrust upward, filling her with my cum until she collapsed over me, her body limp where she straddled me.

I wrapped my arms around her, holding her as tight as I could, needing the connection with her. I'd always need this. Even if I couldn't fuck her, I'd always want my bare body pressed against hers.

Neither of us moved other than to just fucking breathe. It was a short encounter, but all the sweeter because she'd started it and taken what she wanted. She'd given me so much these last few days. More than I'd ever thought she would. She'd given me... *everything*.

I snagged a blanket from the back of the couch and draped it around Venus. It was a long time before either of us moved after that. When she finally raised her head, she smiled down into my rapt gaze. This was Ulyana the woman. Not Venus the warrior. And I was completely and utterly in love with both.

"Much as I'd prefer to stay here with you the rest of the week, we need to finish this. What's our next move?"

The second the words were out of my mouth, my phone buzzed. I reached for it where it lay on the couch beside me and glanced at the screen. I turned it around so Venus could see the name.

"Giovanni." She chuckled. "Wonder what he wants?"

"Probably wondering if we've left yet."

"Well, I can answer that question for him." She took the phone from me and answered it. *"What?"*

* * *

Venus

There was a short pause. "Venus? Why haven't you guys left yet? Did Piston not explain what you needed to do?"

"He did. I chose to ignore you."

"Venus, now's not the time. Victor wants Katya back. He's coming for you."

"I'm aware. I also have plan and it does not involve going back to Palm Beach."

"You can't take him on yourself. He will kill you." Giovanni sounded sure of himself, and I knew he wasn't wrong. Victor was very dangerous man. What both men failed to understand was I was even more dangerous.

"I have no intention of taking him on alone."

"Tell me what you're going to do."

"I'm going to invite Victor to dinner."

As I knew it would, that got Giovanni to shut up. For a brief moment at least. "I... don't understand." He spoke slowly. I could practically the look of utter confusion on his face.

"Dinner? Evening meal? Ring a bell?"

"I know what dinner is," he snapped.

"Good. Should alleviate confusion. I'm assuming you're in Palm Beach now?"

"I am. At the Bane compound. You know. Where you're supposed to be headed."

"If you'd wanted me there so fast, perhaps you should have picked me up in chopper you flew down on?"

"I was in Miami, Venus. Christ!"

"Good. Stay put. Will call you with instructions." Before he could respond with what I'm sure would be scathing commentary, I ended the call. "This should be fun."

"Sounds like you have a plan." Piston grinned up at me. He was still inside me and his cock was getting hard again. I had to smile. I never thought I'd enjoy sex with another person as much as I did with Piston. It all had to do with trust, too. I'd never trusted anyone enough to let my guard down and enjoy the moment. It wasn't that way with Piston.

"Before we do anything else, I want to know something."

"Anything, Shortcake. Name it."

"What's your real name?"

He barked out a laugh. "Yeah, I can see how that would be something you'd want to know. But honestly, Piston is my name. Only one I've ever had."

I jerked back a little. "What?"

"Yeah. I was an orphan. Don't remember my parents. Lived in a group home my whole life. Everyone there called me Piston. No idea why, and I really don't care. It's who I am. They gave me the last name Brown but I have no idea if that's what it always was or not. I'm guessing not."

I gave him a solemn look. "Piston it is, then."

"Can I ask you a question?"

"Of course."

"How'd you get the name Venus?"

"Was given to me by FSB handler. My code name. They stripped away our identities when we first entered academy. They trained us in combat and all other kinds of battle and spy skills, but academy was more about brainwashing than anything else. When I made it to US, I decided to keep name. Silly risk, I guess, but after Millie took off, it was all I had familiar to me." It was hard to admit how weak I sounded, but I didn't seem to have a filter where Piston was concerned.

I thought about what to tell him next but knew there was no way I could keep it from him. "There's something else."

"What is it, baby?" He leaned in to kiss my lips softly, lingering precious moments before pulling back and stroking my cheek with his thumb. "Whatever it is, I promise it's not gonna be as bad as the look on your face thinks it will be."

I had to give him a weak chuckle at that. Because, it was big deal to me. Had always been big deal. I took a breath. "I can't have children." He stared at me, still stroking my cheek but said nothing, like he was waiting for something. So I added, "Ever. At all."

He frowned, a confused look on his face. "OK. Is that it?" He wasn't making light of situation; instead, he looked confused.

"Isn't that enough?" I snapped, my reply sharper than I intended. Closing my eyes I took a deep breath. "Was one of first things they did to me when I went to academy."

"I see. Makes sense even if it is barbaric." He leaned in again to kiss me, but I moved back.

"Why would you say it makes sense?"

"They had no intention of you leaving their service, did they?"

"Not in program I was in," I muttered.

"No kids, no distractions. Nothing would be more important to you than the task at hand."

"Oh." I slumped, allowing him to pull me close once more. This time, I let him kiss me. Mainly because I needed intimate contact with him. "Sorry. Thinking about that time in my life makes me feel weak and defenseless. No matter how many ways I was taught to kill and torture, I always felt powerless. FSB had complete control."

Piston cupped my face in both of his hands. "Until you took back control. You left them."

"And I've been in hiding ever since."

"Hiding in plain sight isn't an easy task. Considering how long you've lived in the States and not had someone from that agency kill you is a testament to how good you are at what you do."

I had to smile. This man…

"I hadn't thought about it that way."

"Because you're out of sorts. I threw you a curve ball and you're adapting."

"You?" That wasn't what I was expecting him to say. "Why would you say that?"

He grinned softly at me. "You love me."

"So?"

"Other than your sisters, how many people in this world will you admit to loving?"

I started to respond with how much I cared about people in my club, but I realized he was right. "It's not that I don't love anyone," I muttered.

"Not at all. But I forced you to admit to yourself you didn't just care about me, but you love me."

"Arrogant man." But I felt smile tugging at my lips.

"You love my arrogance." He wasn't wrong. "So, what's your plan? How do you want to work this?"

I stared at him several seconds, my mind working through a few possible solutions. "I'm going to call him. If everything goes well, Victor will come to me. Then I'm going to kill him."

Chapter Thirteen

Venus

"Why the fuck did no one think to call this bastard before now?" Ripper, the tech guy for Salvation's Bane, grumbled as he rattled off Victor Zaitsev's phone number. Though I hadn't wanted to involve Giovanni out of spite, I was smart enough to know we'd need his help. He was at Bane. I knew Ripper would stand up to the man if he tried to take over. Other clubs' tech people would too, but Ripper could be special kind of scary if he wanted to be.

"I never wanted to call him before now," I said, waving off Ripper's blunt and disgruntled question. I had to grin at expression on his face during video call. The man was always sour on the outside, but I saw the way he treated Emmanuell, his woman and daughters. Man was big softie. "Now I do."

"Keep him talking as long as you can." Giovanni moved into the camera view. "He has a secure phone, but me and Ripper together should be able to find his location, then hack into the security system. It's not going to be a simple, straightforward job though, so keep the call active."

Ripper snorted, rolling his eyes and giving the other man an impatient look. "It'll be more than just me and you, scooter." Apparently, Giovanni was getting on Ripper's nerves as well. "Venus, every single person with technical and advanced computer skills in every one of our clubs is networked and working on this. I'll let you know when we've got him pinned. When we're done, we'll have access to every fuckin' thing the man owns connected to any kind of network. Including his ride." Ripper's grin was positively evil. "You get him in any kind of self-driving vehicle, and this whole thing just got way the fuck more simple."

I raised my eyebrows at that. "Seriously?"

"Oh, yeah. I can lock him in and drive him anywhere you want him to go. All from the comfort of my gaming chair."

"Assuming he has a self-driving vehicle," Giovanni qualified.

Ripper gave Gio side-eye. "Because it's questionable whether or not one of the richest men in Europe has a self-driving car, or that he'd prefer to drive himself when Venus baits him into meeting her?" I had to bite my lip to keep from smiling. Luckily, Giovanni was too busy blustering to notice.

"Bastard," Gio muttered.

"All right." Ripper sat up straighter and cracked his knuckles before starting to work. "I have a secure video conference with each club's command center. Bones, Tzars, Bane, Grim, and Black Reign. We're live."

"Do we know where he is now?" I didn't want to do this in Nashville. Giovanni was right that Bohannon didn't have everything we needed for something like this yet.

"He's in London, Kentucky. Likely on his way to forcibly remove Katya from Bones." Millie had taken responsibility for our half-sister because Katya was more comfortable with her. After our father died and our mother married Victor, Millie had raised Katya practically on her own.

"I don't want him anywhere near Katya," I said immediately. "We need to meet away from Somerset. London is less than hour from Bones compound."

"Do it in Evansville." Sting appeared alongside Wylde on the team conference, leaning over the other man so he was in camera frame.

"You sure?" All the presidents must have been close by because Rocket now came into camera behind Crush. "Grim Road is as private as it gets. Bit far, though."

"I'm sure," Sting said, crossing his arms over his chest. "Bring him here to the barn, Venus. Take as long as you like."

"Appreciate it, Sting," I said, sincerely.

Sting raised his chin, a cocky smirk on his face. "Got purely selfish reasons for the offer, Venus. We'll talk later."

"Good." Ripper waved us on, not inviting Sting to elaborate. "We'll set up a meeting with him in London, then transport him to Iron Tzars once we have him." He did something on his computer before continuing. "As each stage in this takeover is complete, let me know in the chat window. If anyone needs help in their area, communicate that to me in the chat also. Questions?" When there was none, Ripper turned it over to me. "Whenever you're ready, Venus."

I looked at Piston for reassurance. He gave me nod of encouragement and I punched in number, putting call on speaker. Call was answered on second ring.

"*Da?*"

"Victor Zaitsev," I said in a silky purr. "So glad I caught you. I hope I'm interrupting something very important."

There was a pause. "Ulyana?"

"You were expecting someone else?"

"I'd hoped you'd be dead by now." His voice sounded strained, which was good. I wanted him to know what he'd unleashed.

"Hope in one hand, shit in other. See which fills up first."

"*Suka*. What do you want?"

"I want you dead."

"Good luck with that," he snapped. "I will kill you before you even know I'm around."

"Word is you're in US to get Katya back."

"She's my daughter. My property. You took what didn't belong to you and you'll die for it. Give her back to me and I might let you and Millie live."

I bared my teeth on instinct but kept my breathing smooth and even. Last thing I needed was to let Victor know he'd gotten to me. That threat to Millie had been to get reaction from me. I absolutely would not give it to him.

"Millie can take care of herself. I'm calling you now because, for reasons she won't divulge, Katya says she wants to go back with you." A blatant lie, but I knew Victor well enough to know, if I stroked his ego hard enough, he'd fall for any trap I set hook, line, and sinker. He was intelligent, but always thought he was smartest man in room when he was nowhere near.

"Because she knows I can give her whatever she wants. She misses her creature comforts."

"You and I both know you terrorized her. Katya was isolated in what amounted to prison cell when we rescued her from you. Whatever you're holding over her head, don't. You'll only piss me off and that's not something you want to do." Too late, but I wasn't telling him that.

"No. Give me my daughter. She wants to come home. If you love her like you say you do, you'll honor her wishes."

"She is child, Victor. She's scared. If not for her fear, she'd never want to go back with you. I'm asking you to let her go."

"No. Now, we can do this easy or hard way.

Choice is yours."

I'd never wanted to kill someone so badly in my life. Ripper, still in the background but ever alert, started tapping at his keyboard with an increased urgency, the clicks sounding like rapid gunfire. I winced, hoping Victor didn't hear. Piston muted the volume on the conference call before I could indicate he should. Giovanni's face was mask of concentration mixed with determination as he watched on in background.

I let out a slow breath, keeping my voice steady. "Victor, you're not understanding. This isn't negotiation. Is ultimatum. Leave. Katya. Alone."

Victor laughed loudly, his humor laced liberally with disbelief. "You really are full of yourself, aren't you? You've tried several times to take me down and missed, Ulyana. What makes you think anything will change?"

"You can only run for so long. Eventually, I will find you. When I do, I'm going to kill you."

"You're as delusional as you are stupid," he snapped. "Give me Katya and I'll leave you and Millie alone. You can live your life as you wish, not looking over your shoulders anymore."

I didn't respond for a moment, giving the illusion I was thinking when I was really stalling. I glanced at Ripper on video call. He held up one finger, indicating they were close. Moments later he gave me thumbs-up. They were in.

"Fine, Victor. She wants to go with you, I'll bring her to you. But I want your word you won't harm her."

"You're in no position to demand anything, girl." He was angry now. Likely because he knew he was on the verge of getting what he wanted, but thought I was holding back his prize out of spite. "Now, bring her to me. I'll text you a location."

"I don't think so. We meet at time I set and place of my choosing. You will come alone, or I keep Katya with me."

"Time will depend on where. Regardless of what you might think, I can't be everywhere at once."

"Tell me where you are, and I'll choose reasonable place and time."

I thought I heard him growl in frustration, but he said nothing for several seconds. Then, he capitulated. "Fine."

Ripper gave fist pump. I'd led Victor exactly way we wanted him to go. He gave up his location without fight, so we didn't have to show our hand. At this point in time, Victor had no idea we knew exactly where he was.

I gave him address. It was bogus, of course, but I just needed him in vehicle team could control. I knew Victor well enough to know any vehicle he owned would have absolute latest technology. Including self-driving.

When call ended, I heard Wylde in background. "Got that son of a bitch! I'm in his phone and can hear everything he says while he has it on him. He's slumming it at a big-ass estate farm he paid a boatload of money to rent for a few weeks. Private and out of the way. I'm into every smart device on the place's personal network or the local cellular network. His phone is a satphone. He's using a Russian satellite network with that. It's the phone Venus just called. I can hear, see, and control everything around him."

"I've got Trucker and a team on the way to meet him," Ice said in a low voice. When we get there, can you drive his vehicle into the back of the trailer?"

"No sweat. I'm following your team, too. We'll

get him loaded. You get him to Evansville and the party will begin."

"Sorry I'm gonna miss this one, Venus." Lemon grinned at me from where she stood next to Rocket. "I'm there in spirit. Cut off his nuts for me, 'cause if I was there, that's the part I'd take." She gave me a bright smile and a big thumbs-up.

"I will most certainly take care of that for you, little sister." I chuckled.

"OK," Piston said as we ended the connections. "We've got a two-and-a-half-hour ride to the Tzars compound. You ready?"

"I've never been more ready in my life." I wrapped my arms around Piston, resting my head on his shoulder and turning my face up to press my lips to skin of his neck. "Let's go kill son of bitch."

Chapter Fourteen

Piston

Venus was more relaxed than I'd ever seen her. Well, other than after I fucked her into oblivion. We rode side by side to Evansville, her on a bright red Harley instead of her usual pink. I kind of missed the pink.

We rolled into the compound right behind the truck and trailer with Victor Zaitsev inside the back. Venus's smile widened when they opened the back. Sting's men weren't stupid; they'd taken precautions in case the bastard had gotten out of his car and starting shooting at them.

"Do you have any idea who I am?" Victor yelled as he struggled to get free from Atlas and Brick. Once outside the trailer, Atlas zip-tied his hands behind his back and his ankles together, leaving Brick to heave the bastard over his shoulder and drop him into the back of the side-by-side that would take them to the barn the Iron Tzars used as an interrogation room. And to torture when necessary.

Spoiler alert… It was gonna be necessary.

"You're all dead!" Victor spat as they tied him to a chair. His hands were freed only to be zip-tied to the chair arms. They did the same with his feet, securing each ankle to a chair leg.

"Yeah," Sting said with a grin. "Heard that one a couple hundred times. This week."

"Do you have any idea who the fuck I am?"

"Yep," Roman said as he pulled out a rolling cart with all kinds of instruments on it.

"If you let me go now, I'll make sure your families aren't harmed. If you don't, my people will decimate this hick place."

"You're assuming anyone knows where you are," Sting said as he picked up a nail gun. Without warning, he shot a nail into Victor's right hand.

The squeal he got from Victor was a very satisfying sound. I glanced over at Venus. She was smiling from ear to ear, her clear blue eyes dancing with glee.

"That was for threatening our families, no matter how emptily." Sting spoke casually, even as he shot Victor -- in both knees this time. "That was for coming after Katya." He followed up with both shoulders. "That was because you caused Venus a lot of trouble. Do you know how difficult it was for her to get you to come visit us? I'll tell you. Not at all. She made one phone call and had five clubs with more resources than most small countries. A couple hours later, here you are."

By this time, Victor was screaming non-stop. When he finally stopped, sweat saturated his clothing and plastered his hair to his head. Venus had pulled up a chair and casually crossed her legs, swinging the top one up and down. She looked for all the world like she was watching some kind of sporting event. "Perhaps you should ask who Venus is, because clearly you have no clue the type of bear you've been poking."

Roman moved in front of Victor as Sting moved back. "Do you know why you're here, Victor?" The other man just panted. Spit frothed at his mouth and snot dripped from his nose. Tears streamed down his face. I was pretty sure he'd pissed himself. "You're here because Venus says it's time for you to die."

"Please," he begged. "I'll give you anything you want."

"News flash, bro," Wylde said cheerfully as he walked up to Victor, drawing his gun. "You've already given us every fuckin' thing you have. Every dollar, franc, euro, pound, and ruble. I've put in process the liquidation of all your assets and properties. In a couple days, everything will be in bank accounts we control." Wylde casually shot Victor in both feet. "Thanks for the offer, though." Wylde winked at Venus. I would have bared my teeth at the other man, but I knew he was doing it just to get a reaction from me. Fucker loved goading people until they popped. Kinda like his woman's sister. Lemon. The woman wasn't much more than a teenager who was now vice president of Grim Road as well as the president's old lady. Wylde might not have raised Lemon, but he and the young woman were exactly alike.

Victor's screams were constant now, so everyone stood back and waited for him to calm down. All the while, Venus looked like she was having the time of her life, just sitting there watching as the men of Iron Tzars took shots at Victor, all while they gave her every bit of support they would any member of their club.

Finally, Venus stood and walked to the table. She casually picked up the nail gun Sting had started with. She turned it over a couple of times, studying it from different angles. Victor's breathing was coming in gasps, the air wheezing in and out of his lungs in small pants.

She smiled at him. "You seem to be having bad day."

"I'll give you anything, Ulyana. I'll go back to Russia. You'll never see me again."

"Now that I know for fact. After today, I'll never see you again." She pointed the nail gun at Victor but did nothing else. He screamed, then whimpered pitifully. It was easy to tell the second he believed she might not shoot him. When she saw him relax marginally, she aimed at his crotch and pulled the trigger.

I winced. "Jesus," I muttered, though the noise Victor was making probably made it impossible for anyone to hear me. "I thought he squealed like a pig before. This is torture. For me."

Wylde handed me his gun. "I know, right?"

I moved up beside Venus and raised the weapon. I squeezed off a round into first his right elbow, then his left, before handing the gun to Venus.

"Poor little Victor. Are you finally realizing just how fucked you really are?"

"Please..." His pitiful begging might have swayed me if I didn't know how much he deserved everything he was getting.

"You sold me to state government so you'd have an ally on inside of FSB. You were going to do same with Katya. You buy and sell boys and girls as playthings for people who sexually and physically abuse them before killing them. For fun! You are in middle of everything our collective clubs fight against daily. Especially Iron Tzars. They've fought for longer than you've been alive. And you expect we're just going to let you go?"

I raised an eyebrow. Venus was talking like she was part of the Tzars. I glanced at Sting who had a satisfied smirk on his face. Yeah. He heard it too. I knew then I needed to pack my shit. Looked like we were moving to Evansville.

"You can't! Please! Don't!"

Venus cocked the gun and pointed it at Victor's head. "I can. I will." She pulled back the hammer. "I am." Then she shot him in the head.

There was silence in the barn. Blessed silence.

"I'm hungry," Wylde said. "Anyone want a

pizza?"

"Fuck." Mars chuckled. I hadn't really been paying attention to anyone but Victor, but it looked like most of the patched members of the club were here to witness Victor's demise. "That's just wrong, Wylde."

"What? I love pizza!"

"Just for that," Sting said as he tossed a rag to Wylde. "You're on clean-up duty."

"Oh, man…"

Brick clapped the other man on the shoulder. "Good luck, man. Mop's in the corner by the pitchfork."

Wylde looked like a child told to clean up his room or go to bed without supper. "I just wanted something to eat," he muttered. But I noticed the way his lips curled. The man had no reverence whatsoever. Then his smile brightened. "Good thing I have a couple prospects who need to learn how to do this shit."

Venus went to Sting. The two sized each other up for a few seconds before Venus stuck out her hand to him. "I will put in a formal request to patch in with Iron Tzars. I'm not the type of prospect you normally recruit, but I can be asset to you."

Sting grinned. "Come with me."

He took us to Wylde's office where Danica, Wylde's woman, was talking to her sisters. Lemon and Apple were chatting away while Danica smiled and laughed. There were several feeds open on the call, not just the one from Grim Road. It looked like every club in the circle was in on the call. Bones. Salvation's Bane. Black Reign. Grim Road. Even Kiss of Death and the fucking Shadow Demons.

"Hey, guys." Sting said, after the women finished their conversation. "Deed's done. Clean-up's underway."

"Good." Thorn grinned. "Good to see you, Venus. When Giovanni flew in here like a bat outta hell, we were a little worried about you."

"Shut up." Giovanni grumbled. He looked as disgruntled as I'd ever seen the man. It looked almost like the bastard was pouting.

"Hey. It wasn't my fault. I tried to tell you she could handle herself."

"I can't believe you were willing to take that kind of a chance with a member of your own club."

"What kind of chance?" Thorn actually scowled at the other man. Giovanni was with Thorn at the Bane clubhouse, likely in Thorn or Ripper's office.

"Victor Zaitsev isn't the kind of man you fuck around with. He will destroy you and have the backing of the entire Russian government to do it."

"Would have tried." Venus said. "He would have tried to destroy me." She shrugged. "He did try, actually. I'm here. He's not."

"I was just looking out for you, Venus," Giovanni pleaded his case. "That's what I've done since the first day we met you."

"You've looked out for yourself," she countered. "You found out Victor was tracking me, then you sent me off. You know. Away from your precious company and home. News flash! I survived on my own until I found place to call home. I found that with Thorn and Salvation's Bane. And then I met all kinds of other people in clubs who work closely with Bane. I may not have fully appreciated it at time, but in my heart I knew I was never alone."

"For what it's worth, I'm sorry. I should have at least told you. I honestly thought you probably knew."

"Whatever." She pointed a finger at Giovanni's image on the screen. "You're still on my shit list."

Thorn grinned. "I talked to Mama." I had to wonder if the change of subject was intentional. Knowing Thorn, probably.

The smile Venus gave Thorn was tentative, but she didn't demur. "I'm sorry I didn't tell you everything. Just never seemed like right time."

"Doesn't matter because I've always thought of you as family. You've been a wonderful asset to Bane."

"Thanks."

Thorn opened his mouth to say something else, but El Diablo, president of Black Reign MC and former assassin, spoke first. "I never thought I'd see this day, Venus." The enigmatic man had a warm, welcoming smile on his face. "But what we're all about to propose benefits us all and, because it was my idea, I'm butting in to make the proposal myself."

There was a collective groan from the monitor's speakers. El Diablo just smiled even bigger. I didn't know him very well, but I'd heard he'd mellowed somewhat since he and Jezebel married. He mellowed even more when their adopted daughter, Dawn, married Ice, the new president of Bones MC. I'd heard he'd actually said "please" when Dawn had gotten herself in trouble and El Diablo had needed help retrieving her.

"Daddy, you're doing it again." Dawn was beside Ice on the call. "Don't be that guy."

"What guy?" He looked genuinely puzzled, but his wife rolled her eyes.

"Liam, hush. Venus belongs to Bane so let Thorn do his thing."

"Fine. But just so you know, I had rehearsed a whole thing. I'm sure I'd be better at this than Thorn."

To my surprise, Thorn just chuckled. "He's just happy because he's finally going to be able to claim

Venus as one of his club family."

Venus stiffened. "What?"

"What we're all trying to say is, we all want you to patch in. With all our clubs. You and Piston both, if you agree."

"Huh," I said, scrubbing a hand over the back of my neck. "Wasn't expecting that."

"It's a simple thing, Piston," El Diablo said with a wave of his hand. "You both become patched members with all the clubs, and you work on keeping us together. Ambassadors, if you will. We're spread out over the southeastern part of the country, but we can be great assets to each other during times of trouble."

"Times of trouble." Thorn chuckled. "You sound like you have a giant stick up your ass, El Diablo."

That got laughs from everyone. Dawn had her hand over her mouth as she turned her face against Ice's shoulder, her own shoulders shaking as she tried not to laugh. Even Jezebel barked out a laugh before she clapped a hand over her mouth.

"Not cool, Thorn." El Diablo pointed at the screen, like he was going to poke Thorn in the chest.

"As such," Sting said, picked up the narrative. Probably because it had gone way the fuck off course. "We've made you both vests to reflect all our clubs. Even the Shadow Demons, though, I want to point out they aren't technically MC."

"Are too," Giovanni muttered.

"Riding a ninety-two-thousand-dollar Indian Challenger doesn't mean you're an MC, Gio," Thorn said, helpfully. Judging from the look on Giovanni's face, he didn't appreciate it.

"Anyway." Sting chuckled, obviously enjoying the bickering. "Here." He handed us both vests. Mine was the usual black. On the back all six clubs had their patch. The rocker above said, *Southeastern MC Alliance* while the bottom simply said *United States of America*. The front had our usual name designation on one side. The other patch said *Ambassador*.

Venus blinked rapidly as she studied the vest, her lips parted in surprise. She looked up at me helplessly, her eyes glistening with tears I knew she didn't want to shed. Time for me to take over.

"I think I can speak for both of us when I say it will be an honor to serve in this capacity. Thank you."

There was a collective cheer from the speakers. Apparently, each club had assembled everyone for the big announcement. I saw Mama and Pops. Mama looked so proud I thought she might burst. When Venus met her gaze through the monitor, the older woman blew her a kiss. Pops simply smiled and gave Venus a respectful nod.

"Sorry to ruin the party, but I need a shower and some rest. I'm too old for torture and mayhem on little to no sleep." I wanted to get Venus out and in private. Not only would she not appreciate it if she cried in front of everyone, but I wanted some quiet time with my woman.

We said our goodbyes, shook Sting's hand, then accepted keys to a little house the club had designated as ours. It was partially furnished, which was easily remedied. Most importantly, it had a bed someone had already made up with clean sheets. I was only partially exaggerating about being tired.

The second the door to the house was shut and locked, Venus jumped into my arms, kissing me like she meant to devour me. I chuckled and followed her lead. Until I decided I wanted to lead.

As always, the sex was explosive. How the fuck I'd lived my entire adult life and not experienced sex even close to this intense I had no idea. But I knew in my heart it was all Venus, the strong, fierce woman with a vulnerable streak she hid well from everyone but me.

"I know I haven't said it yet. But I want you to know how much I love you, Piston." Her voice was soft in the quiet of our bedroom.

I had to grin. She was such a treasure. "Figured."

She snorted. "Think you are that irresistible, do you?"

"Not at all." I did chuckle then. "You haven't killed me in my sleep yet, so I figured it had to be love."

That got what sounded suspiciously like a giggle from my warrior woman. Not that I'd point it out. I wasn't stupid. "You're not wrong." She shifted so she lifted herself up to look down at me, bracing her arms on my chest. "I do love you, Piston. With all my heart. You've helped me see I have family all around me. With you in the center of my world."

"I love you too, honey. Have for a long fuckin' time. I'll always have your back. No matter what."

"I'll have your back too. Thank you."

"For what?"

"For giving me back my life. I never knew how much I tried to keep myself apart from everyone until you made me see you for what you are. And that's man I always want in my life. That means I risk my heart, I risk it. You're worth the risk."

"It's not a risk, Venus. Because I'll never betray you. I'll never hurt you. If anyone else does, all you have to do is tell me who and they're dead. No questions asked."

She smiled. "Such romantic words."

"More than words, baby. I mean every one of

them."

She settled back with her head on my chest. Then with a deep sigh. She stilled. When I looked down at her, I realized she was asleep and smiled at the trust she showed by that simple act. Venus wasn't a woman to make herself vulnerable intentionally. With me, from the very first time we'd fallen into bed, she'd slept like the dead. Her trust made my heart swell with pride. And love.

Venus. My very own deadly, scary, beautiful love goddess.

Yeah. I was totally putting that on a shirt. If nothing else, it would make her smile. After she threatened to cut my throat. Totally worth it, though. Besides. That was just our version of foreplay.

Mama & Pops (Bones MC Legends 1)
A Bones MC Romance
Marteeka Karland

Somerset, Kentucky. My home. Or it was. Coming back from Nam was a friggin' shock. No one wanted us there, but no one really wants us back here, either. In their eyes, we're all guilty. Guess I feel the same way about them. I don't belong anywhere. Maybe I never really did.

Except with Mama. For me, meeting Mama was like a dime novel. Fell for her almost the moment I laid eyes on her. Knew she'd be mine after our first kiss. Of course, convincing her took a little time. But it's because of Mama I have a home and people I care about now. I may be a badass soldier, but she's the hardest, coldest warrior I ever met. Yet she has more compassion in her than any ten people I know.

This is the story of how Bones MC was born, and why Mama and me keep to the shadows. Since we met, we've always had each other's backs. No one knows all our secrets, not even those closest to us. Other people have come and gone in our lives, but it's always been me and Mama. This is our story.

Chapter One
Sgt. Michael (Mike) Wilbanks
Louisville, Kentucky, 1968

"This right here is some happy horseshit."

I glanced at the woman beside me who spoke in a low, wistful tone. She'd been on the same plane as I had coming from San Francisco. Though the bag she carried had an Army medical insignia, she'd dressed in street clothes. There was a hard look about her that I'd seen many times during my tours in Vietnam. We hadn't spoken during the flight, but she was hard not to notice.

She looked to be in her mid to late twenties, carrying herself with the confidence of a warrior. My eye had been drawn her way automatically from the moment she'd stepped on the plane. I'd pegged her as the most dangerous person on the plane -- other than myself. Looking at her now, I was reevaluating that notion. The woman might be even more dangerous than I was.

"One'd think those people had jobs to go to." I wasn't sure if that was the "happy horseshit" she was referring to, but I chose to make it about the protesters. I'd encountered groups like this in every fucking airport I'd stopped in on my way back. To say I was spoiling for a fight was the understatement of the fucking century.

"One would think." The woman didn't look my way or seem interested in conversation. Instead, she was scanning the crowd. Not like she was looking for someone in particular, though. I'd seen that look many times. She was looking for a threat. *VC on the trail*!

I shook my head, shaking away the memory. The war wasn't over yet, but it was for me. "You expecting trouble?" Her vigilance -- and my own demons -- had my radar pinging.

"Always."

I had travel plans, but there was something about the woman that made me walk beside her through the Louisville terminal instead of making my way to my own gate. She was tall, maybe five-ten, with shoulder-length strawberry-blonde hair. She wore a sleeveless shirt that showed off lean, muscular arms. Everything about her screamed confidence, strength, and control. I'd met a few Army nurses who had similar looks about them, but this woman was different. She carried herself with purpose, her duffle slung over her shoulder like my own. Like she was on a mission and no one was going to stop her, even if she had to kill to get them out of her way. She didn't speak again or acknowledge me, but she didn't tell me to back off, either.

The terminal wasn't particularly crowded, though there might have been a hundred people in the area. All I wanted to do was secure the bike I'd procured the second I'd gotten back to the States and fucking *ride*. I'd been offered a chance to join an MC called Iron Tzars, but I wasn't sure they were really my thing. Their causes were noble and any killing they did wasn't indiscriminate, but I'd had my fill of death in country. Even for those who needed killing.

Boom!

A shot rang out and all around us people screamed, ducking for cover.

Boom!

A nearby window shattered as the round hit, sending glass shattering to the floor and the concrete outside. I scanned the crowd for the shooter before glancing where I knew the woman had stood. Same as me, she was looking around for the shooter. I saw the exact moment she spotted him. Her features hardened and she looked angry as fuck as she squatted next to me, behind the nearby counter. "Fucker's military."

"Can't say I blame him given the reception we got when we landed. Wouldn't be my first choice of things to do, though."

Her gaze went to mine. "You any good in a fight?"

I shrugged. "Good as any, I guess. Ain't armed."

She shook her head. "Me neither."

"Got a plan?" If she didn't, I'd come up with one, but this woman looked like she'd been expecting trouble and knew how to deal with it. If she knew the soldier in question or had known this was going to happen, she'd have a plan. I'd follow her lead until she proved she didn't know what she was doing. One thing I'd learned in Nam was that often it wasn't the most educated man or the highest-ranking officer who could get you out alive.

"He's not aiming at anyone in particular. I'll talk to him. See if I can get him to surrender peacefully. You position yourself behind him and be ready." She gave me a pointed look. "I'll be counting on you to take him down before he shoots me."

"Fuck," I muttered. "Maybe *I* better try to talk to him."

She gave me an exasperated huff. "Do you honestly think I can take him down myself? I'm strong, but he's easily twice my size."

"You ain't makin' this easy, woman."

"What's so fuckin' difficult about it?"

Her scowl was hard enough to trigger my well-trained instincts. I wanted to snap a salute and bark out, *Yes, sir*!

"Be ready. Take him down if he looks like he's gonna shoot me or anyone else." She tilted her head, giving me a puzzled stare. "You ain't got battle fatigue, do you? You don't act like you've had all you can take."

"No. I'm good." I scrubbed a hand over my face. "Just don't like puttin' a woman out front to use as bait. I should be the one takin' the risks."

"Well, I mean, if you want to risk your life when he'll probably be able to shake me off the second I go for him, fine by me. But I trust you in that regard more than you should trust me. The odds of you gettin' killed are way higher than me."

I stared at her until another *boom* went off followed almost immediately by another window shattering. "You're gonna give me all kinds of fuckin' trouble, ain't you?"

She grinned. "Trouble's my middle name. Get in position. I'll wait until you're behind him." She pointed at the barrier next to the stairs and I saw where she meant.

"Yeah, that's where I thought I'd wait. I'll let you know when I'm ready."

We stared at each other hard for a moment before she spoke. "What's your name, soldier?"

"Sergeant Michael Wilbanks. At least, that was my rank when I was discharged."

"Honorable?" She raised an eyebrow.

I rolled my eyes and pointed at my Army issue fatigues. "Of course. Still wearin' the uniform, ain't I? Re-upped after my initial tour. Not this time, though. Had enough of the killin'."

She nodded. "Dr. Josephine Peyton, Captain, US Army. Or I was. You can call me Jo. I got a four-six-one discharge for 'inadequate personality' 'cause I told a general touring our field hospital to suck my dick when he said the men in my ward were sacrificed for the greater good, then couldn't tell me what the fucking greater good was."

I couldn't contain my bark of laughter. "Promise me when this is over, you'll let me take you out on a date."

Josephine smirked. "Well, I guess that depends on whether you're able to take this guy down or not. I won't go out with a pussy."

"That sounds like a challenge."

She shrugged. "If it gets this guy to stop shootin' the place up, take it however you like."

Another *boom* broke the moment. People screamed all around us, but the only person I saw was Jo and her pale blue eyes. Before I could think too much about it, I leaned in and wrapped my hand around the back of her neck, pulling her in for a hard kiss.

At first she stiffened, then seemed to melt into my touch. We crouched there behind a fucking counter. When she gave a soft gasp, I thrust my tongue inside her mouth. I tasted the sweetest woman I'd ever had the pleasure of meeting. She smelled like wild honeysuckle and citrus and I knew I'd never live through another spring without remembering this scent. My cock shot hard and I growled when she whimpered under my touch. Josephine didn't seem like the kind of woman to whimper much, so I hoped I was doing something right. I wasn't sure I'd ever wanted a woman more than I did at that moment. I knew nothing about her other than she had a smart mouth and a keen mind. She'd said she was a doctor, but I knew she was much more. She was a warrior through and through. And I wanted her for my own.

The kiss lasted only a few seconds before I broke it off. She looked adorably dazed, a soft look of pleasure on her face. When she opened her eyes, it took her a brief moment to focus and she almost smiled… Then she scowled again. Seemed to be her default setting. "Do that again without permission and I will fuckin' bury you."

I tried my best not to smirk at her. Not sure I succeeded. Then, with one hard look into her eyes, a promise as well as a warning to be safe, I ran for my cover at the top of the stairs.

Once I was in place, I made eye contact with Jo. She gave me a crisp nod, then moved closer to where the shooter had taken his stance at the top of the stairs. It was eerie how he calmly fired his gun. Round after round. He didn't shout or scream or demand anything, but the report of his shotgun echoed in the vast terminal, speaking volumes for him.

"Hey, soldier!" Jo called to the guy from her cover at the bottom of the stairs. "Hold your fire."

"Ain't takin' orders from no one no more!" the guy screamed in Jo's general direction. He didn't appear to be looking for her so much as he was looking for the next target. A pillar in the middle of the room caught his eye and he fired. Dust and shrapnel exploded around the area, sending the few people hiding behind it screaming and scurrying off to find better cover.

Jo had to yell to be heard over the shouts of people running for their lives. "I know you don't wanna kill no one here. If you've been to 'Nam, I know you've had enough killin'. I sure as fuck have. Come on. I just wanna go home, man. Have a beer. Maybe get laid."

"Ain't been to 'Nam yet, but I ain't goin' back to

base neither."

"No one said you were." He'd stopped firing momentarily, likely to reload. Jo took that opportunity to talk to the guy. "Where you stationed?"

"Fort Knox." The guy's voice was quiet now. I wondered if he was scared to go back or if he was thinking about his buddies. I could see now he was black. Light-skinned, but black just the same.

"Gettin' picked on by white boys who think they're better'n you?"

I hadn't expected Jo to go there, but I'd seen it more times than I cared to admit. Especially with younger soldiers who had no idea what they were getting into when they signed up. We were all warriors, brothers on the battlefield, but in the barracks, prejudice was alive and well. She must have hit the mark because he was silent a long while before speaking again. He didn't start shooting, though.

"Ain't all I thought it was gonna be. My dad was in France during World War II. When the draft started, he said I should join the Navy. Said I wasn't smart enough to go to college so I should go ahead and join the Navy before I got drafted to the Army. Only, the Navy didn't want me on account 'a I didn't get no high school diploma. When the Air Force wouldn't take me neither, I was gonna go on back home, but the guy at the office took me next door and the Army signed me. I didn't want to sign up, but they said I'd have a better chance of gettin' to stay home if I volunteered. I think they tricked me."

"They sendin' your brigade to 'Nam?"

"Yeah. Dad says I ain't smart enough to not get my head shot off." There was a loud sob as the kid broke down. "I don't wanna get my head shot off, lady!"

"I know. How old'er you, honey?"

"Eighteen."

"Joined the second you left school?"

"Yeah. But I didn't want to be in the Army." He sniffed once and I thought the kid was probably crying.

"You don't wanna hurt these people." Jo's voice was calm. She spoke to him like a mother. Firm but loving, like she truly felt sorry for the kid. "Put your gun down and let me take you to the police. You might not have to go to 'Nam, because they'll probably put you in jail, but you'll survive. And if you do it now, voluntarily, you won't hurt anyone and maybe you can get a service lawyer to negotiate a less than honorable discharge so you can go home after you serve your time."

That was promising a little much, but it was possible the military had more important things to worry about than one scared teenager in over his head. The kid stood there with his head down. I could see him where I crouched behind the barrier to the stairs, maybe twenty-five feet away. He had the shotgun in one hand at his side, not like he was ready to start shooting again.

"No. I don't wanna really hurt nobody. Was kinda hopin' what you said'd happen. They'd just kick me out. Maybe put me in jail for a while, then I could go home."

"Put your gun down, honey. Lay it at the top of the stairs and put your hands behind your head. Can you do that?"

It was hard to reconcile the Jo who'd threatened to bury me if I kissed her again without permission to this soft-spoken, motherly woman trying to talk down an airport gunman. My hackles rose when she came out from her hiding spot, her hands up in a non-threatening gesture. I didn't like her being away from cover, so I slowly stepped out into the open, keeping my hands palm up and out to my sides.

"I got a buddy behind you to your left, kid. He ain't gonna hurt you, but he's gonna get your weapon and stay at your side. If you've got any other weapons or ammo, we'd appreciate it if you'd lay them next to your shotgun and back away. Do it slowly so everyone knows you ain't gonna hurt no one."

"Ain't got nothin' else," he said. "Just this one. Ammo's in the bag beside it."

"That's good. Very good. Now, can you put your hands behind your head and take five steps straight backward? My friend Mike's gonna be right with you."

"You ain't gonna shoot me, are you?"

"No, honey," Jo said. "We've both had enough shootin' to last a lifetime."

"I'm right here, buddy," I said, letting the kid know where I was so I didn't startle him. "What's your name?"

He sighed, putting his hands behind his head. "Alex."

"I'm Mike. I ain't gonna hurt you, but I need to come to you and pat you down. That way when the police get up here, they'll know you're not a threat anymore. Will you let me do that?"

The kid looked so defeated I felt sorry for him. I'd seen that look in every new soldier who set foot in my battalion. Fear. Resignation. Everyone knew your life expectancy plummeted the second you got your draft notice. Sounded like this kid was just like all the others.

He didn't give us any trouble after that. Jo climbed the stairs and secured his weapon before approaching us. "Thank you, Alex. It was very brave of you to trust us. Do you want me to call your dad?"

Alex shrugged, shaking his head. "He'll just box my ears. I ain't supposed to do nothin' to get sent up to 'Nam. He said once the war ended, I might have a future if I kept my nose clean. 'Course he don't know we got ordered to ship out."

"Right now, I think he'll tell you the most important thing is that you're alive." Jo smiled at him. Again, it was a kind smile, so at odds with how I'd first pegged her. She said she was a doctor. Maybe this was her bedside manner.

Alex met Jo's gaze with a frightened but grateful one of his own. "I ain't smart, but I know what you done, ma'am. You saved my life."

"I've seen more than enough death to last me a lifetime, honey. Just remember this. Take your punishment like a man, then go home to your family and take care of them."

"I will. Thank you, ma'am." He glanced in my direction before lowering his eyes again. "Sir."

I cringed inwardly, trying not to let Alex see. Last thing I wanted was for him to feel like he'd done something else wrong. I'd feel like I was kicking a fucking puppy.

We waited with Alex until the police had him cuffed. Every time one of them would get a little rougher than Jo thought strictly necessary, she'd calmly say, "That's enough. He's going peacefully." When one of them called Alex a yellow-bellied nigger, Jo stepped up to him and grabbed him by the scruff of the neck and got right up in his face. "You say one more word to that kid tryin' to provoke him, and I'll cut off your nuts. Then I'll take my jail time with a fuckin' smile. I may be in prison for a while, but you'll be minus your balls. *Forever*. Get me?"

Surprisingly, the officer backed down. Probably because this was a completely different Jo than the woman who'd been so kind with Alex. She also looked scary as fuck. Even more so than when I first pegged her on the plane.

For his part, the boy looked startled, like he hadn't expected anyone to take up for him. As the police led him down the stairs, Alex turned his head over his shoulder to look at us.

"Kid's gonna be lucky to survive the next few days. If his CO will get him back to Fort Knox to await trial, he might have a chance." She spoke absently. I could almost see the wheels turning in her head.

"What'er we gonna do?" I asked. Because I just knew Jo wouldn't let this go.

"Nothin'. Ain't my fuckin' problem." She snarled her words a little too harshly to be believed.

"Nope. It ain't." I had to bite back a smile. I had the feeling the next few days were going to be interesting.

Chapter Two
Dr. Josephine (Jo) Peyton
Captain, US Army (Mama Jo)

The kid -- Alex -- did indeed get taken back to Fort Knox. Two days later. There were a whole slew of charges against him. I had no doubt he'd end up in Leavenworth before it was all over. The only question was how much time he'd get. There wasn't much I could do about it, but it was obvious the kid wasn't all that bright. He wouldn't have survived a tour in-country. I was surprised he'd managed to last in any form of armed services as long as he had. Something about the kid had me needing to help him as much as I could, though.

Though Mike and I had just met, I was reluctant to leave his company. For one, we *fit*. There was a fierce sexual attraction, but we both chose to let it simmer a while. Mike had expressed his intention of going South to a little town in Kentucky called Somerset which I'd never even heard of. That was fine by me. I wasn't fit for the big city anymore. I wanted to make a home somewhere peaceful and quiet.

We stayed in Louisville. I tried to be nice. Go through the proper channels without stepping on toes or anything. After two days of waiting with minimal to no response from Fort Knox, I'd had enough. I was done being nice.

"Well?"

Mike was right beside me. I almost jumped because I hadn't heard him approach. I scowled. Not paying attention to my surroundings could get me killed. Except this wasn't 'Nam. And Mike had my back the way I'd never completely trusted anyone else to. There was something different about that man and it wasn't just my attraction to him -- which was something I'd definitely have to analyze. I filed it away for later.

"You ready to get the fuck outta this place?"

"And leave that kid alone?" I answered him with more irritation than I should have. This whole situation was a shit deal for Alex, even if it was one of his own making. I knew I would do something. I had no idea what, but I could make sure the kid got an adequate defense and that his CO didn't cut corners and trick him into a plea deal or something that would put him away for the rest of his natural life. He'd have a better chance of having a life after this if he were tried in a military court than he would a civilian court, especially in Louisville after Martin Luther King, Jr. had been assassinated. At least, I hoped so.

"Well, if we leave, that's what we'll be doin'. You finally ready to shake things up a bit?"

When I glanced over at Mike, a smile tugged at his lips. How could the man have my number so early in this game? I could tell he knew I wouldn't let this go. And he'd go along with anything I decided.

"We don't know each other, Mike. So don't pretend you can read my mind." I was trying to push him away. Had been trying for two days. I'd kicked him out of our hotel room three times yesterday alone. I worked better by myself anyway.

"We went through something together." He grinned. "I think that warrants a little commiseration. We can talk about our feelings and shit. And you can tell me what's goin' on inside that pretty head of yours." He winked at me.

I scowled at him. "What's going on is I'm trying to decide if I'd have a better chance of successfully killing you if I slit your throat while you sleep or shove you in front of a fucking bus."

"If I were you, I'd go with slittin' my throat in my sleep. But only if I get to play with you a bit before I go to the Hereafter. Hell, you let me show you a good time, and if you still want to kill me, I'll furnish a fuckin' rusty, dull-ass knife and let you saw as long as you need to for me to die."

"Wow. Been a long time there, soldier?"

He shrugged. "Didn't say *that*. Just that fuckin' you would be worth any punishment."

No one talked to me that way and got away with it. I tried to scowl at him again. Except I felt my lips twitching, trying to grin at his audacity. "Keep it up, man. We'll find out who's the better fighter."

Mike chuckled as he put his hand on the small of my back and led me from the motel. It was time to swing by Fort Knox. If I was right, it was the 138th who were stationed there and getting ready to deploy. I just happened to know the commander and he owed me a huge favor. Official channels weren't working. It was time to use the backdoor. No pun intended.

"Come on, Mama Tiger. You got a ride?"

I shrugged. "Figured I'd get a taxi. Ain't no biggie."

"Ride with me. I'll take you anywhere you want to go."

"I suppose I could do that."

He grinned and took my hand and led me out of the little motel we'd been crashing in. I was surprised when he led me to a Harley Davidson Electric Glide. Black with silver accents. Subtle, but beautiful. We hadn't gone anywhere that required more than walking a short distance since we'd been here, so the bike was a pleasant surprise. I couldn't help the slow smile that spread my lips. "Where the fuck did you get this? And how did you get it *here*?"

He shrugged. "A friend from Nam. Dropped it off for me last night. He'll be meetin' us in Somerset."

"So sure I'm coming with you? I don't even know where that place is."

"Good. When I get you home, you won't be able to find your way out."

I gave him a hard look, hoping to bend him to my will. When he smirked at me, I knew he was on to what I was going to demand next. I decided to sweeten the pot. "How about *you* ride with *me*. I'll give you all the sexual favors you want."

That got a deep, amused chuckle from Mike. "Baby, I'll charm you into the sexual favors. I don't need to bribe you."

I bristled a little. Not because I was upset with him, but because I knew he was likely right. Mike was tall and broad-shouldered. His nut-brown hair was still regulation, but more than a little scruffy around the edges. He didn't have a full-on beard, but he sported a few days' growth on his face. For Mike, he was letting his hair go just because he could. For me, I refused to take orders from anyone I didn't trust and respect, or who I thought was a dumbass. Mike didn't fall into any of those categories.

If he gave an order, I would bank on him knowing exactly what he was doing. It was easy to tell in the short conversation we'd had and the input he gave which meant he was definitely not a dumbass. The way he'd followed my lead without question earned my respect. Not many battle-hardened men I knew would willingly take orders from a woman. Instead of arguing, however, Mike had offered his own opinions, building on mine and making it possible for us to get Alex out of here in one piece. He'd worked *with* me and hadn't tried to dominate the operation.

"So sure that's a foregone conclusion?" Inwardly I sighed. Because he *might* be right.

"Yep. I knew it when I kissed you. You want me nearly as bad as I want you." He threw his thick thigh over the seat of the Harley. "Climb on, Mama Tiger. You ride with me this one time. After this, if you want to ride up front, I'll let you." He handed me a helmet. "Told my buddy I might have a passenger. He packed accordingly."

I snorted. "Will not." But I climbed on behind him. Instead of wrapping my arms around his waist, I placed them on my thighs. I could grab on to him if I needed to, but I wasn't about to let Mike know how drawn to him I was. And it wasn't only physical. Sure, I wanted him with an ache I'd never experienced before -- felt like I might die if I didn't have him soon. He ticked every box I had in my mind of what a man should be. And that wasn't something I wanted to think about. I didn't need a man. Least of all one I hardly knew.

Mike started up the bike and revved the engine a couple times. Before he took off, he reached for my hand and tugged me to him, holding my hand against his rigid stomach.

"Hold on, Mama Tiger." That deep chuckle of his was going to get me in trouble.

He took off, and I slid my other arm around his waist. I could still fight this attraction. Just... maybe not right this second.

The warm breeze felt good on my face and Mike's clean, warm scent teased my nose where I was close against him. Occasionally, he'd pat my hand with his big one.

Then I remembered I wanted to go to Fort Knox.

I'd gotten so wrapped up in the experience of riding behind him with his scent blowing all around me that I forgot where I wanted him to take me.

When he stopped at the next light I tapped him on the shoulder. He turned his head to look at me over his shoulder. "We need to go to Fort Knox."

Mike gave me a crisp nod, revving the engine a couple of times while we waited for the light to change. When it did, we took off quick enough I had to hurry and wrap my arms around his waist once more. I might have let out a girly squeak, but I'll never admit to anything of the sort. He chuckled lightly, letting me know he'd been teasing me even as he effectively refused to let me back off touching him.

What surprised me the most was the fact that Mike didn't demand to know why I wanted him to take me an hour away. Just like before, he was willing to follow my lead. I knew he'd want to know the plan when we got somewhere we could talk, but for now he was giving me what I wanted without arguing.

Once we got on the open road, it was all I could do to keep from squealing in delight. I wasn't a novice. I'd been riding motorcycles since the first time I stole one. But this experience wasn't something I was prepared for.

"Wooooo!" With the sun on my face, the wind in my hair, and my thighs cradling Mike's delectable ass, I raised my hands in the air and whooped my excitement. When he chuckled, my whole body heated. He reached back and ran one hand down my leg to squeeze my knee before putting that hand back on the handlebar.

For the better part of my life, I'd been the adult. The grown-up. My pa disappeared before I was born, and my ma couldn't have told you who he was to begin with. She had seven other children, some of them older than me, some younger. I was the one everyone went to, though. From the time I was old enough to stand on a kitchen chair and cook a meal, it was me taking care of my family.

Now? For the first time since I could ever remember, I was living in the moment and not worrying about the next move. *Joy. Pure bliss.* It would be so easy to wave him off the exit and just keep going South. This wasn't my fight anyway. I'd done what I could to keep the kid alive. He was back at his barracks until they'd finished the fucking paperwork, then he'd be shipped off to a disciplinary barracks. Likely Leavenworth, as I'd thought earlier. I could… just keep riding. Let Mike take me away somewhere we could spend some time seeing how attracted to each other we really were, or realizing we hated each other and have a fight to the death. I had to grin at that. For the first time in my life, I thought I might have found a man who could take me in a fair fight.

As we neared the exit, I was about to say fuck it all and tell Mike to keep going. But he squeezed my knee, harder this time. He didn't look back at me, but kept going until he'd pulled off the interstate and onto the exit ramp. He didn't say anything even when we stopped at a light just before we got to the post. Instead of pulling to the visitor entrance, he pulled into a gas station to top off the tank.

"What are you thinking?" I asked as Mike handed the service guy a five-dollar bill. It wouldn't take that much, but I imagine Mike wanted the guy gone so we could talk.

"Just wondering what your plan is. If we're gonna get shot at, I'd like to know now." He grinned as he spoke, but the smile didn't quite reach his eyes.

"No plans on getting shot at. I know a colonel there. He owes me a favor and I'm gonna to try to collect."

"What are you hoping for with the kid, Jo? You know he's gonna do time. If nothing else, they'll put him in a mental institution."

"I know that, Mike," I bit out, a little harsher than I should have. "I just want the kid to get a fair shake, OK? Yeah, he has to do time. And he'll get a dishonorable discharge. I'd just like to make sure he gets what he needs while he's there, especially the means to contact any family who need to know where he is. Maybe some psychiatric help."

"OK. Fair enough." Mike finished fueling the bike before securing the pump and climbing back on in front of me. "Let's see what we can do for the kid." A few minutes later he pulled up to the visitors' entrance. The gate was manned by several MPs who looked no-nonsense. I'd have trouble getting in if Colonel Gill decided to renege on our agreement.

"Military ID, please." One guard approached us while three more kept watch.

"We're both recently discharged." I pulled an envelope from my jacket pocket with my paperwork inside it and handed it to the guard. Mike raised an eyebrow but did the same. "I'm here to see Colonel Gill. He's not expecting me, but tell him it's Dr. Josephine Peyton."

"Pull over by the guard tower while I look into this." The guard gave me a disgruntled frown. Doubtless the man didn't like a change in routine. Most men who took their responsibilities seriously when on guard duty weren't fans of the unexpected.

Mike took us to the area the guard indicated. There were several parking spots for people to pull over and wait, though none were taken. It gave us another few moments to discuss our next move. Which, I admit, might have been smarter to have done at the gas station. Or in the parking lot before we left. Or any number of places other than outside the guard tower at Fort *fucking* Knox.

"I hope you know what you're doin', Jo. You on good terms with Colonel Gill?"

"Not at all. In fact, he hates my guts. Only problem is, I saved his life more than once in Laos. *He* may be an insufferable, know-it-all, condescending bastard, but he always repays his debts. And he's not a bad man. Just tends to be a rule follower, even when he knows he needs to make his own rules." I was betting this kid's life with my belief on the strait-laced bastard, but someone needed to look out for the youngster.

It took far longer than I expected. That was understandable given the importance of Gill's job as CO of one of the most secure buildings in the world, *and* the fact that the last time I saw him I'd called him a coward. I was betting the delay was more because of the latter than the former. An hour and a half later, I was fuming, but one of the guards came over to us.

"Sorry, ma'am." The young man was tall, blond, and skinny. He looked like a stiff breeze would blow him over. Not to mention he didn't look comfortable at all with having to deliver the news. "The Colonel says he's busy and can't receive visitors."

I opened my mouth to give the guy what for -- even though I knew it wasn't his fault -- when Mike lay a hand on my thigh -- a clear signal to shut up if I ever saw one.

"Can you please tell the Colonel it's a personnel matter? Dr. Peyton and I have information on a soldier named Alex. Not sure of his last name, but he said he was stationed here. We were the ones who got him to the police."

The young man's eyes widened and his lips parted in an "O" of surprise. "Oh, man. Give me a minute." The kid turned and ran back to the guard post.

Mike commented on their animated conversation. "They probably don't want to bother the Colonel again." Mike brushed his hand over my knee casually as he gave me the rundown. Even if it was through my jeans, I still soaked up his touch. He had to know I could see what was going on just fine but was using his voice as a distraction so he could touch me. I'd have called him out on it, but I was afraid he'd stop so I let it go.

As a general rule, men and I didn't get along. Not because I wasn't attracted to them, but because men in the military tended to be too alpha to tolerate a woman who outranked them. Though it was against the rules for officers to date enlisted personnel, I'd have chucked that out the window if I'd found a man I was even remotely interested in fucking. There been a few men who were comfortable with my rank, but those guys usually weren't alpha enough for me. I wanted my man to be strong with a take-charge kind of personality, but not so much he resented me for my education. Mike… Yeah. He was that alpha. But he also took in stride the fact that I was a woman and still knew my shit. He seemed willing to follow my lead instead of trying to bulldoze his way to the front.

"If they don't let us in, I'll call Gill myself. And if I have to do that, I'll be fuckin' somebody up." My irritation was coming through in spades, but I didn't care. I was going to do my best for Alex and make sure he had everything he needed. Normally, I'd have said good riddance and just killed someone shooting up an airport. I guess I'd seen too many young soldiers dead, dying, and with battle fatigue so profound they'd gone mad. I had no idea what the kid's story was -- other than he seemed a little slow. That could be his mental capacity, or it could be as a result of knowing he was going to be deployed to Nam. Whatever was going on inside that kid's head, he needed help coping. Not to spend the next couple of decades in a prison cell.

"You know, your vicious side turns me the fuck on, Josephine." Mike's lips quirked up at one corner. He didn't look at me or take his eyes of the two men talking. "When we get this settled, you and I are gonna have a nice long chat about what happens when you get all bloodthirsty around me."

"You're on dangerous ground. Keep talking and you might find you're in way the fuck over your head." I tried to sound menacing, but I'm pretty sure it all came out all breathless and shit. Like I wanted him the way he claimed to want me. Which wasn't true. Not at all. It wasn't.

His warm chuckle was his response. Also, that hand on my knee squeezed once before he moved it. Probably thought I'd bite or something. Or he could be freeing up his hands because the first guard was now approaching our vehicle and he didn't look happy.

"No fighting," I muttered. I couldn't help it. It just slipped out.

Mike glanced at me sharply. "Really?" He raised an eyebrow. I shrugged.

"We've told you. The Colonel is not taking visitors." The guard looked supremely pissed off. It was obvious he had no intention of checking with anyone else or relaying the message Mike just issued.

"I'd get your name, rank, and serial number, but

reporting dumbasses ain't my thing," Mike told him. "You tell Colonel Gill that Dr. Josephine Peyton is here to see him. You tell him she ain't forgot about Laos and has come to collect a debt. You tell him that word for word, then come back and tell us he won't see us."

The guy looked wary now. Like he knew he'd just sprung a trap but couldn't see it or figure out a way out of it before it closed in on him. "If you're wasting my time, I'll arrest you both."

"I'll waste your fuckin' time," I muttered before I could stop myself. Mike clapped a hand back on my knee. "What?" I tried to look all innocent but neither man was buying it. "He's being stupid."

"Jo…" Mike gave me a warning glance. Which just made my chin go up.

"Bitch," the guard muttered.

To my surprise, Mike climbed off the bike in one smooth move, reaching the guy's retreating form in two long strides. He grabbed the guard's shoulder and spun him around, catching him with a right hook.

"You don't talk to a lady that way, soldier. I don't care what the fuck she says or does. Do it again and you won't have to worry about getting called to Nam. I'll beat the fuckin' shit outta you right here in the good ol' U. S. of A. so bad you'll be lucky to walk again."

Several other guards in the vicinity ran toward us. The guard in question rubbed his jaw but had only staggered back before regaining his balance. He gave Mike a withering look but backed off.

"There a problem, Sarge?" one of the other men asked. He didn't look at all ready to take on Mike. I mean, Mike's a big guy. Tall and thickly built. But there was a total of four guys surrounding him. None of them looked like they were eager to take him on.

Which meant I needed to get a look at my new friend, because I had a feeling whatever I saw on his face might just be panty melting.

"No. I was just going to give the colonel's secretary a message." He waved a hand toward us. "Let them wait here until I get off the phone."

The guards each took a few steps backward, not turning around, not standing down a single bit. Mike waited a couple of heartbeats before reaching out to rub my upper thigh in a soothing gesture. Wasn't sure if it meant to soothe me or him. Then he crossed his arms over that mouthwateringly thick chest. He planted his feet shoulder width apart and stood there, staring at the group of soldiers. Finally, he turned his head to look at me, and the fierce expression on his face made my breath catch.

Mike nodded at me slowly. "You like seeing me all riled up on your behalf?" The man obviously saw way more than I wanted him to. Which made him doubly dangerous.

"I ain't your problem. You didn't have to do that." I knew I sounded breathless. Hell, I was breathless. The man's swift defense of me with such passion that he looked like he was ready to kill a motherfucker went straight to my clit and *throbbed*.

"You're my woman. That most definitely makes you my problem."

I shook my head. "I never agreed to that."

"Yes, you did. When you didn't castrate me after I kissed you."

Chapter Three
Mike

It didn't take long before Colonel Gill instructed the dumbasses at the gate to escort us in. OK, so I wasn't being fair. Those guys weren't dumbasses. They were doing their job. Besides, I wasn't too high and mighty to admit that, had I been in the sergeant's position, I wouldn't have bothered a colonel either. What I took exception to was the disrespect to Josephine. I wasn't above killing a woman if necessary. Lord knew I'd done it more than once in Nam. But even if a woman needed killing, I did it as quick and painless as I could. A simple bullet to the head. The sergeant wasn't impressed with Jo's credentials and probably thought he could get away with disrespecting her because she was a woman. Not on my watch.

Once inside the reception area of the colonel's office, Josephine sat stiffly on the edge of her chair. She'd worked herself up to a good pissed off and I found myself looking forward to the confrontation that would soon follow. While I hoped she didn't get us landed in jail, I'd enjoy the shit out of seeing her spar.

"This way, please, Dr. Peyton." A tall, thin man with sharply pressed service greens approached us. He was perfectly groomed, not a hair out of place. The poor guy had a shave so close it had to have hurt. He didn't smile but was completely professional. I pushed off from the wall where I leaned, watching from the background. "Not you, sir. Only Dr. Peyton."

"Where I go, he goes," Jo barked out.

The guy stiffened but nodded his head once. He gestured to the massive wooden door that led to Colonel Gill's office. He opened the door and we stepped inside.

Colonel Rylan "Ry" Gill was a huge man with a permanent scowl on his face. At least, that's what it looked like. He shot Josephine a look when she entered. The cursory glance he gave me might have been insulting if he hadn't looked at Jo with a wary expression. Like he'd sized us both up and knew Jo was more of a threat than me. He'd be partially right. Under normal circumstances, Jo was definitely the one to worry about. But not at the moment. I was pissed. If this guy gave Jo the slightest bit of lip, I was ready to throw him a beating like he'd never had.

"Sorry for the way the guards were at the gate with you, Dr. Peyton." Gill's expression was still one of vast disapproval, but his tone and words were respectful so, for the moment, he got to live. "They were only doing their duty. I'd left orders I wasn't be disturbed."

OK. No self-respecting Colonel explained himself to just anyone. Yet, this guy was treating Josephine like she was his superior. Either he owed her a really big debt, or he knew exactly how dangerous the woman was. This guy went up a few notches in my estimation.

"We need to talk about Alex. The kid who got arrested a few days ago."

With a sigh, Gill reached for a file on his desk and opened it. He flipped through the pages like he was reviewing it. I could tell it was more something to do with his hands while he gathered his thoughts.

"Alex Brown. The kid shot up an airport. What do you expect us to do with him?"

"Just give him a fair shake. He's not cut out for this and if you're the same man I knew a few years ago, you know every man under your immediate command and what they're capable of."

"Alex Brown. Born and raised in Sparta,

Mississippi. Left high school when he turned eighteen without graduating. Got duped into joining the Army, but Uncle Sam needs recruits so they wouldn't let him out of his enlistment." He looked up at Josephine. "Kid couldn't kill a bug much less a person, even if they were shooting at him." He sighed and dug his fingers into his eyes. "When they told me he shot up the Standiford Field terminal, I couldn't believe it. He's as gentle as they come. Simple, maybe, but the only trouble he's ever been in was a direct result of his lack of intelligence."

"Kid doesn't need to be in the Army, colonel." Jo leaned over and placed her palms on his desk, looking straight at the man. "I realize he'll have to do some time for what he did, but make it minimal jail time and an other than honorable discharge. Let him go back home to his family."

"Believe me, I'd love to do nothing more. Unfortunately, the JAG prosecutor is out for blood with this."

"Because he shot up an airport filled with civilians? That would make sense."

"With all the racial tension happening all over the country, JAG's taking a hard line with anything that even remotely smacks of racial violence."

"This wasn't about anything to do with that." I knew there was no way Josephine was going to let this go easily. We both knew the kid would have to do time, but she wanted to give him a fair chance. "Kid's scared and, like you said, a little on the simple side. Surely you have some sway. Get them to sentence him to a couple years. No one was hurt or killed. He surrendered peacefully. That has to count for something."

"I'll try, Dr. Peyton. I've got a buddy willing to

take his case. He's really good at what he does. If anyone can get him a fair shake, this lawyer can do it. That's all I can promise."

"Ian McGregor," she said.

The colonel tilted his head at her. "Yes. You know him?"

"He's my half-brother. I'll talk to him when we get done here. Can we talk to Alex? I want to make sure he has a way to contact his family. If he doesn't, then I'll get them a message."

"You know you can't have contact with a prisoner, Jo." It was the first time the colonel had used anything other than a formal address when speaking to Josephine.

"Today I can, Ry. Ten minutes. That's all I'm asking for right now. The kid needs a way to let his family know where he is and what's going on."

With a sigh, he nodded. "Ten minutes. Not a minute more. I'll even give you another ten minutes when you get his family here. But Jo?" When she raised an eyebrow at him, he continued. "This evens us out."

"No, it doesn't," she said, with a lift of her chin. "Not by a fuckin' long shot." She stood to leave without another look at the colonel. He sighed but followed her to the door.

As Jo marched out of the office and started down the hall, Gill spoke to the aide who'd shown us to his office. "See to it Dr. Peyton and her escort are shown to a holding area. Have Private Brown brought to them. Tell the guards they have ten minutes with the prisoner."

"Yes, sir." The aide rose and headed off. Josephine and I followed at a discreet distance. I liked to blend in and I didn't like being outnumbered, even if this was a US post on US soil. I wasn't sure what Josephine had in mind, but it was my job to make sure she got what she wanted.

The aide placed us in a room with a steel table and two chairs. I moved to the far corner and did my best to become part of the wall. As much as I was itching to take charge of the situation, this was Jo's deal. I was there for moral support and backup. Jo sat quietly in one of the chairs provided, lacing her fingers together and placing her hands on the table. She was perfectly still. Like she was lying in wait for the enemy when I knew she didn't see Alex that way. Likely, she was getting ready to lay into some dipshit dumbass for abusing the boy, 'cause that was Jo. A mother hen. Or, rather, a mama tiger.

A few minutes later, two guards escorted Alex to the holding cell in handcuffs with which they fastened him to the table. Poor kid looked terrified as hell. Also looked like he'd taken several blows to the face.

"What happened?" Jo asked without preamble.

Alex shrugged. "Same thing always happens. My face got in the way of some guy's fist." He didn't seem like he was upset, just stating a fact. "It's better here, though. That was the folks in the city jail."

Jo took a breath and let the silence linger for a moment before she reached out and covered Alex's bound hands with one of her own. "Have you called your pa?"

Alex shook his head. "They said I could later, but ain't never let me yet."

"What's the number? I'll get in touch with him so he knows where you are and what's happening."

Alex gave her the number, but Jo didn't write it down. The kid noticed and gave her a disappointed look. "You ain't gonna call my daddy," he muttered.

"What makes you say that?" Jo didn't move and her facial expression didn't change.

"You didn't write it down. You ain't gonna call him."

"Oh?" Then she repeated the number back to Alex. "I have a photographic memory. I remember everything I read and most of what I hear. I won't forget, Alex. Now. Is there anyone else you want me to get a hold of?"

He studied her for a long moment, then nodded. "My girl. Her name's Gracie. Last time I talked to her, she got throwed out the house 'cause she was my girl. Her pap's pissed."

"Tell me where I can find her. An address. A phone number."

He gave her an address and phone number. Again, Jo didn't write anything down. Fortunately, my memory was as good as she said hers was, so I was pretty sure between the two of us we'd remember.

"You promise you'll let her know what happened?"

"I will, Alex. Assuming you get a military trial, I don't know that she can be there, but I'll make sure she gets to see you at some point if she wants to." Jo squeezed his hand. "She love you, Alex?"

He shrugged. "Said she did. She didn't back down when her daddy said he'd throw her out. I give her my pay so she can have a place to live. I don't know what she'll do now." The big kid sniffled once, his lower lip trembling. "I wanted to be a good man to her. I know I could be. She's got a little one on the way too." He met Jo's eyes, and I knew I was fucked. "How'm I gonna take care of her and my kid from prison?"

Jo shook her head once like she was arguing with

herself. I had to grin, though I put my hand up to hide it. If she saw me smile right now, she'd castrate me on the spot.

"I'll figure something out, Alex. Whatever happens, I'll make sure to get word to you. Might take a while. In the meantime, the colonel is trying to get you a good lawyer to help you out. Someone I know. I'll put in a good word for you."

"Why you helpin' me?" Alex looked equal parts hopeful and wary.

"Someone needs to, kid. Just so happens that someone's gonna be me." She stood just as the guard opened the door.

"Time's up," the guard said. "The colonel's aide will escort you out."

"Hang in there, Alex. I can't tell you everything will be all right, but I can promise to look after your girl and to get a message to your pa."

"Thank you, ma'am. Ain't worried 'bout me. It's Gracie who's gonna suffer the most."

"You have my word I'll do everything I can for the girl."

With a nod, Alex let the guard lead him out of the holding cell and down the corridor.

I kept silent, watching Jo like a hawk. I didn't want to miss even one facial expression. It was easy to see how determined she was. I just wasn't sure what she'd do next. God knew I was looking forward to finding out.

Chapter Four

Mama Jo

Mike and I spent the better part of the day traveling to the Eastern part of the state. Not the most common place for a black man to live in Kentucky, but not unheard of either. Also, it couldn't have been easy. Alex's father owned a garage with an impeccable reputation. The person we talked to when trying to find the place had told us, "Don't hold it against the garage for having a colored owner. He does top-notch work."

We got a hotel room. I wanted to get two, but Mike insisted we only needed one. I was pretty sure he intended to make some kind of move on me and couldn't say I was too broken up about it. Still, I put up what I thought was an appropriate protest. He just grinned and got one room.

The next day, we found Alex's father. Job Brown had been distressed but resigned to learn what had happened to his son. And no, the Army hadn't notified him in any way. A transplant from Jackson, Mississippi, Job was a hard-working man just looking to make a living. He and his wife had nine kids with Alex being the oldest. "I was afraid somethin' like this'd happen. He OK?" Job gave me a concerned, anguished look.

"Got a little roughed up in the city jail, but he's back at the barracks now. Fort Knox. Colonel Gill is getting him a good lawyer. I know both men personally. They'll do everything they can for your son, but you have to understand there's gonna be no way for him to avoid prison time and a dishonorable discharge."

"Yeah. Figured." He scrubbed the back of his

neck. "Least they ain't sendin' him off to Nam. Alex has a good heart, but he's not real good at followin' orders. Not 'cause he don't want to. Just gets mixed up sometimes if it's more than something real easy. Gets nervous. Bit… simple."

"He's a good kid, Mr. Brown. Just scared. I think learning he was getting deployed pushed him past his breaking point. From talking to him, it sounded like he had a lot on his plate even before that."

"Yeah." He frowned. "I told him not to get mixed up with no white girl. Her daddy had it in for him from the first day he found out. Now he done went and knocked her up."

"I take it you're not happy about it either?" Mike stepped in, probably figuring I was getting ready to give the guy a piece of my mind. But I got it. It couldn't be easy for any of them to have a son involved with a white girl whose parents didn't approve. Not in the current environment.

"Of course, I ain't happy," Job barked. "You think I want to see my son havin' to fight every single day to defend his wife's honor? It ain't as bad in Kentucky as it was in Mississippi, but they still get harassed. And now they got a baby they bringin' into it? No. I ain't happy. I'm just tryin' to look out for my son, is all."

I sighed. "Ain't we all. Look. Alex has been giving Gracie his pay to keep a roof over her head and food in the house. He's not gonna have that much longer. I ain't talked to the girl yet, but Alex said she can't go back to her parents." I had a habit of falling back into my southern accent when I was agitated or talking to someone with a similar accent. I inwardly cringed but decided to just roll with it. Besides, Job Brown would be more inclined to cooperate fully if he didn't think of me as a white woman with a silver spoon up her ass.

"Nah. She got throwed out. The whole town was talkin' 'bout it. Said he don't want no nigger baby runnin' 'round his house. Called her white trash and said she could damned well get her stud to take care of her. He was done. Girl's mama tried to talk sense to him, but the man's as mean as they come. Next time anyone saw his wife, Luellen was havin' to explain how she'd run into a door that got her face all bruised up."

A woman stepped out of the little house. Her sundress had roses crawling over it with green leaves and a white background. She smiled but had a concerned look on her face. "Job don't mean anything by that. But that Danny Braxton's a mean man. He hits on his wife all the time, and I'm pretty sure Gracie wasn't spared. I'd take her in, but I ain't got room for my eight other kids as it is. Gracie's a good girl. Works hard and she loves my Alex." The woman -- obviously Alex's mother -- smiled sadly. "We'll help where we can, but her situation could be trouble for my other kids."

"I understand," I said. "We're headed to find Gracie now. If you see her, tell her Josephine Peyton and Michael Wilbanks are looking for her on behalf of Alex. We're staying across town. I promised him we'd talk to her. We intend to do our best to see she's taken care of."

"Do you know when Alex will get to come home?" His mother looked hopeful but resigned.

"No, Mrs. Brown. I'm afraid it might not be for a while. I'll do my best to keep you informed, but I want you to have this." I handed her an envelope. It had Ian McGregor's office phone number and address along with my full name. "This has his lawyer's contact information. When you get in touch with him, you tell him Josephine Peyton is your friend. My name's in there too. Don't have a phone yet, but I'll let you know when I do. Until then, you get in touch with Ian." I pointed to the envelope I'd given her. "Do exactly what he says. Once he's gotten better acquainted with the case, he'll tell you what you can expect. He's a good man. He'll do right by your son, I promise."

We said our goodbyes and left. Once we climbed back on Mike's bike, he started it and took off but didn't go far. He stopped at a little diner in the middle of town. We sat there for a long time, not saying anything. He was likely as deep in thought as I was.

The delicious smell coming from the diner finally got my attention. "I'm hungry."

"Figured." Mike turned to look at me over his shoulder. I gripped his arm as I climbed off, bracing myself so I didn't fall. The man had some serious muscle going on. Made me wonder what he'd look like naked. Feel like, his skin pressed against mine. I shook my head. Now wasn't the time to go there.

How long had it been since I'd been seriously attracted to a man? In the past, any man I'd thought about getting with had ruined any attraction I had the first time he opened his big fucking mouth to tell me I was a woman and needed to know my place. Mike hadn't done that. In fact, the man had followed me all on his own. Until we'd actually talked in the airport, I'd never seen the man before.

Shaking myself mentally to focus on the problem at hand, I approached the diner. Before I could open the door, Mike reached for the handle and pulled, stepping aside to let me enter. I swallowed as I looked up at him. At five feet ten inches tall, there weren't many men I couldn't look in the eyes without craning my neck. Mike was a good six-six, at least. He met my gaze with a steady one of his own. Yeah. I was in trouble.

I put my shoulders back and did my best to blank my expression. The smirk on Mike's face told me I hadn't done it fast enough. The bastard knew the effect he was having on me and was biding his time.

Once we were seated, I scanned the menu, ordering a burger, fries, and sweet tea before handing the menu back to the waitress. Mike ordered the same, never taking his eyes off me. I was sorely afraid the man saw more than I wanted him to. He certainly had my number so far.

"If we're gonna go find that girl, we're gonna need more than a bike." He watched me carefully. "Unless you plan on leavin' her here?"

"She ain't got no future here," I found myself saying softly. Shit. I'd let my hillbilly out again. I seemed to do that a lot around Mike. "Not if she wants to make a life for herself."

"What do you want to do, Jo?"

"Don't know. First, we find Gracie, then we'll figure out what to do next."

The waitress brought our drinks. Mike took a sip of his tea. "Good. If she's willin', you think we should take her back to Somerset with us? It's in a better part of the state. Still ain't great for a white girl raisin' a black baby, but with us there to help…"

"Yeah. If she's willing, that's the best choice." I raised my head and frowned. "Not sure I agreed to stay in Somerset with you."

He grinned. "Not sure you didn't either."

"Asshole." I took a sip of my tea.

The food was wonderful. Or maybe I was just

hungry. I ate everything on my plate and drank another two glasses of tea. By the time we were finished, I was feeling every hour we'd spent on Mike's bike.

"We gonna try to find Gracie tonight?" Mike wiped his mouth and snagged the check before I could. I frowned at him.

"No. I need rest before we face this. Got a feeling it ain't gonna be pretty."

Mike shrugged. "Not sure why. Girl's dad kicked her out. She has no idea she's not gonna have income from Alex so she'll have trouble keeping a place to stay."

"I need to think," I muttered. "To do that I need rest."

"I know exactly what you need, Josephine." Mike stood and slapped a few bills on the table before snagging my hand and pulling me to my feet. "Come on."

I wanted to argue with him just because he was trying to take charge. Thing was, I found I was OK with that. I was exhausted. Mentally and physically. And more than a little heartsick. For some reason, Alex Brown had wormed his way inside my heart and I couldn't let this go until I was certain I'd taken care of the kid as much as I could.

Once we got back to the hotel, Mike shut the door and hung the security chain. When he turned around, there was hunger in his gaze. Hunger, and a knowing so deep I was sure he could read my mind.

"While we're in here, in this room, you're gonna let me worry about everything. You're gonna rest and recharge, and I'm gonna take over. You're also gonna let me comfort you."

"You've lost your Goddamned mind." He was

delusional. "Don't think you know me or what I need," I spat, though I had the feeling my outrage stemmed from the fact that he *did* seem to know me. "Comfort is for the weak, and I'm not weak."

He raised his eyebrows. "For the weak, eh? You think you don't need someone to comfort you?"

"Absolutely not." I scowled at him as I backed across the room. He moved toward me like a predator stalking his prey. "Why would I need comfort? These people are nothing to me."

"Right. That's why you went toe to toe with a colonel in his own territory. That's why you threatened to cut off that cop's balls. That's why we're on our way to find a white girl pregnant with a colored boy's baby. Because these people are nothing to you." He looked angrier than I'd ever seen him, even out front of Fort Knox. "You, Josephine, are a mama tiger. You see this kid as someone who needs your help, and you're takin' care of him in the only way you can. I got no problem with that. Admit it. Own it. But do *not* lie to me, Josephine. Ever."

I'd backed up until I was against the opposite wall. Mike caged me in with his superior height and muscle. I placed my hand on his chest, unable to drag my gaze back to his face. His T-shirt molded that wide, muscular chest to perfection. I'd never felt threatened by Mike, no matter his size. Not even now. Oh no. Definitely not now. What I did feel was an intense lust threatening to swamp me and have me throwing myself into Mike's strong arms to see what he could offer me.

"Oh yeah, Jo. Mama Tiger. I see you. You're a hair's breadth from takin' what you want from me."

"You sayin' I couldn't?"

"I'm sayin' all you have to do is tell me what you

- 172 -

want."

"Ain't beggin', bastard. Not for any reason."

"Did I say you needed to beg? No, Jo. I said to *tell me what you want*. Tell me. I'll give you the fuckin' *moon*."

Before I could stop myself, I nodded. "Kiss me then. Kiss me like you mean it."

Mike covered my mouth with his almost before I got the last word out. The first kiss we'd shared was spontaneous. I think it'd shocked us both. But this one... Mike completely dominated me. His body pressed me close against the wall, mashing me against his chest in the most dangerous and delicious way. Tongue sweeping inside my mouth, he invaded my senses, consuming me. And I didn't put up a fucking fight.

His hand came around my throat, holding me steady while he continued to kiss me. I arched my neck, giving him better access. Why, I have no idea. I wasn't the submissive type.

"That's it, Mama Tiger. Let yourself go."

The embarrassing whimper that escaped barely registered as I did exactly what he told me to do. I surrendered myself to him. Let him take control. Mike grunted his approval before squatting and lifting me into his arms, urging my legs around his waist.

Next thing I knew, Mike was laying me on the bed and following me down. He covered my body with his bigger one and the weight of him was... *sublime*!

Moaning and rubbing myself against him wasn't even something I tried to prevent. At this point, there was no use denying either of us. He wanted me and I Goddamned sure wanted him.

With a resigned sigh, I pulled his shirt from his

pants and found his skin with my fingertips. The hollows and valleys that played over his skin were sexy as fuck. I wasn't certain I'd ever seen a man as muscular and strong as Mike. He moved with fluid grace but had raw strength and power in his body that was ambrosia to a woman like me. He was powerful without smothering me. I could quickly tell this was going to be a relationship where I might control things in the real world, but in the bedroom, Mike would be firmly in charge. The surprising thing was, I found not only didn't mind, I might even prefer it.

It wasn't long before we'd managed to rid each other of our shirts. My bra followed, and Mike cupped one breast in his hand, his thumb feathering over my nipple in maddening caresses.

"You're beautiful, Mama Tiger. So fucking beautiful and responsive." As if to punctuate his statement, he twisted my nipple in a teasing caress and I cried out. Not in pain, but the most exquisite pleasure. "Let me have you." His growl sent shivers through my body. As I clung to him, I panted, trying to get my mind straight when his scent muddled any coherent thought I might have tried to hang on to. All I wanted was what Mike was doing to me. Giving me pleasure I'd never imagined existed.

When he kissed his way down my neck to my chest and took a nipple between his lips, I was gone. With a sharp cry, I wrapped my legs around his waist and ground my pussy against his very hard cock. Our jeans might have separated us, but I took what I wanted just the same.

"That's it, Mama Tiger. Take what you need. Take it from me and come." He hissed the command as he looked up at me from my breasts. His dark eyes and intense gaze pushed me over the edge from reality to some place I'd never been. It felt like a detonation inside me. A bomb searing me from the inside out in immeasurable pleasure. And still, I needed more.

"Mike!" I screamed his name as he unwound my legs from his waist and quickly moved down my body. He sat back and unfastened my pants before tugging them down my hips and thighs in snappish movements until he flung them and my panties to the floor.

"You want to take me inside you?" He lifted an eyebrow as he shoved his pants over his own hips and fisted his cock. "You want me to fuck you?"

"Yes! Oh, God! Please Mike! Please!"

With a grunt and a shove of his hips, Mike sank inside me in one smooth stroke. Again, I screamed, another orgasm overtaking me almost immediately. He was thick and pulsing inside me, and I thought he cried out with me.

It took several seconds to realize he was holding himself deep inside me but not moving. I shook my head, trying to think. Shouldn't he be moving? I was pretty sure…

"Mike?"

"Hush, Mama Tiger. Hush…" He kissed my lips. It was then I realized he was sweating, his breath sawing in and out of his lungs in a ragged pant. "Just hold still a moment, honey."

Hold still? What the fuck was he talking about? I didn't want to hold still. "Fuck me!" My demand was like steel. I met his gaze with my own, hoping he could see the determination and need to have him give me what I wanted.

"Is that what you need?"

"Yes!"

The next instant, he rode me hard, looking

straight into my eyes as he took me ruthlessly. Breath exploded out of my lungs with each surge forward. I hung on tightly, gasping with each time his cock slammed home.

"Come, Josephine." His hoarse whisper was a harsh command I was helpless to resist. The second the words were out of his mouth, I obeyed. My screams were as loud as his shouts. As I clamped down around him, I felt his hot seed shooting inside me and something settled in my chest. My breathing was fast and deep, like I'd run a race, but I felt at peace. Like the interlude we'd just shared was an integral part of my life. I felt... complete.

"You good, Mama Tiger?"

"Why do you call me that?" I was good, but I wasn't ready to admit it to him yet.

"Because that's what you are. A mama tiger protecting the cubs she sees as hers."

"Cubs?"

"Yeah. Alex. His girl. Their child."

"No one said I was protecting them. And I've not met the girl yet."

He smirked at me. "But we'll be taking her to Somerset with us to our new home."

I scowled and shoved him off me. Immediately I felt the loss of his warmth and had to fight myself to keep from whimpering and pulling him back. The smirk on his face said he noticed, though. "I've not got any intention of keeping Gracie with me. God knows I've got enough on my plate just adjusting back to civilian life. And who says I'm going to make Somerset my home? *Our* home? You've lost your mind."

Mike rolled over on his back with a groan. His cock was still high and proud, ready for another round.

"That thing ever go down?" I raised an eyebrow.

"Only when there's not a desirable woman in the vicinity."

"Guess you're up all the time then, huh." I gave him a disgusted look. It wasn't that I wanted to think I was special or anything, but it still hurt to know I was just one in a long line of women this guy had had. I likely wouldn't be the last.

"Nope. Ain't been this hard this long in my life. Not even sure I was this horny even as a fuckin' teenager. Not to mention the fact I just came a flood for you."

That surprised me. On many levels. But I wasn't about to say so. Of course, Mike glanced my way and winked at me.

"Look," I said as I snagged my clothes and started dressing with jerky movements. I needed to clean myself up but didn't want to look like I was running away. Also didn't want to stand there naked while he looked his fill. "I don't care if we're fuck buddies. We can both scratch an itch when necessary. But you demanded I not lie to you, so I want the same. I don't need your flattery or pretty words. Just your dick."

Instantly, his gaze grew hard. "I never say anything I don't mean, Josephine. Not for you. Not for anyone." With that, Mike sat up slowly before retrieving his own clothes.

Yeah. I might have overreacted. But Goddamnit, the man appealed to me on more levels than I could count. He ticked every single motherfucking box I had. Michael Wilbanks was not only my match in every way, he complemented me like no partner I'd ever had. Who was I kidding? I'd never really had a partner. Not like I thought of Mike. He got me. And that scared the fuck outta me.

Chapter Five
Mike

Backing off and giving Josephine space was the hardest thing I'd ever done in my life. If I was going to keep her I had to do it, though.

She avoided looking at me or talking to me the rest of the evening. I lay down and pretended to sleep so she'd relax a fraction. Either I fooled her or she was so exhausted she couldn't help herself, because ten minutes after she lay down, Josephine was out cold. I couldn't help but smile. She might not want to feel secure in my presence, but she did.

I dozed on and off throughout the night. When I woke, I'd glance at Jo to find her sleeping contentedly. She looked so fucking young when she was asleep it was hard to reconcile that with the seasoned warrior I knew her to be. Which was odd, considering she was medical. She'd be in the middle of a combat zone, but not in an active combat role. I'd bet my life that woman had seen more than her fair share of fighting and that wasn't something that happened in the U.S Army. I wondered if that was what Col. Gill owed her.

Just before daylight, I roused myself. She was on her side, facing me on the second bed in the room. Her hand rested under her cheek on top of her pillow. Strawberry-blonde hair fanned out around her like a fiery halo. She was the most beautiful woman I'd ever seen in my life. And she was all mine. She just wouldn't admit it to herself. Yet.

Careful not to rouse her, I dressed and slipped out of the room. I wanted to give her something to think about. Let her wake up without me. See what she did. If I was right, she'd be cranky as fuck the rest of the day. I grinned. It'd make the night even better.

Sure enough, an hour later, I watched from the car I'd had a friend drop off as she stomped out of the room and looked around. "Michael, you motherfucker!"

I barked out a laugh. She immediately zeroed in on me and scowled, flipping me off as she marched to the car, opened the door, and plopped inside before slamming the door.

"Motherfucker," she muttered. "You coulda told me you were gonna go get a fuckin' car."

"Just givin' you time to yourself. Seemed to be what you wanted."

"I did!" she yelled. "But you should tell me when you fuckin' leave! I thought you'd fuckin' gone."

"I ain't leavin' you, Jo. Not ever. Might as well get used to it now." I started the car, and we took off. Finding where Gracie lived wasn't that hard. Everyone knew her and her family. While a couple of her neighbors tried to help her out occasionally, most of them didn't want anything to do with her. She was the white girl pregnant with the colored boy's child. *Persona non grata.*

We sat outside the tiny shack for a full minute before Josephine shook her head. Opening the door, she stepped out and slammed it shut, not looking to see if I followed her. She rapped on the door three times before stepping back to give the girl room to open the door if she answered.

It wasn't long before the slender brunette opened the door a crack. She looked terrified. "What do you want?" Her voice was strong, if a bit shaky. She had a black eye, and I noticed finger-shaped bruises on her upper arm.

"My name's Jo. I'm here on Alex's behalf."

"Oh no." Her whispered response was an

anguish plea. "I know his unit got called up, but…"

"He's all right, honey." Jo tried her best to reassure the girl, but really. What could she say? Alex wasn't dead, was no telling when he'd get out of prison, or if Gracie would ever see him again. "Can we come in?"

Gracie shook her head. "I'll come out. If you're gonna hurt me, you'll have to do it in front of God and everyone." She lifted her chin as she exited the house and stepped onto the porch.

"Christ." I shook my head as I took her in. Bruises on her face and arms were likely just the tip of the iceberg. I noticed she had one hand holding her side. Probably had damaged ribs.

"We're not gonna hurt you, honey. We'll back off further if it makes you comfortable." Jo moved her hands to the side, palms up so the girl could see she was unarmed.

Gracie wore a yellow maternity sundress that should have looked pretty on her, but the material was dirty and threadbare, and every inch of skin that showed had bruises on it somewhere. The girl clutched her belly tightly, as if protecting the baby she carried inside her. I saw Jo clench her teeth. The muscle in her jaw ticked like a son of a bitch. I knew the feeling. Mine was doing the same thing.

"Who did this to you?" I couldn't stop the growl in my voice. It made the girl flinch, and I had my answer before she gave it.

"My father. My brothers." She gave us the information in a quiet voice, then shrugged. "I learned not to answer the door when they come by."

"Go pack a bag," Jo ordered. "You're comin' with us."

Gracie lifted her chin as she shook her head. "I

don't know you."

"No, you don't," Jo bit out. She closed her eyes and took a deep breath, obviously trying to rein it in. The mama tiger in her was surging to the fore. "But I guaran-damn-tee you we won't be as harsh as this." She waved her hand to indicate Gracie from head to toe.

"I'm not giving up my baby." The girl's hands clutched her gently rounded abdomen, her slender arms circling her belly even tighter than before. "People don't understand, but I love Alex. He's kind of simple, but he's been good to me since the day I met him. He works hard and has the biggest heart of anyone I've ever met." She looked off. "Much better than my own family."

"Ain't askin' you to give up your child, Gracie." Josephine softened her tone, stepping closer to the girl. "We're here to make sure you and your baby get a decent start. Come with us. You can stay until you're back on your feet. Longer if you want. But Alex wouldn't want you livin' in a place like this if he could help it."

"He gives me his Army pay but I don't spend it. We're not married. And I might need it for the baby. I won't spend his money on myself, but I'll do whatever I have to, to protect our child."

"I know you will." Jo took the opening Gracie had just given her. "He'd want that too. Which is why you're going to come with us to Somerset. This is for your child."

That made the girl blink. Obviously, she was carefully considering her decision. "How do I know you're not trying to trick me?"

"Honey, I promised Alex I'd find you. I'll tell you everything that happened on the way. I've got you ten minutes of privacy to talk with him. Well, as private as I can get. You discuss it with Alex. After that, I'll do whatever you want. But I promise you, Alex is gonna want you to come with us."

She gently rubbed her rounded belly again, as if soothing her child. Likely, it was to soothe herself just as much. The sheen of tears in her eyes made me wince. This woman was just a terrified kid. Same as Alex. Two kids together battling a world of hate. I thought Jo was about to force the issue when Gracie put her chin up. Her lower lip quivered but she stood her ground.

"OK. I'll go with you. But I want to know what's going on and what you intend to do with me."

"We're going to bring you with us to South Central Kentucky. It's still Kentucky, but the area is a little more... friendly." I could tell Jo was trying to be careful about her wording. She even winced slightly. Neither of us wanted to insult the woman or make her uncomfortable. Just the opposite. Josephine had a mothering instinct inside her she couldn't seem to fight. I knew the feeling, only my instinct was protective. I wanted the right to protect Josephine and anyone else she brought into her family.

"Fine. I want to go see Alex now, please."

Jo nodded once before showing Gracie to the car. When we were all in the car, I started it and took off. Jo explained what happened and about Alex's legal issues. Silent tears flowed down Gracie's cheeks, but she said nothing. Only clutched at her belly and rubbed small circles over it.

When Jo finished, Gracie silently wept but kept her head up. "Do you think I'll ever see him again after today?"

Jo smiled but shook her head. "I don't know,

honey. But I promise you I will do everything in my power to help him. I've already got a good lawyer willing to take his case. He'll have to do some time and he'll get a dishonorable discharge, but hopefully he'll be out in a few years."

She shook her head slightly, denying what she was hearing but wanting with everything in her to believe my mama tiger. The hope on her face was plain for anyone to see. "I'll figure it out."

"We'll be here to help you." I added my support to Jo. "I've got a place where you can stay and be safe. Me and some of my buddies have a place we're turning into clubhouse. It's an old hotel and we're hoping to make it into several rooms where we can have a place to crash. Jo and me are gonna live there until we decide what we want to do from there."

"You mean, I could live there?"

"Yes. Absolutely." I gave her a slight smile. "Jo and me'll stay with you as long as you need. You can count on us."

Chapter Six

Mama Jo

I managed to bully Colonel Gill into giving Gracie and Alex as much time as they needed. He scowled at me and bitched and moaned the whole entire time, but he didn't try to break it up. The couple discussed everything for over an hour. Most of it was Gracie feeling out Alex's trust of me and Mike. Some of it was Alex making sure Gracie knew she was to use the money he'd given her to take care of both herself and the baby.

Once they'd finally made their decisions and Gracie felt comfortable with Alex's instructions, they held each other. Gracie cried and promised to keep in touch with him so he knew where she was and how to find her. I gave the colonel the information Mike had given me about where we were going.

"Yeah. I know that bunch of guys." He grinned, chuckling to himself. "Good bunch." He looked to Mike. "How close are you with them?"

Mike shrugged. "Close as any. Served with some of 'em. Worked with others --"

"Good," I interrupted. "Then you know how to find us if anything at all changes with Alex."

"Relax, Jo. I'll make sure the kid is treated fairly and is able to communicate with you and his woman. I've got all three of you listed as his next of kin. That satisfy you?"

I gave a crisp nod. "Perfectly."

Gracie gave Alex a tearful goodbye but left with us willingly. Once we were all in the car, I turned to her. "Is there anything you need us to get before we get the hell outta Dodge? Anything from your place or your father's house?"

"No. And I don't want them to know where I'm going, either."

"I can respect that." I reached back and squeezed Gracie's hand. "I swear to you, everything will be all right. We'll protect you and your child. You're family now."

The second I uttered the words I realized two things. First, fucking Mike was right. I couldn't help myself. I'd claimed those two kids and their unborn child as my own. Second, I knew they were absolutely true. As I figured he would, Mike chuckled.

"Mama Tiger. Told you."

"Bastard," I muttered. Gracie didn't comment, staring out the window, oblivious to our little tiff.

A little over two hours later, we pulled up to a chain-linked fence with a gate. A man approached us, much as the men at Fort Knox had, holding up a hand for us to stop.

"Private property, brother. Sorry."

Mike had on an Army jacket with his rank and company, so the guy knew he was military. This guy had long, shaggy hair with an equally shaggy beard. Muscular arms had a smattering of service tattoos beneath the sleeveless shirt and vest he wore. Three motorcycles were parked by the gate where he and two other men stood guard.

"I'm here at Taz's invite. Check with him."

The guy gave a crisp nod before going back to the other two. He picked up a CB radio and called the man in question.

"Who's Taz?"

"Knew him in Nam. Wasn't in my unit but was a good man. Tried to take care of all of us when our commanders went nuts. Name's Rodrigues. Never knew his first name. Just Rodrigues."

"Taz... Rodrigues?" I sat up straighter. "Theodore Rodrigues. Taz."

Mike shrugged. "Dunno. Only ever knew him as Taz Rodrigues. He pushed me to apply for the Rangers. Said I had a good head for war."

"Sounds like the man I knew."

We waited until the guy came back to us as the other two opened the gate. He waved us in. "Hey, Pops. Welcome. These your women?"

Pops? What the fuck?

"This one is." He jerked his head at me. "Name's Mama. The other one's Gracie. She's under our protection."

The guy gave Gracie a quick look before nodding. "Taz says he'll meet you at the clubhouse. Says to tell you he has your bike in the garage."

"Good. Thanks."

"Straight ahead, over the rise. It's not far."

Mike took off down the gravel road. I gave him a sidelong look. "Mama? Really?"

He shrugged. I could see his lips twitch and didn't appreciate it. At fucking all. "Seemed to fit. I'm Pops. You're Mama."

I narrowed my eyes. "You've been leadin' up to this for a while. That was your play all along. Mama and Pops. Like we're a couple already."

"Seemed better to avoid any motherfucker makin' a pass at you once we got here."

"I coulda not gone with you."

"But you did. Now, everyone here knows you're with me and not to be fucked with." I grinned.

"Oh, they'd'a found out on their own I ain't to be fucked with if they had. I don't need to be linked with you to protect myself."

"I know that. Unless you want some horny

motherfucker gettin' killed when he makes a play for you, you needed to be linked with me."

I sighed, needing to change the subject before I lost my Goddamned mind. "How'd you get the name Pops?"

"'Cause I don't sweat the small things, but I protect the people in my life who are important. That included my unit and the kids we were stationed with."

"Good to know." I had no idea what to do with that because I had seen that protective streak in spades since I'd met Mike. It made me feel claustrophobic and maybe... cared for? I'd never had that in my life, and I had felt it with Mike since the first moment I met him. Knowing that was his default setting took a little of the wind out of my sails, though. That was when I finally admitted to myself that I wanted this man. But on my terms. I wouldn't take a back seat to anyone. Not ever again.

Once we reached what I assumed was the clubhouse, since it looked like the old hotel Mike had described, Mike parked the car but didn't get out. He seemed to study the building for several moments before turning to me. "Stay here. I'll feel this out, then come back for you."

"You're kidding, right? Surely the fuck you're kidding."

"Mama Tiger..."

"No, Mike. We're both coming with you. Me because you need backup. Gracie because I'm not leaving her by herself in this place until I know more about what's going on."

"Taz was always congenial. He invited us here. He provided me with a bike, then the car. I trust him, but I don't like taking the two of you inside until I know what's in there. Taz is a good man, but he's ultimately out for himself."

"You said he tried to protect the men in your unit. When things went to shit."

"He did. But there was always a reason he did everything." Then Mike gave me the side eye. "How exactly do you know him?"

"I pulled his ass out of an ambush when we first got to Nam."

Mike's gaze snapped to mine. "That was you?"

I raised an eyebrow. "So he told you about that."

"Told me his platoon was saved by the most vicious killer he'd ever seen." Mike tilted his head, studying me but not surprised. Which was... puzzling.

"He must not have told you everything."

"Why?" Mike grinned at me. "Because I'm not afraid of you?" When I shrugged, he gave me a cocky smile that threatened to melt my panties. "Make no mistake, Mama. I know exactly what you're capable of. The first time I saw you, I pegged you as the most dangerous person in the room. Even more than me. As to being a vicious killer? I'm sure you are. Aren't all mama tigers?"

I gave him a disgusted snort. "You have no idea what I really am, *Pops*." I spat out the name he'd used, meaning it as an insult. "You should be afraid of me. Very fuckin' afraid."

If anything, his grin got wider. "You're not gonna hurt me. Not because we've fucked either. You're not gonna hurt me because I've not broken your code. And I'm pretty sure you know I never will."

"You're so fuckin' frustrating." I muttered my complaint as I opened the door and got out of the car. Poor Gracie sat there, not saying a word. She hadn't spoken since the beginning of the trip. Even now, she looked like she was in her own world. Likely deep in thought about what she was going to do with her life in the foreseeable future. I opened the back door and jerked my head for her to get out. "You don't need to stay by yourself until I'm sure of everyone in this place, Gracie. Come with me."

"I don't want to cause trouble."

"You won't." Mike and I spoke at the same time. I scowled. He smirked.

"Fucker."

Mike just chuckled. "Come on, Mama. Let's get this over with so we can all have a rest." He made me crazy, but I kind of had to admire him. I knew the man saw me for what I was. It was why he'd willingly followed my lead in the airport and at Fort Knox. He knew I was capable and more than a little ruthless. Yet he stayed with me. Supported me when I'd never asked him to. He was an enigma and a refreshing change all at the same time.

Gracie followed me, her arms wrapped around herself protectively. The clubhouse looked like some old hotel they were fixing up. Men were everywhere, working. There were at least fifteen or twenty. None of them paid us any attention. Well, except one guy. And he was most definitely the Taz I knew.

"Jo?"

I lifted my chin. "Taz."

He turned his attention back to Mike. "You didn't tell me you knew Dr. Peyton." Taz's slight English accent always threw me. Although his parents were Brits, he'd been born in the U.S., yet managed to pick up a bit of their accent. It wasn't pronounced, but there all the same.

Mike shrugged. "Just met her when we landed in Louisville. You hear about what happened?"

Taz nodded. "Yes. You there when it happened?"

"Yep." Mike nodded in my direction. "Mama here talked the kid down."

"Where's he now?"

"Holding cell at Fort Knox, where he was stationed," I offered. "He'll be moved at some point, but Ry and Ian are going to try to keep him there until his trial is over."

"Rylan Gill and Ian McGregor?" When I nodded, he snorted. "If it can be done, those two will do it." Taz turned his gaze to Gracie. "And who's the girl?"

"She's the soldier in question's woman. She's pregnant with his child."

"I see. She got any place to go?"

I took a threatening step toward Taz. "She stays with us."

Taz chuckled. "Pops give you the name Mama?"

"He did. Don't mean I accepted it."

"Well, he named you well."

"What the fuck is that supposed to mean? Just because you guys think you have me figured out doesn't mean you do."

"Oh, I think we do, Mama." Taz sobered then. "You're the most ruthless warrior I've ever met, but only when someone you love is threatened. In my case, it was my whole company."

I sighed. "They were just kids."

"They weren't any younger than we were."

"They weren't as prepared as we were, Taz." This was fucking exasperating. "I had a demon for a stepfather and you grew up on the streets. We were at least a decade older than those kids in life experiences."

"Whatever. You took them all under your wing and when they were threatened, you did what you could to protect us all. Myself included."

"Then my temper got me a dishonorable discharge."

Taz just grunted. "Controlled yourself better'n me."

"I heard you killed that fucking general."

"Maybe."

"Then you disappeared off the face of the fuckin' planet. Until now."

"It's amazing what you can do when you're willing to lie low." He tried to give me a superior smirk, but I could see the underlying tension in the set of his jaw.

"I heard you had some help." That wasn't all I'd heard. If the rumors were to be believed, Taz was in deep shit. "An organization older than the fuckin' country is what I heard."

"Not a discussion I can have, Jo. If you've heard anything accurate, then you know I can't talk about it."

I nodded. That was exactly what I'd heard. "What are you gonna do?"

"Not much I can do. But there's more than just me to think about."

"Oh?"

Taz turned his gaze to the back of the room, to the shadows the sunlight couldn't quite reach. "Liam. Come meet my friends."

A skinny kid of about four or five moved into the room. His gaze was fixed on us like he was studying us, even though he was just a kid. His gaze moved from me to Mike, then to Gracie. When he finished, his gaze returned to me and he narrowed his eyes. He said nothing but stayed at Taz's side.

"My son."

That shocked me. "Your son?"

"Yes. Unfortunately, his mother was killed in Laos."

As I'm sure Taz knew, my heart ached for the child. The kid tilted his head at me, like he knew I was the person he had to win over. Not Mike.

"Yes." Taz grinned. "Liam has you figured out."

The kid took a step forward. Then another. Then he walked straight toward me. When he stood in front of me, he looked up. There was weariness in his eyes. "You know my dad?"

"Yeah, kid. I do."

"You gonna take me when my dad leaves?"

I glanced up sharply at Taz. "Leaves?"

He nodded. "I can't take Liam with me where I'm going."

"You can't abandon your son, Taz."

"And I can't take him with me."

"Then don't fuckin' go. This is crazy."

"I don't have a choice, Jo." Taz raised his voice in proportion to my own. "I took their help so I could find my wife. But I was too late. A group in her village executed her because she'd given herself to a man not her husband and had his child. Probably woulda killed Liam too, except he was a boy."

"She was killed because of me," Liam said. Hearing the kid say that so casually sent chills down my spine.

"Not because of *you*, Liam." Taz's voice was firm, his features hard. "Because of me. If I hadn't left her, if I'd brought her back with me…"

"And how would you have done that, huh, Taz?" I was losing patience with this whole conversation. It was also hurting my heart. Just a little bit. "You couldn't just waltz out of the country and hop a plane back to the States with her."

"I should have tried to figure out a way. If I'd known she was pregnant, I might have managed it."

Mike remained silent. These were men he'd agreed to meet, the men who'd invited him into their club. He hadn't been in their unit, but he'd obviously made an impression on them if they wanted him to be part of something this close knit. I only knew Taz. But once more Mike had my back and let me take the lead.

Liam moved to stand beside Gracie. The boy smiled up at her. "Hi. I'm Liam." Just like his father, the kid had a slight British accent, though his coloring looked like it might have come more from his mother than father.

"I'm Gracie."

"Are you with Mama and Pops too?"

I gave Taz an exasperated look. "Really? You told everyone to call us that?"

He shrugged. "What would you prefer to be called? Figured with you guys being here, you wanted to disappear."

"Not a bad idea, Mama." Mike spoke for the first time in a while. "We could just lie low here. Forget our past and everything in it."

"My past made me who I am. Besides, I don't think you really want that."

"Maybe not for myself, but I get the feeling there's more to your story. I also get the feeling that the two of you would be much better off disappearing. For a multitude of reasons."

"He's right, Mama." Taz handed me a manila envelope. It had my name on it. "I ran into a couple of guys after I made it back from Nam. Word got out. What you did."

I opened the envelope and my jaw tightened. "CIA? What the fuck?"

"If my sources are right, they want to recruit you for special ops inside Vietnam for the remainder of the war. They need a woman and think you've got most of the training you need already."

"Well, with my less than honorable discharge, I'm sure they've rethought that position."

"Or they could have been the reason you got that discharge."

"As opposed to the general I told to suck my dick? I don't think so."

Taz barked out a laugh while Gracie gasped before letting out a small giggle. "Yeah, I guess it could have been that." He sobered, his smile fading slowly. "But I think you know it wasn't."

"Yeah."

"I had no idea I was hookin' up with a real badass." Mike grinned, even as he stepped closer to me. I didn't miss that he put his body slightly in front of me and between me and Taz.

"You stayin' with her, Pops?"

Mike nodded. "Yeah. Thought I might."

"She's the real deal. Skilled surgeon and one of the deadliest people I've ever met. Don't fuck with her."

The grin Mike gave Taz set my teeth on edge. Like this was all a big joke to him. "Fuckin' with her's half the fun. I like living dangerously."

"Just have her back."

Instantly, Mike sobered. "Always."

"Will you take my son? Keep him safe?"

"Taz --" I started to tell him to fuck off, but the bastard interrupted me.

"Just until I come back. Once I figure out exactly what this group wants from me, I'll be better able to protect him. I don't want to take my only son into a situation I can't control or predict."

I wanted to punch the bastard in the taint. But I got it. What he was asking wasn't unreasonable. "Fine. We'll take care of him. But you can't abandon that kid. You have to swear on your life you'll come back for him."

"Give me three years, Jo. Hopefully it won't take that long, but I have a feeling it will."

"Who are those people?" It wasn't like I'd know them, but if I could find out, maybe I could help Taz.

"Not here." He jerked his head to his office. "Gracie, why don't you let Liam show you around. Son, take her to the room I had the boys get ready. Either one."

"Yes, sir." The kid took Gracie's hand. "Come on, Gracie. This place is really cool."

I looked at Mike and he nodded, indicating he thought it was safe. I agreed but wanted his input. *Why* I wanted his input was a pain in my ass. I trusted Mike -- Pops -- with my life. Maybe it was the airport confrontation, but I didn't think so. He was the first man to ever treat me like he knew my worth. Sure, he tried to protect me when I was perfectly capable of taking care of myself, but I kind of found that endearing.

We both followed Taz to his office where he shut and locked the door. When he turned to us, I could see the strain on his face I'd missed earlier.

"They call themselves the Brotherhood. When they told me what they wanted in exchange for getting me to Jazeera and Liam, I promised them anything they wanted if they'd help me. Now I'm rethinking that promise."

"The Brotherhood." I thought back. The name tickled something in my brain, but it was elusive, gone before I could nail it down.

"They go back a long fucking way. Longer than the U.S. has been a country. I don't know everything -- that won't come until I'm fully committed. They're vigilantes, but more on a global scale."

And then it hit me where I'd heard of them. "That Vietcong general said something about them. The one I killed."

"The Brotherhood is the reason we won't win that conflict. They've got people deep in both governments pulling the strings and guiding everyone else where they want them to go. They want control over that region. Therefore, the U.S. can't push the communists out and take over, even with a puppet president. The communists like to keep secrets. The U.S. has a very savvy and efficient press corps that hates secrets as much as the communists like to keep them."

"So they need Vietnam united, but under communist control." Mike stroked the scruffy whiskers at his chin as he voiced his thoughts.

"Yes. While money paves the way for every government, the Brotherhood feels Vietnam being under the control of a non-democratic country would better serve their interests. Also, the money trail is less likely to be followed."

"That's why the CIA wants me in Nam, isn't it?" My gut was tightening. While I had the feeling something might come back to bite me in the ass, I wasn't expecting this. I mean, one didn't fuck with a general and get away with only a less than honorable discharge. No. Taz was right. I'd given them the excuse they needed to kick me out of the army and be ripe for the picking for the CIA.

"That's my guess. Understand me, Jo. Under no

circumstances can you let them recruit you. It'd be a death sentence, even for someone as skilled and deadly as you are. You do not want to take on these guys. Not for something like this. That country is going to be what it is. The Brotherhood might nudge it in the direction they want it to go for a while, but it's not something they can sustain. Eventually, the people of Vietnam will govern themselves again. That's the way it works."

"I'll think about it. But I think you're right on this. Besides, I have no desire to get caught up with the spooks."

Taz let out a sigh. Relief? "Thanks, Jo."

"You act like I'm doing you a huge favor. What's going on?"

"This goes with you to the grave, Jo. I'm telling you because I need you to know what I'm up against so you can protect Liam if need be." He glanced up at Mike. "You too. To the grave."

I widened my stance and crossed my arms over my chest, lifting my chin. "Give it to us."

"They want me to be an assassin for them."

"Jesus, Taz." Pops stepped forward again, putting himself between me and Taz one more time. "What the fuck?"

"If I can't get out of this and you're actively working against them, they will set their sights on you next. I don't want to go up against you, Jo. No matter if I was able to get the best of you or not, I'd still lose. And that's a mighty big if, and I'm not too proud to admit it. But these guys would never stop, even if I failed. They have one assassin over a very small group. He controls everything. And he never misses. They call him El Diablo, but I think with them it's more a title than a name. It's passed down from one assassin to the next."

"Fine." I tried to ignore Pops, but it was hard. He was head and shoulders taller than me and probably outweighed me by a hundred pounds. All of it muscle. Kind of hard to ignore when he didn't want to be ignored. "But you have to keep your promise. No longer than three years. Not because I don't want the responsibility or anything. Because that boy needs his father."

"I swear. Give me three years. I'll come back for him, no matter what it costs me."

"And back to your brothers," Pops said firmly. "Liam's not the only one who needs you. What about the boys here? I saw several who looked like they're barely more than kids."

"All of them served in one way or another. All in Nam. Most in my unit. I promised I'd give them a home and I'm trying. But I could use some help." He looked from Pops to me and back again. "Please. I want to make this a club with its own set of rules. Its own code. We make money, support each other, and stick to our code. If that means we have to skirt the law, we do it. If someone in our territory needs killin', we do that too. As long as it doesn't go against our moral code -- which means we don't hurt innocents and we always protect women and children. It's not about making a living so much as it's to give these guys a sense of freedom and control over their own lives. A sense of purpose. Anything else is an added bonus and will go into a club fund."

"Fair enough," Pops said. "We never harm women or children." I thought Pops repeated that last to reinforce there was a hard line there. I agreed with him about the children and mostly about the women, though I was a firm believer that some of the worst people who needed to die were women.

"Absolutely not. There's a budding drug highway coming through this way. Coming in primarily through military channels, but it's spreading. They're taking it in this direction because it's rural. Most of these guys have problems with heroin. I'd like to keep that stuff out of our territory. And bury any motherfucker who doesn't take the fuckin' hint so no one will find even their bones."

"First thing we need to do is finish building the clubhouse," Pops offered. "After that, we'll work on what we're gonna do with the club. You got a name for it yet?"

"Yeah." Taz grinned. "I'm gonna call it Bones."

Chapter Seven

Mike/Pops

A week later, I was still trying to come to terms with everything Taz had dumped on us. I knew about the Brotherhood. Or, at least, knew *of* them. That last was the worst part. The fact that I knew about the Brotherhood made me a marked man. No one outside the Brotherhood was supposed to know they existed. And I most decidedly wasn't part of them. With Taz being with them now, I worried about his son, Liam. Then there was Gracie and her baby.

At any other time in my life, I might have scoffed at the idea of a family. After my first tour in Nam, I decided I never wanted to have to go through what my mother was going through. I could have a woman and companionship, but I didn't have to bring children into the world. And, honestly, this was the first time I ever realized I could actually have people in my life closer than blood. Not having kids didn't help me at fucking all. Alex and Gracie were definitely tugging at my heartstrings as much as they did my mama tiger's.

Looking at Liam as he made his bond with Gracie warmed my heart. The pair had both seemed more than a little lost, but they were helping each other. Along with Mama's gentle insistence they be together, they seemed to genuinely like each other. Mama said it helped Gracie learn what she'd need to do after her baby was born, and Liam needed a mother figure. I suspected it was a way to help both our young charges feel normal again.

In the week since I brought Mama and Gracie to the compound, I could already see signs Gracie was relaxing. She'd stopped jumping every time one of the men barked out a laugh, or spoke to her, or approached her in any way, really. A couple had tried to make a move on her, but she'd shut them down. Then Mama reinforced the shutdown. That always made me smile. They were a good lot, but a little lackadaisical in discipline.

"What the fuck are we gonna do with this bunch?" Mama muttered under her breath as she stomped inside the common room, which was supposed to be under construction. Currently, me and Mama were the only ones working on it. It would be a perfect place for the guys to hang out together and drink beer. Maybe watch a ball game or play pool. Or, as evidenced by the women who seemed to have descended on the place, fuck to their hearts' content. Assuming we ever got the fucking room finished. Currently, they were doing everything ass backward. Pretty sure they'd done it on purpose too. Just because they could.

"I'd say whip 'em into shape like a batch of new recruits, but I'm not sure these guys'd appreciate it." I shrugged. "They just got outta the service. I doubt they want reminders this soon."

She stared at me hard, her gaze contemplative. "Or maybe that's exactly what they need. Lord knows if they don't start working on the clubhouse again, we're never gonna get the rooms done."

I shrugged. "We can try. Taz is leaving today. I'll run it by him."

Instantly, her gaze hardened and she glared at me. "He don't like it, he needs to keep his ass here. He's left us in charge for the time being, he'll have to live with any changes we make."

"God, that tone of voice makes me hard."

She jerked her head up where she'd been scrubbing on a freshly installed counter -- which should have been done last on this job -- to get the gummy glue off of it. No sense wasting the work already done. I thought she might lay into me, but, to my great and utter delight, she stalked toward me, gripped my face, and pulled me down for a heated kiss.

I tunneled my fingers through her hair, fisting the silky strands in a tight grip. The strawberry-blonde curls sifted through my fingers as I adjusted my grip. Mama clawed at me, trying to get my shirt off. Her little grunts of demand were music to my ears.

When she finally did get my shirt off, I pulled her to me, looping my arm tightly around her back while I found the crook of her neck with my mouth and sucked. She cried out, leaning her neck back to let me have better access while she raked my skin with her nails.

"Guessin' I ain't the only one horny as a motherfucker."

She grunted, her hand going to the front of my jeans where she squeezed and kneaded my cock. I found her breast with my hand under her T-shirt and gave it my own rough squeeze. This was the woman I knew was inside her. She was aggressive. Dominant. And I'd let her be because she needed to be.

Until it was time for me to be even more dominant than she was.

I shoved her bra over her tits to grip soft, warm flesh in my palm. I squeezed roughly, a grip that might well bruise. It was a test. To see how hard she needed this to be. I wanted to give this woman everything I was, and I needed her to know I could take charge when she needed me to.

Mama's hands went to the fastener of my jeans, undoing them and shoving them down my hips. "Get inside me, Pops." Her voice was a husky groan. There was still that demanding bite that made my cock ache, but there was also a helpless lust she didn't even try to hide.

My hand shot to her neck and she tilted her head back, baring more of her skin to me. My gaze bore into hers. "You're not in charge, woman."

"I said fuck me, you bastard!"

"Oh, I'll fuck you all right. I'll fuck you hard and messy. That what you want?"

"Just give it to me!"

I spun her around and bent her over the counter she'd been cleaning, holding her shoulders down when she would have pushed up. "Stay." I bit out my command at the same time I swatted her ass.

With one hand I unfastened her jeans before pushing them past her ass. Once I got them down far enough to swipe my fingers through her pussy lips to test her wetness, I made my cock follow the path my fingers had taken, slowly shoving myself inside her hard and deep.

Mama screamed, pushing back against me as she gripped the countertop. I supposed this moment made it worth the fact that the guys had built it before they should have. I gripped her shoulder in one hand, her hip in the other, and fucked her. Hard. Letting loose all the pent-up lust and longing and joy and gratefulness I had inside me. How the fuck had I done enough right in my fucking life to be given such a woman as this?

I continued fucking her, both of us grunting with each jarring, staccato smack of flesh on flesh. She screamed again. This time her pussy clamped down on me, squeezing and squeezing until my cock exploded with cum inside the haven of Jo's body.

Mama.

I knew the names we'd taken would stick. I also had the feeling Jo and Mike would cease to exist, and it would be Mama and Pops in this world we were being dragged into. Surprisingly, I found I was looking forward to that.

When we both finally came to our senses, it was to catcalls and whistles from a few of the men who'd finally shown up. Likely not to work.

With a vicious snarl, I bared my teeth to all of them. "Get the fuck out. Line up outside the garage in five minutes. Things are gettin' ready to fuckin' change 'round here."

"You don't get to tell us what to do, Pops." One of the younger, smaller men smirked. "You might be all badass and shit, but we're younger and stronger."

I tucked my cock away and stalked toward the kid with every intention of throttling the little bastard. Thankfully, the kid and a couple of his buddies around him weren't complete dumb shits. They all backed up several steps. I still got in the punk's face, shouting at him like any drill sergeant at a new recruit.

"You wanna stay in this outfit, boy? Do you? Because I got no problem sendin' your fuckin' smart ass out the fuckin' gate."

"You're not our leader."

"Yeah? You might wanna tell Taz that. He's leavin' for a while. Puttin' me and Mama in charge o' you fuckin' dumb shits until he gets back. That fuckin' makes me the fuckin' leader of this fuckin' heap of maggot shit." The kid looked surprised and wary, but didn't push back. Probably because I could be a scary motherfucker when I wanted to be.

"Right. Yeah. We'll get everyone together at the garage."

"You'll fuckin' line up in two Goddamned lines

at attention. Then you will wait for Taz and me and Mama. You will not say a fuckin' word and you will not fuckin' move. If you do, I'll take it as a sign you don't wanna fuckin' be here."

"Yes, sir." The youngster snapped to attention before spinning around and marching double time out the door. Everyone followed him without question.

"Well. That was… surprising." I wasn't sure if I wanted to laugh or shake my head in amazement. "Don't let anyone ever say you can't read people, Mama. You knew what these kids needed."

"They didn't realize it when they were in the service because everything went to shit over there. In Nam. I suppose some people know what we were fighting for, but I just wanted to get out alive. Guessin' these guys felt the same way."

"What did you do over there, Jo?" I reached out to stroke her wild hair away from her cheek. "Why does the CIA want you? And why do I get the feelin' you were more than a doctor?"

"Because you're smart." She sighed, straightening her clothing. I expected her to be embarrassed to have been caught by the kids fucking. And, let's face it, that's exactly what this group of hooligans was gonna be to us. Our kids. Yeah. For someone who never thought he'd have a family, I was acquiring family by the gaggle. "Rest assured, I did nothing through official channels. When the orders coming in for the unit I was with ceased to make sense and men were being thrown up a hill for nothing, slaughtered for nothing, I took matters into my own hands. We rescued more than one unit from ambushes when intel was bogus and they walked into an area that was supposed to be cleared, only for the VC to start a killing field. A bunch of 'em in Colonial Gill's outfit. Can't say we saved more than we lost, but we managed to get a few out who might not otherwise have come home. That was why the general was *really* at my field hospital. Taz is right. I'm sure that fuckin' general baited me. I was never quiet about my opinions and my opinion of leadership was that they were fuckin' shit. Now? I guess I know why."

"You think people in the government know about the Brotherhood?"

"Not sure. My gut says no, but there's always that possibility. At least, anyone who knows of them doesn't know the full extent of what they do and how much power they really have. If we're aware of them, there have to be more who know. How *much* they know is anyone's guess. I'm guessing anyone in the government knows just enough to think they can control the Brotherhood. They can't."

"Which, again, might be the whole point. The Brotherhood wants to recruit you. Get you to go back. Then you either join them or disappear."

She shook her head immediately. "No. If they know me at all, the Brotherhood knows I'm not the kind of person they want in their ranks. I think too freely and I'm not too great at taking orders. Especially if I don't agree with them. If they're trying to get me there, it's to take me out."

"You think Taz will tell them about you?"

Mama gave me a hard stare. Yeah. She would make sure Taz never said a word.

"Understood." I grinned at her. I might have been mistaken, but I was pretty sure I saw her lips twitch before she finished straightening her clothing, then stormed outside to face the "recruits."

Yeah. I was looking forward to this.

Chapter Eight

Mama

I'll admit, I didn't expect the club to be lined up outside the garage like Pops had told them to be. And when the fuck had I embraced these stupid names everyone had started calling us? I wasn't anyone's mama. Wasn't ever gonna be.

Heavy sigh... Except I was. Started with Alex. Then Gracie and her unborn child. Now this whole fucking club. I was getting soft. Which pissed me off to no end. Sure enough, when I got out to the garage, there they were. Every single one of them was at attention like it was the second day of basic training and they were determined not to give the sergeant any reason to get all up in their shit.

Pops stalked past me, his game face firmly in place. "Gonna be some fuckin' changes around here. Startin' this very fuckin' second." A couple of them glanced at each other, and Pops jumped all over that shit.

He moved quickly, like he was expecting this very thing and was ready to shut it down. Getting in the faces of the two in question, he yelled as effectively as anyone I'd ever met in the Army.

"You two got a fuckin' problem?" When one of them opened his mouth, Pops continued, his voice carrying all over the compound. Almost made me wince. Almost made me smile, too. "No one cares if you've got a fuckin' problem! It's my way or the highway. Hell. Ain't even no highway option. You will do what the fuck I say and you'll fuckin' like it! You clear?"

"Sir, loud and clear, sir," he yelled back, staring straight ahead.

"Don't fuckin' call me *sir*."

The guy faltered, looking up at Pops instead of staring straight ahead. "Uh… Pops?"

Pops was silent for a long while, staring both those fuckers down like they really were back in the service. These two were Marines. Most of the others were Army, but there were a smattering of Navy and Air Force. And why the fuck had I made it my business to know that shit? Christ.

"Good. Listen up because I'm only gonna go over this once."

Taz chose that moment to enter the yard. He stood beside me and nudged my shoulder. When I looked up at him, he appeared to be struggling to keep the amusement off his face. Which made me scowl all the harder at him.

Pops continued. "Taz has a situation he has to deal with. He'll be gone for a while. Ain't sure how long. He's leavin' me and Mama in charge." Surprisingly, no one gave any side looks or showed any surprise, their training kicking in as I'd hoped it would. This was, after all, basic stuff. "He let you be laid back and adjust for a while, but I'm done with that. We got shit to do around here to make this place livable and we're gonna get it done. Anyone who ain't on board, get the fuck out."

No one moved. Taz cleared his throat and stepped forward. "Not sure how long I'll be gone, but there is no negotiation. You do what Mama and Pops say or you're out. I don't care why, or how unfair you think it is; if they say you're gone, you're gone. Even if I don't agree with them, they're still in charge. I will not override their decisions." He glared at each of them for a long moment before continuing. "A word of advice to all of you, and I suggest you pass it on to anyone and everyone who comes to this place looking for a home. Of the two of 'em, y'all might think Pops is the bigger threat. He's not. Mama will have your balls sliced clean from your body before you even know she's near you. Don't fuck with either of them, but especially don't fuck with Mama."

"Now you're just taking away all my fuckin' fun," I muttered. I was secretly pleased he'd done it, but I also knew there would be a couple who'd test me. There always were.

As I glanced around, I found two, possibly three, who would test me. I could see it in the way their gazes slid to me. They were all young -- none of them over twenty-three or twenty-four -- but they had been on their own long enough to not take kindly to a woman giving them orders.

I walked up to the biggest of them. He was a good three or four inches taller than me, but I managed to get in his face. "I see you got a problem with me bein' in charge." My voice was quiet, as deadly as I could make it. "You gonna test me, do it now. I won't have anyone claimin' I snuck up on 'em before I nutted 'em." I stepped back a couple of steps and held out my hands to my sides, raising an eyebrow. "Take your best shot, motherfucker."

As I expected, the guy lunged for me, going for his arms around my waist, probably to take me down in a football tackle. Amateur. I went down to one knee and uppercut his crotch with as much force as I could. The guy let out a startled yelp, then went down to his knees, clutching his privates.

I spun out of the way so he couldn't reach me if he tried. Immediately, the other two charged. One of them I punted on the side of the knee. The other one wrapped two brawny arms around me from behind. I snapped my head back twice, my height letting me catch him in the nose. He staggered back and I nailed him with a spinning kick so my heel connected with his jaw.

"Who's next?" I glared at the three men on the ground before staring down the rest of them. Mike, bless his heart, stood with his arms crossed over his chest, a big-ass shit-eating grin on his face.

He looked at Taz. "That's my woman."

The men on the ground groaned, looking to Taz for... something. I had no idea what, but this would define our relationship with this club. If it wasn't to my satisfaction, I'd take Gracie and Liam and we'd get the fuck out. Start our own fucking club.

Taz shook his head. "Don't look at me. I tried to fuckin' warn ya."

I waited until the guy whose knee I'd taken out attempted to stand. He looked up at me, pain on his face. "Sorry, ma'am."

"Mama. My name is Mama."

I reached down to offer him a hand up. The kid nodded as he took my hand and stood. "Mitch Bohannon. They call me Brutal."

The one I'd kicked in the face was already on his feet, holding out a hand to me. "Mason Gray." He shrugged. "Gray."

The poor guy I'd nailed in the balls had made it to one knee, but he didn't look like he was ready to go farther. "Gerald Ferguson, ma'am."

"Mama." I grinned, holding out a hand to him. "Got a road name?"

He gasped for air. Though he took my hand, he couldn't seem to get to his feet. Kid shook his head before dropping my hand, one arm braced on his knee, the other went back to his balls. "Nah."

"How about Squid?" someone called out. The guy on the ground threw a scowl over his shoulder. Or tried to. He ended up groaning, but finally managed to get to his feet. He still bent over, sucking air.

"How about you shut the fuck up." Pops took charge, angry scowl firmly in place. "He needed a demonstration. He got one." He tilted his head at Gerald. "How about we call you Mo." Pops shrugged. "Seems fitting."

"Mo?" One of the other guys barked out a laugh. "What does that even mean?"

Pops looked at me, grinning before shrugging his shoulders. I rolled my eyes but couldn't help the twitch to my lips. "The Mighty Mo."

"What does the USS Missouri have to do with Ferguson?"

"Jesus, man." Brutal gave the guy an irritated look. "Missouri is the fuckin' *Show Me* state. Maybe you're the fuckin' dumbass."

"Oh." The other guy looked a little deflated but didn't protest. "Yeah. That's pretty good."

"Mo it is then." I clapped the guy on the shoulder. He grunted, but actually attempted to chuckle. Straightening slowly, he extended his hand to me. I took it in a firm grip. "Mama."

I grinned. "Good." Looking around the rest of the group I raised an eyebrow. "Anyone else need a demonstration?"

When no one answered, Pops took over again. "You all are gonna get to work. We've got a place to clean up and remodel. And build. We can't have a proper home until we get it finished."

"We've been working."

I winced, almost feeling sorry for the guy. Pops growled and stomped toward the guy in question.

Immediately, the guy backed off. "I'm sorry. I'm sorry!"

"You got a problem with working harder?" Pops was back to yelling again, right up in the guy's face. "Do you? 'Cause I won't allow no deadbeat pussies in this fuckin' outfit!

"No problem. No problem at all, Pops."

Taz got a kick outta that. "Yeah. Things're gonna be just fine while I'm gone."

* * *

Taz left the next morning. He spent the whole evening with Liam, preparing his son for his absence. The boy was resistant, but agreed he'd stay behind if he could stay with Gracie. Kid might have thought he was negotiating, but it was exactly what Taz wanted.

Gracie was more than agreeable. The girl seemed to have latched onto Liam the same as he had her. I knew they needed each other. I got the impression Taz thought so too.

"You know, this is a good thing. Right?" Pops pulled me aside and wrapped his arms around me from behind. His mouth found the side of my neck and he sucked ever so delicately.

I shivered, trying not to show how much he affected me, but it was a losing fucking battle. "I know they're gonna be a pain in my ass. Solidly."

Mike chuckled. "Not disagreein'. But you're good with this. Right?"

I turned to look at him over my shoulder. "Of course, I'm fuckin' good with this! These guys are a fuckin' mess!" I snapped my outrage, turning around completely to glare at him. "With Taz leavin', who the fuck else is gonna save these bastards from themselves?"

Mike lifted his hands in surrender, an amused

smirk on his face. "Just makin' sure, Mama. No need to go all mama tiger on me."

"Good." I turned back around, giving him my back. I reached back for his hands and tugged him to me. "Now. No one told you to stop what you were doin'."

Mike chuckled against my neck, sending electric zings down my spine. I wanted to melt into him. I wanted him to bend me over and take me right here. Fuck me. Show everyone who happened upon us that I was his and no one else's. "Demanding little thing, ain'tcha." God! The man knew how to push every single one of my buttons!

"I am. Ain't apologizin' either."

"Never said you had to."

"Good. 'Cause if you don't satisfy me, I'll find someone who will."

With a growl, Mike spun me around, slamming me against a nearby wall. When I went to shove him away, he grasped my wrists in one of his big hands, pinning them above my head. A wild, frenzied lust punched me in the gut, taking my breath. When I parted my lips, Mike descended on me, taking my mouth in a hard, controlling kiss.

His tongue thrust deep, his other hand squeezed my breast hard. He pinched my nipple roughly, twisting it once. Then again. I cried out with the third twist but not in pain. Sure, it hurt, but the pain morphed into something I wasn't sure I was prepared for.

The pleasure was sharp, intense, making my knees buckle. Mike steadied me with his body, his breath hot against my cheek as he whispered, "You want this. You need this."

I couldn't deny it. The mixture of pain and

pleasure was intoxicating. Every harsh touch was a message, every tender brush a contradiction that drove me wild. Mike's hands roamed over me, exploring as if he had all the right in the world -- which, in this moment, I might have given him.

Then the hand holding my wrists tightened and his other hand went to my throat. It was a threat pure and simple. Except... it wasn't. Instead, it was a dark temptation I'd never thought I'd even contemplate going down.

"Tell me what you want," Mike murmured, his voice low and husky, filled with an unspoken promise. "Ask me for what you want." He looked into my eyes, studying me. Withholding my reactions from him was impossible, but I tried to keep my gruff, demanding exterior so he didn't get the idea he could push me around. Or take the lead. Except, wasn't that exactly what I wanted? Needed?

"Fuck me, you bastard." I bared my teeth at him. Mike tightened his grip on my throat just that little bit. He was a big, strong man. While I was tall, fit, and a seasoned warrior in my own right, Mike towered over me and was easily twice my size. Had I been in this position with any other man, I'd have been worried for my life. The expression on his face was hard. Calculating. And so very dominant it curled my toes.

"You don't get to dictate. You're not in charge here." His voice was gruff, husky with steel in his tone. "Ask me." He gave me an almost evil grin. "Nicely."

"You've lost your mind," I bit out. "Put up or shut up."

He fused his mouth to mine, never letting up on his grip around my throat. With wicked flicks of his tongue, he proceeded to set my body ablaze with sensation. The contrast between the pleasure of his kiss and the aggressive hold he had on my neck was a confusing mix of fear and overwhelming lust.

"Little witch." His lips still brushed mine as he growled out the words. "Fuckin' little witch."

"Are you gonna fuck me or not?" I tried to sound angry. I mean, angry sex was always good sex. But, if I was honest with myself, I sounded every bit as breathless as I felt. My head was swimming with all the sensations he effortlessly created.

"Like I said. You gotta ask nicely."

"Like hell." I tried to shove him away, but Mike was having none of it. He just continued to kiss me. The more he did, the feebler my efforts to get away from him became. I didn't really want him to stop, but I couldn't quite make myself actually ask him to fuck me.

I watched in fascination as his hard, dominant expression turned into an almost evil grin. As he kissed me, I kept my eyes open, looking into his gleaming eyes watching me back. It felt like he was the predator who'd caught me as his prey and was just waiting to go in for the kill.

God, the man was skilled with his tongue! He kissed me like no man had ever before. I'd never even imagined kissing could be so exciting! And we'd had sex regularly since we'd started. It wasn't like this was all new. Mike -- no. He was Pops now. And Pops was different from Mike. I saw it in the way he took charge of the men in this club, and many of them were definitely alpha. Pops was the top alpha. And he was slowly but surely asserting dominance over his very alpha mate.

I continued to shove at his chest, trying to get free. Though, I had to admit, I wasn't trying as hard as I should have. Not if I'd felt threatened. Did I really want him to dominate me on some level? Did I want to submit to him? But that was crazy. Right?

The sharp scent of lust hung heavily in the air, making my thoughts and feelings all the more a chaotic mess. A window somewhere let in a sweet summer breeze smelling of the rain about to come.

The taste of his lips and tongue was a strange mix of the whisky he'd sipped earlier and his own intoxicating, unique taste. It was aggressive, sweet, power and tenderness rolled into one that left me breathless, wanting more. My lips tingled from the force of his kiss. There was the faint essence of his cologne mixing with the other scents and tastes until my head spun in a dizzying high.

My breathing was strained, ragged as I struggled against him, needing to assert some kind of dominance before I completely lost myself in this erotically tantalizing madness. My gasps and moans were muffled by his kiss as he literally stole the breath from my body. Our mingled sighs, grunts, and growls were the music to our cacophonous dance.

No matter how much he kissed me, no matter how I halfheartedly fought him, Pops's grip around my throat was unyielding, his touch both arousing and infuriating.

Just as I thought I might succumb completely to the bewildering storm of emotions he was stirring within me, Pops suddenly pulled back, his eyes burning into mine with an intensity that both scared and excited me. He loosened his grip but didn't let go completely. There was a slight smirk playing around the corners of his mouth as he watched me catch my breath, panting.

"You're a wild one," he murmured, his voice low and teasing.

"That may be. But if you think you're going to tame me, think again."

"Got no desire to tame you, Mama. I like that you have fire. I hope you always do."

I glared at him, not fully believing he could actually want me to fight him. And I would. I would always be dominant. But for Pops, I thought I could let him take control. Sometimes.

Maybe.

"I'm not some pet to be domesticated," I shot back, my voice husky with need.

"No. You ain't. But the fight is half the fun. Make no mistake, Mama. In any battle with you, I... will... win. I will win because you won't have a man you can't respect. And you won't fully respect any man you can best. Giving you up isn't something I'll ever be able to do, so I'll do whatever it takes." He lifted his chin, looking down at me. "So, I'm going to ask you once again, Mama. What is it you need?" It was a demand pure and simple. A command.

I swallowed. No doubt he could feel the movement of my throat with his hand still a tight, unbreakable band. Then I closed my eyes and exhaled slowly before obeying him. "Please, Mike," I whispered. "Please fuck me. And that's as much as I'm capable of. I won't beg. I can't."

He grinned. "Never said you had to beg, darlin'. Never that. But you need to know I can and will take care of you. If I step in, you need to know I can enforce my will if necessary."

"We'll have words," I threatened, but I was pretty sure it came out a breathless protest more than an actual warning. "I won't roll over for anyone. Not even you."

"Which is where you're going to trust me to have

your back. I will never take over unless I feel you're being too careless with your safety, or I think you need it. Then, in private, we can hash it out. But I want you to understand, from this point on it's me and you. We have each other's back. We are united."

God, what he was saying appealed to me. Not only did the relationship he described appeal to me, but also, wasn't this how a mother and father should be? United in the eyes of the children so they couldn't play one of us off the other? I knew in my heart we were better together than we ever were separately.

After giving it thought, I nodded my head slowly. Only then did Mike let up on his grip around my neck. "I like the sound of that." I didn't look away from him. And though he eased his grip, he didn't let me go.

With a grunt of approval, Mike bent his knees and wrapped his arms around me, lifting me so I had to wrap my legs around his waist to hang on.

He carried me to a nearby door and opened it, taking us inside. He locked the door before kissing me again. I knew the room was being used as an office at this point. It was unfinished and smelled of sawdust, drywall, and paint. The desk in the middle of the room was littered with papers and notebooks that Mike brushed away with one swipe of his arm.

Setting me on my feet, Mike whipped my shirt over my head before moving to my jeans. His movements were swift and jerky in his haste. I unfastened my bra and reached for his shirt, tugging it from his jeans, running my hands up his hair-dusted torso as I pulled the material from his body.

While he shoved my jeans and panties over my hips, I leaned in to take one of his nipples between my teeth, nipping at the bit of flesh. He barked out a sharp yell before he pulled away to lift me to the top of the desk. Shoving my legs apart, Mike unfastened his own jeans and pulled out his cock.

The next thing I knew, Mike had shoved himself inside me and began a brutal ride. He slammed into me with explosive force. Our flesh slapped together loudly in the small room. With each of his thrusts, my body shook, forcing the breath from my lungs. I clung to his shoulders, trying to ground myself until he shrugged off my grip and grabbed my throat again. This time, I wrapped my hands around his thick wrist. Only thing is, I wasn't sure if I was simply holding on to him, or making sure he didn't abandon this aggressive, dominant position. My entire body was consumed in a firestorm of lust and need. His cock filled my quivering pussy, stretching and burning even as he pounded inside me with bruising force.

Mike's body was a work of art as he moved over me. Muscles played under his skin, heavy and strong. A man able to protect his family.

With a cry, I went limp beneath him. I laid my arms out to my sides and let my legs fall wide open. That seemed to be exactly what Mike wanted because he snarled loudly before fucking me even harder. Faster.

"Gonna come with me, woman. I'm gonna put my cum deep inside your pussy and you're gonna take it from me. Now. Fuckin' come on my cock, Josephine. Now!"

I did. God, I did! My body fragmented into a sensory explosion the likes of which I could never have been prepared for. Each time Mike took me seemed to be better than the last. Each time he took me, I fell for him that much more. He was a force to be reckoned with, but beneath his gruff exterior he had a soft side.

He slipped up on you when you weren't expecting it and completely took you over. At least, that's what he did for me. The thing was, I surrendered willingly. And I knew I'd never regret it, and never look back.

Chapter Nine

Pops

Weeks turned into months. Months to a couple of years. Gracie had her baby and took in Liam as a second son. Liam took the role of big brother to little Abraham very seriously. Colonel Gill and the lawyer, Mama's half-brother Ian McGregor, had gotten Alex a sweet deal. I had no idea how they'd managed it, but I'm sure bullying and threatening were involved. Alex got sixteen months plus four years' probation for shooting up the airport. Well, that and community service. Which, surprisingly, he took to with gusto. Kid thrived on helping people. He'd joined us only a week ago and was still trying to adjust to his new life. But he was good for not only his own son, but Liam too.

Mama and I sat on the porch of the big clubhouse, watching as a couple of the guys worked on their bikes in front of the garage.

"Five bucks says Brutal's gettin' ready to kick somethin'," Mama muttered to me, never taking her eyes from the group.

"Nah. It'll be Mo." I took a pull from the beer I'd been nursing for the last fifteen minutes. The sun beat down on the group, likely making them sweat even though it had started out as a crisp, fall morning.

"Motherfuck!" Mo fell back on his ass and threw the wrench he'd been using at the bike. Unfortunately, his aim was too high and it sailed over the seat and hit Brutal in the back of the head. The other man stumbled forward with a sharp yelp, only to turn and throw the wrench he'd been using at Mo.

Aaaand the fight was on.

Without looking at me, Mama held out her beer in my direction and we clinked the glasses together before taking another pull.

"Tie?" I continued to watch the kids wrestling. Boys will be boys after all.

"Sure."

That was the moment Gracie stepped outside the small house she and Alex had been given. Abraham stayed with them, of course, but so did Liam. Did my heart good to see the kid find a sense of belonging I wasn't sure he'd had with just him and his father. Even though he'd lived here longer than me and Mama, it had taken the kid a couple months after his father left to relax and actually act like a kid.

"What on earth?" Gracie stopped, her hands going to her cheeks as she frantically scanned the crowd gathering to egg on the fight. "Alex?" When she didn't see him anywhere, she ran forward. "Alex!"

The big black man poked his head out from the shed near where the men were working outside and his gaze settled on Gracie and the boys. He raised his hand to his ear, like he was trying to hear whatever she wanted to say to him.

Gracie visibly relaxed but there was still tension in her body as she made sure she had a hand on each child, preventing them from running into the fray. She looked seconds away from bursting into tears. No doubt the fighting distressed her, given her background. The girl had known nothing but violence for a long time because of her relationship with Alex.

Alex gave her a crisp nod before hurrying over to the fight. I glanced at Mama who'd sat forward in her chair just that little bit, watching intently while trying to prevent herself from jumping up and going to the guys.

When Alex reached the group, he inserted himself between Brutal and Mo, shoving the two men apart. "That's enough!" His voice carried easily over the entire area, clear and strong. "No fightin' in front of the kids."

Mo and Brutal were winded and looked ready to do murder, but to each other. Not Alex.

"Come on, man!" Brutal pointed an accusing finger at Mo. "He started it!"

"And I'm finishin' it. No fightin' when the kids are in the compound."

"But they never leave the compound," Brutal complained.

"Then take it someplace else," Alex insisted, not backing down an inch. "Don't want my boys thinkin' it's OK to lose their tempers." He lifted his chin. "S'what got me in trouble. I don't want that for my kids."

Immediately, Mama sat back, a satisfied smile on her face. I chuckled, reaching over to grip Mama's hand. She didn't look over at me, only turned her hand so she could lace her fingers through mine. God, I loved this woman!

"Mama and Pops didn't say nothin' 'bout it." Mo looked disgruntled as he glanced our way. "I say it's OK to fight."

Alex grabbed the other man's shirt front in one fist and jerked him closer. "No. Fuckin'. Fightin'. In. Front. Of. The. Kids." He spoke each word slowly and distinctly. It was so unlike Alex. He never brought attention to himself. If anything, he kept his head down and did whatever was asked of him, no matter the task and did it without complaining. He never half did anything either. Kid might be a little on the slow side, but he was a stickler for details.

Whatever Mo saw in Alex's face must have clued the man in to the fact he was very deadly serious.

"Yeah, man. You're right. We should set a good example for the kids."

"They don't need to think violence is OK," Alex replied in a gruff voice. "It distresses their mother, and I won't have her upset."

All the men immediately looked around for Gracie. Once they spotted her, with the grip she had on the kids, they immediately settled.

"Sorry, man," Brutal said, sticking his hand out to Mo. There was no hesitation on either man's part. They immediately shook hands.

"Yeah. My fault. I got frustrated and meant to hit the bike."

"Don't take it out on the poor bike either." Brutal grinned. "Let me help. Then we'll do my bike together too." He shrugged. "Take half the time."

"Thanks, man. I owe you one."

Alex gave the men a nod, slapping Brutal on the shoulder as he left to go to Gracie. The young woman immediately threw herself into her man's arms.

"I thought they were beating on you," she whimpered. I could barely hear her. She was far enough away I couldn't hear whatever Alex said to her, but I could hear his deep voice as he tried to soothe her.

Liam looked at the group of men with a scowl. He marched over to the group and I started to intervene. Mama gripped my hand tighter, a signal to stay where I was. The kid went straight to Mo and Brutal, his little fists clenched tightly.

"Hey, buddy," Mo said by way of greeting, obviously trying to pretend nothing had happened.

"You upset my mom." That got a raised eyebrow from me. Gracie had same as adopted Liam, but the kid usually called her Gracie. This was the first time he'd referred to her as Mom. "Do it again and I'll hurt you."

Instead of scoffing at Liam or waving off the threat, Brutal crouched down to be on Liam's level. "You're right, Liam. I'm sorry. We shouldn't bring violence home to our women. I'll go apologize to Gracie."

"Yeah," Mo agreed. "Me too. I'm sorry I upset your mom, Liam."

The two big men hung their heads, appropriately chastised, and shuffled over to where Gracie was clinging to Alex and quietly crying. There was a soft, gentle exchange while they spoke to both Alex and Gracie. Alex had picked up little Abraham in one arm while he held Gracie with the other. Gracie looked up at the men while they spoke and nodded her head as she swiped her eyes with the back of her hand. Brutal then stuck out his hand to Alex. The other man hesitated but took his hand, then Mo's.

Mama let out a little sigh and sat back in her chair. I squeezed her hand and she looked over at me. We shared a satisfied smile. Our boys were definitely growing into themselves. They were going to make fine men. Already were fine men. But they were going to be better. The guys needed direction and a lot of structure, so Mama and I provided.

Then, almost three years to the day, Taz showed back up. Changed in ways I didn't want to think about. He was harder. Colder. It felt like death followed him. When he met us, we did so on neutral ground. Just me and Mama.

"Back just like you promised." Mama might have smiled at Taz, but it didn't reach her eyes and she didn't move to shake his hand.

"I am. You kept my son safe?"

"You know we did, and I'm trying not to take offense at the implication we might not have." Mama's expression never wavered. Her tone was congenial, but I could feel the underlying tension and a healthy dose of anger radiating from her.

"I meant no offense, Mama. I think you know that." Taz spoke slowly, using the name everyone had given Jo, not addressing her in a way that might seem familiar. He was dancing around us, being very careful about what he said. We were the ones who suggested a place away from the compound, but Taz hadn't balked or even tried to get in to see the men he'd taken in as family. Which sent up all kinds of red flags. I also noticed that, since the very first message when he contacted us to let us know he was back, he'd always used our club names, but hadn't thought anything of it. I was thinking about it now.

"What's going on?" I moved slightly in front of Mama. If she minded, she didn't let on. Which told me all I needed to know about what Jo thought of the situation. She would never go against anything I said or did in the presence of an enemy or someone who was questionable, no matter if she didn't like that I was taking the lead. Or protecting her when she was perfectly capable of protecting herself. Taz realized it too.

"Good." He nodded to both of us, a silent acknowledgment he knew we saw him as a threat. "I've come to take Liam with me."

"Not sure that's the best idea." Mama spoke but didn't try to move around me. "He's grown roots. He's happy."

"I know. I'm still going to take him."

"You're not staying?"

"No, Mama. You and Pops have done exactly

what I'd hoped you'd do. Made Bones into a family."

"Keepin' tabs on us?" I wanted Taz's focus back on me. If he was here to take out either of us, I wanted to give Mama her best chance to take him out first. While I was a warrior through and through, she was just as skilled and even more cunning than I was.

"Always. Bones is family."

"Then come home," Mama said softly. "Liam's made a home here with Gracie, Alex, and their son. He's a bright child. Strong and skilled. He'll make a fine warrior one day."

"I know how special my son is." Taz leveled a look on Jo and I had to stop myself from stepping completely in front of her again. "That's why I need to take him with me."

"Where are you taking him?" This time, Jo wasn't playing nice. I could almost feel her protective instincts kicking in as she prepared to fight for the little boy in our care.

"I don't have to answer to you, Mama. Liam is my son. You'll give him to me willingly, or I'll take him from you."

The two must have faced off or something. I wasn't about to take my attention from Taz and couldn't see Jo, but the tension was so thick I could have cut it with a knife.

"He's a good kid, Taz. If you can't give him a safe, loving home you need to leave him here."

"I can. I will." Taz's expression didn't change but I trusted what he was saying.

"I have no doubt you'll keep him safe, but I'm having trouble believing the loving home part is something you're capable of now. You've changed."

Taz nodded slowly. "I have. But not so much I can't show my son how much I love him. I swear to you, he'll know."

"What have you gotten into, Taz?" Mama's voice was so soft it was nearly a whisper.

Taz shook his head before stepping closer. When he spoke next, it was so low I had to strain to hear him. "What I'm doing is for the greater good. I'll teach Liam to handle himself, how to fight and protect those weaker than him. But he has to sever all ties with you. It's for everyone's safety. His included."

"This has to do with *them*, doesn't it?" Jo kept her voice as low as Taz did. There was no doubt who she was referring to, but if she wasn't going to say anything more, I wasn't about to.

"It is. Trust me when I say, they'll need both myself and Liam to balance them out. I'll build that foundation, and it will be up to Liam to continue. He'll take my place when I no longer can. Until then, he'll train. Study. Go out into the world and prepare himself once he's reached an age he can do so on his own."

"That's a hell of a thing to put on a kid, Taz. Do you honestly think you can get the upper hand with them? Really, Taz?"

"No." There was no hesitation in his answer. "But the cost if I don't at least try is too great."

"That's fine. *For you*. But what about Liam? He doesn't deserve that life."

"No," Taz agreed. "He doesn't. Doesn't change the fact he's going to have it, though."

"I'll fight you for that child." Now the mama tiger I knew and loved was baring her fangs and claws.

"I know you will, Mama. It's how you got your name. Fighting for those who need help. But I'm asking you not to. Trust me to know what's best for my son."

"If they're holding his safety over you --"

"They're not. I've looked at the situation and all the possibilities I can imagine. This is the best solution for him."

"For him? Or for you?" Yeah. Mama wasn't pulling any punches. If Taz was going to do this, he'd answer to Mama first.

"For both of us."

There was a long pause. I wanted to look back at Mama but didn't dare take my eyes off Taz. He was always dangerous. Now, I got the feeling he was even more so. And, let's be honest, if he had formed any kind of tie with the Brotherhood, he was one of the most lethal men on the planet. "Fine." Whatever Mama saw when they studied each other must have satisfied her. If not completely, enough to let Taz have his son. "But if you hurt that boy in any way, Taz, I will make you beg for death before I fuckin' kill you."

"I'd expect nothing less. Bring Liam back here. Don't tell anyone I'm here. Again, for everyone's safety."

"This is horseshit, Taz." Finally, Mama pushed past me. If I thought she was angry, I'd have been dead wrong. Mama was fucking *furious*. "You know it as well as I do."

"I do. Doesn't change my decision."

Without another word, Mama spun on her heel and went back to her bike. I backed away from Taz, not wanting to turn my back on the other man until Mama was safely away. I took a tentative step toward Taz, looking at him hard and holding his gaze. I needed to know if we were being observed. If the conversation was private. Taz nodded his head slowly before muttering softly. "Ask. Keep it down and don't move your mouth much."

So, observed, but not with a listening device.

"They want Mama?"

"Yep."

"They know where she is?"

"No."

Fuck. I needed more, but how to ask without giving anything away...

Taz shook his head. "They don't know what she looks like since she left the service. Glad she had her hair up when you guys came here or they might have figured she was here. I have them looking for her in Nam. They think she's with an MC called Iron Tzars. Not a club that's off-limits to them, but one they leave alone."

"Tzars reached out to me when I first got out of the service, but I declined."

Taz nodded. "You'd be the kind of person they'd want."

"Were Mama and I on the plane together intentionally?"

He shrugged. "Might have thrown you together to see what happened, but I didn't set up the airport thing. That was a happy coincidence."

"Don't believe in them." The hair in the back of my neck was standing up now. "Don't like being manipulated either."

"You weren't. At least, not wholly. I wanted you with her, but I never dreamed she wouldn't kill you."

"You didn't know where I was going."

"Knew you were headed in the same general direction as Mama. Knew enough to know you were the only person who could pull off this job."

"What fuckin' job?" I was growing angrier by the second. In the years I'd been with Jo, I'd grown to love the woman, prickly personality and all. I wasn't sure I could take it if this was all some kind of setup. I

- 230 -

thought she loved me too, but she wasn't a very demonstrative person.

"The job of keepin' Jo safe and away from... *them*."

"Why me?"

"Because I knew you'd be protective without reining her in. You can't force her to your will, and you'd never try. Knew you'd let her make the decision, then deal with the fallout."

"Why does she need protecting?"

"They want her, Pops." Taz dropped his voice even lower, almost to a whisper. "She'll never be their puppet and they'd kill her. She's one of the very few people they believe can achieve their goal, whatever it is. Not only is she smart and cunning, she can get into places others can't. You've seen the connections she has. The people she knows. By themselves, those people might not be much, but each of them has skills and credentials that make them dangerous to someone willing to put them all together. *They* want those connections."

Again, we stared each other down. I got that he couldn't elaborate. Had probably said more than he should as it was.

I gave him a slow nod. "What do I need to do?" Because there was no way I was *not* going to protect Mama, no matter what.

"Disappear. Stay with the club if you want but stay under the radar. Disappear Jo and Mike and become Mama and Pops."

I thought about that until I heard the rumble of Mama's bike in the distance. She was back with the boy. "OK." I'd figure it out. It would be tricky, but I had an idea. Now, if only the man I needed would meet up with me.

The boy rode behind Mama. He had a backpack on his shoulders, his arms wound tightly around her middle, and a big smile on his face. The second Mama stopped the bike, the kid was off and running to his father. "Dad!"

"Hey, sport." Taz smiled, but it didn't reach his eyes. Liam, already the most observant and intelligent kid I'd ever met, noticed.

He slowed just before he was close enough for Taz to reach out and grab him, actually taking a couple steps backward. "Dad?"

"It's OK, Liam. Remember I told you I'd be back and what would happen?"

"Yeah?" The kid looked wary.

"It's time."

Father and son seemed to communicate silently before Liam finally nodded, putting his shoulders back proudly. "All right. I'm ready."

"You don't have to go if you really don't want to," Mama said before Taz could reach for the boy. "You can stay with me and Pops."

Liam gave her a look so adult it gave me a pang in my chest. No kid his age should have that look. Like he was preparing for battle and had no doubt in his mind he was up for the task. And he knew it was to the death. "Yes I do, Mama. I have to go."

"Liam --"

"Let it go, Mama," Taz said gently. "I will protect him with my life. I swear it."

"You fuckin' better, you son of a bitch," she bit out.

"Taz, are you sure?" I asked. "Really fuckin' sure?"

"I am, Pops. And I'm no longer Taz. You can call me El Diablo."

Chapter Ten

Pops

Once back at the clubhouse, I hurried her back to our room where I locked us in. Then I explained what I'd learned from Taz. El Diablo. Whatever. She was understandably furious.

"If I found out you had anything whatsoever to do with this, Pops, I'll fuckin' kill the fuckin' fuck outta you." She was trembling with rage. Which was what she wanted me to see. What she likely wanted to keep to herself was the sheen of tears glistening in her eyes and on her eyelashes.

"I swear to you, Jo. I got played as much as you did. More, even."

"How could you possibly have gotten played more?" The look she gave me said she was not only calling bullshit, but she might carve out my liver, cover it in said bullshit, then shove it back inside me just to watch me die from gangrene, then celebrate my death with a gleeful smile. It made me want to grin at her. Which would have probably set her off. So, I did the only thing I knew to do. It might not be the best decision, but it was the only thing I could think of. Probably because it was the thing that was foremost on my mind.

"Because the meddling in our lives put me in a position to meet you. Then you made me fall in love with you. So no matter what happens to either of us from this moment forward, I'm never gonna be the fuckin' same."

Mama opened her mouth, probably to give me a piece of her mind, then blinked as if my confession was the last thing she'd expected. "I… what?"

"You heard me."

For the first time since I'd met her, Jo looked like a young, vulnerable woman. It didn't hold with the confident, powerful warrior I knew her to be, but it endeared her to me all the more. Because, I knew without a doubt, I was the only person in her world who'd ever seen that particular look on her lovely face. She gave that trust to me. No way in hell I was gonna let her take it back.

"You can't love me."

"No?" I stepped closer to her, reaching out to pull her into my arms. She didn't resist, but braced her hands on my chest so I couldn't get as close as I really wanted. "Why not?"

"I'm not a woman a man like you looks for, Mike. I'll never be the obedient wife who defers to her husband. I take charge of my own life and, occasionally, the lives of those around me."

"Fully aware of all that, Jo. You know I can be a take-charge kinda guy, but I'm more than willin' to let you be you. If that means I follow your lead, I got no problem doin' that. I think I've proven that over the last couple of years. I ain't gonna hold you back. I'm just gonna follow where you go and protect you with my fuckin' life."

There must have been a God somewhere smiling down on me, because that must have been the exact right thing to say. Mama threw herself into my arms, tightening her arms around my neck and clung to me, sobbing like I'd never known the woman was capable of. Again, I'd be willing to bet my life she'd never let anyone see this side of her. In fact, I had to wonder if the woman had ever let herself cry like this.

I held her as tight as I could. She seemed to need the support, and I was only too glad to be whatever she needed. I kind of expected her to get herself under control quickly, then brush me off, but she didn't. Jo let out everything she needed to right there in my arms. I felt fucking ten feet tall. No one else in the world could ever be in this position because Jo would never let anyone else this close to her. Which meant, even if she didn't acknowledge it out loud, she loved me.

When she was finally more under control, she pulled back only to pull me down by my beard to kiss her. I would gladly provide her with as many kisses as she wanted. Or anything else. She was my woman. I'd always be her man.

Things escalated quickly after that. It didn't take long for us to be naked and for me to have Mama on her back with her legs spread and my mouth buried between them. I took her up as high as I could without letting her fall. Over and over, she screamed my name.

I had to grin because she no longer called my first name during sex. It was always Pops. I rarely called her Jo, only when we were alone and it was important she listen to what I had to say. While she always took me seriously, I found that pulling her out of the persona she'd become since taking this club under our wing had become our signal for her to focus solely on me. In those times, she knew it was important for her to let me in and for us to make those decisions together. The longer we were together, the less and less it happened.

"Oh, God! Pops!"

"That's my name, baby." I chuckled. "Tell me what you want. I'll make it happen no matter what."

"You. I want you."

"Yeah?" I grinned up at her. I was sure the expression wasn't tame. "I'm right here, baby. What're you gonna do with me?"

"Fuck me, you bastard!" she screamed. "Put your

fuckin' cock inside me and fuck the shit outta me!"

That was all I needed. I took action, guiding my cock inside her and moving in a hard, driving rhythm. Mama wrapped her legs around my waist and dug her heels into my ass. Urging me to move harder and faster, she took what she wanted. She gave me much, much more than she took. I'd had several women in my life. Usually only for a night or two. Never with any expectation either of us would be around in the morning. It was the way I liked my life. I didn't want a woman I had to worry about leaving when I went off to war or anywhere else. I took my pleasures, tried to give her as much as I took, and didn't worry about her beyond the moment.

Not so with Mama.

When she clawed at me, I bared my teeth. I didn't stop fucking her, but I snagged her wrists -- first one then the other -- holding them in one hand above her head.

"You don't get to dictate the pace, Mama. I'm in charge."

"Bastard," she hissed, showing her own teeth. "You said you'd give me what I wanted!"

I had to chuckle. She was just so darn cute when she got all demanding. Mainly because I knew the real her. Mama didn't beg. She took what she wanted. I loved that I could hold her off and she trusted me enough to know I'd eventually give her everything instead of exacting her will.

"I will. But I decide when. You get to lie back and enjoy."

After that, things got worse. By the time I let her come, Josephine Peyton was close to killing me. I think I even had bite marks on my shoulder where she punished me. A few times. When she came in my arms, with my dick deep inside her hot, wet pussy, I lost my Goddamned mind. She took my cum inside her with several ragged screams and a lot of scratching down my back. I'd be wearing those scratches for a couple of days at least. Which was a good thing because I wanted everyone in the Goddamned place to know who I belonged to. Marked her with more than one hickey to stake my claim, too.

If she had bruises on her hips where I gripped her during our hard ride, well, I caught her admiring them in the mirror with a satisfied smirk before she caught me looking. Her smirk turned into a scowl. Our loving was sometimes rough, but it was always satisfying.

"We need to disappear," I told her as I stroked her bare shoulder where she cuddled against me with her head on my chest.

"From the Brotherhood?" She rubbed her face over my skin where she rested. "Not sure that's possible."

"Taz was careful not to say our real names. He indicated we were probably being observed, but that they didn't know you were the woman they were looking for."

"I have no desire to be on that bunch's radar."

"Me neither."

We were silent for a while before she spoke again. "What're we gonna do?" She sounded sleepy. Sated. Made me grin.

"I've been thinkin' on that. I have an idea, but it means giving up everything. Family especially. Family is always the downfall of anyone who tries to hide from these fuckers."

"You sayin' we need to die?"

"That's exactly what I'm sayin'."

"What's the plan?"

"I know a man. He's an asshole, but I ain't ever met anyone as intelligent. I'd like to reach out to him. Meet up and see if he can help."

"OK. Where is he?"

"Rockwell, Illinois. He has a place in Oklahoma too. I thought it would be better to meet him there. Assuming he's agreeable."

"Why wouldn't he be?"

I couldn't help but smile, remembering exactly why Luca Romano was pissed at me. "Because, the last time we were together, I beat him at chess."

There was silence and Mama was completely still. Then she looked up at me. "You beat him at chess." It wasn't a question.

"Yep."

"I take it he's a sore loser?"

I chuckled then. "You could say that. He likes to think he's the smartest man in the room. Usually is. I got lucky, though I'll never admit it to him. Far as he's concerned, every move I made was on purpose."

Mama chuckled too. "Now we're thinkin' alike."

"Honey, I think we always do."

Her smile was so beautiful that if I hadn't already been in love with her, I was now. "You're so fuckin' beautiful, woman."

"I am not." She shoved back to sit up, a fierce scowl on her face. "Take it back." And, God help me, that little bite in her voice made me hard as a motherfucker when I'd already come my brains out.

I barked out a laugh. "I absolutely will not, Mama. You're beautiful like a hurricane. Breathtaking and destructive. A fuckin' force of nature. And all fuckin' *mine*."

She looked appropriately put out but didn't deny

- 238 -

she was mine. I called it a win. "You're mine," she said with a huff. "Don't you dare deny it."

"Never, honey. No matter what, I'll never deny I'm yours."

"Good. Because this is all your fault."

I shook my head, still chuckling. "Not saying it is, not saying it isn't, but what exactly are you referring to?"

"You knocked me up, Mike." There was that vulnerability again. For such a strong woman, she hid what she thought of as weakness very well. She must have been afraid I'd leave if I found out. Or that I wouldn't want her or the child. She couldn't be further off the mark.

"So, another hellion to add to a whole slew of them. Only this one's mine." I grinned. "I hope it's a girl who looks just like her beautiful mama."

I think I kind of expected Mama to frown at me or pretend to be angry at me for implying any child of hers would be beautiful. Or say she was having a boy just to be ornery. Instead, she gave me a soft smile. "She'll be a beautiful girl, and courageous like her father."

"I'll be spoilin' her terribly. And she's never dating."

"I'll teach her how to get around you. She'll give you a world of trouble."

I grinned. "Same as her mother."

"God, Pops. I love you so Goddamned much."

"I love you too, Mama. With all my heart."

Epilogue

Mama

We were on our way back from the West Coast when I realized we'd gone as far as we were going. I led us off the main highway to a rural back road. Took a couple hours to find what I wanted, but it was worth the wait.

We pulled up outside an old barn. Pops stopped beside me before killing the motor. He looked up at the structure with a puzzled expression.

"Why we stoppin' here?"

I shrugged, though I was starting to feel a panic setting in I wasn't expected. "Thought it looked interesting."

"Uh-huh." I could feel his gaze on me as I studied the outside of the barn.

"Looks sturdy enough." I said in a cheerful voice. "Been a while since we camped out. I thought it might be fun to do it one more time before the baby was born."

"Right." He slowly, deliberately climbed off his bike, moving around it to my side. He put a hand gently on my shoulder. "Mama?"

"Hmm?" I looked up at him innocently, trying to keep my cheerful mien.

"You OK?"

"Of course! Why wouldn't I be?"

He seemed indecisive about what to do. Like he was a hunted animal who'd just walked into a trap and was trying to back his way out without springing it. "Camping? You said you hated camping."

"You know I was just joking. It's fun. You know. Getting back to nature. Away from everyone. Out here all alone in the great big Texas sky."

"Right. How about we get inside out of the heat. Yeah?"

"Sounds wonderful." I climbed off the bike carefully. My balance wasn't great with a baby so close to being born, and the last thing I wanted to do was fall and injure myself or my child.

Pops took my elbow gently, probably trying to help without seeming to be helping. I'd berated him for doing that very thing several times in the past. When I didn't react, he scooped me up and carried me inside the barn.

He managed to get me up a ladder to the loft before setting me on my feet while he moved a small wooden crate next to me against the wall and helped me sit.

"Do not move from this crate, Jo." He pointed a finger at me. His use of my real name told me he meant business.

"Wanna add 'young lady' to the end of that?" I muttered the complaint, trying my best to look angry when that panic in my chest was growing. As was the pain in my abdomen.

"I might." His gaze didn't soften. "Stay."

"Yes, master," I bit out.

The second Pops was out of my sight, I wanted to call him back. The cramping pain in my abdomen had me gripping my belly and doubling over. I had to spread my legs so my belly could fit between my thighs.

Which was when I saw what I'd been wanting to deny.

"Fuuuuuck..."

Not three minutes later -- I knew because I was counting -- Pops popped his head up over the side and hurried up the ladder. When he fully took in my appearance, he froze.

"Mama?"

"What!" I snapped. Because the first really, *really* bad pain hit me.

"Maybe I'll just make you a nest. Seems we might need it soon."

"Don't say it!" I snarled. "Do *not* say it."

"Ain't sayin' nothin'. Not a Goddamned word." Yeah. Pops got the severity of the situation. He hurried back down the ladder to get the rest of our things. It took him two minutes this time. Again, I was keeping count.

"Still with me, Mama?" Pops's gaze found mine the second his head was over the ledge on his way back up to the loft.

"Right here." I groaned, gripping my belly with one hand while the other arm braced my weight on the crate.

"Can you give me two more minutes?" He didn't stop to see if I had two minutes to give, but set about making me a little nest to use as a bed while I...

"Sure. Take all the time you need." I tried to be flippant but was pretty sure any humor came out a little maniacal.

"Christ!" Pops swore as he finished. The second he moved me, what I'd been trying to ignore the past ten minutes became impossible to confront. "When did your water break?"

"Um, I'm not really sure?"

"Let's get you undressed so you can be comfortable as you can be. Then I'll get the rest of it ready."

"Might want to hurry." This time, I couldn't contain the cry that tore from my throat. The pain was nearly unbearable. Nothing I'd ever experienced prepared me for what just hit me.

"Yep." Pops's curt reply was all I heard before the pain crested. Someone let out a long, pained yell before gentle hands pulled me upright so they could pick me up and carry me to the nest.

Pops moved over me, propping my head up and putting a blanket over my naked body. I'd put a birthing kit together shortly after we'd left Somerset several months ago. Everything we'd need to deliver this baby ourselves was in a backpack I'd taken great care with. Blankets. Surgical scissors. Umbilical clips. And a gentle cleanser to clean the child after she was born. Because there was no way I wasn't having a girl. Just to annoy Pops. It was the least he deserved for knocking me up and making me go through this horrid pain…

Another hole was ripped in my abdomen. At least, that's what it felt like. The contraction seemed to go on forever and it felt like something was trying to tear me apart from the inside out.

"Mama?" Pops hurried to kneel in front of me, crouching so he could see the gaping maw where a watermelon was trying to push its way out of my fucking pussy!

"Get this fuckin' thing outta me! Fuckin' shit!" I yelled, then strained as I screamed. Pops reached between my legs just as I pushed a second time.

"Hold up! Hold up!"

"Don't you fuckin' tell me to fuckin' hold up! What the fuck, Pops? You fuckin' hold up!" And I pushed again. Until Pops smacked the inside of my leg.

"I said stop!"

"How the fuck am I supposed to do that!"

"You can. Hold your breath five seconds." Then he proceeded to count while he got everything ready to bring our child into the world. I'd coached him on this at least a hundred times. Gone over every possible scenario I thought I could teach him to help me live through it. I knew what he was doing down there and why he was instructing me not to push and enforcing his order. But Goddamn, nothing had ever hurt this bad or been this urgent! I'd delivered a few babies in country, but this was nothing like they teach you. And Goddamn them for not accurately describing the kind of pain a woman is in when she births a baby anyway! Buncha Goddamned motherfuckers every fuckin' one of 'em.

"OK, now push, Mama. Push!" Pops was looking down where his hands were between my legs. As he told me to push, he got this big shit-eating grin on his face. Which was just a little bit more than I was ready to take.

So I kicked him in the face. The bastard just took it and laughed. So, I kicked him again.

"Go ahead, little mama. Kick me if you gotta. But I'd really like to meet my son."

"Not a boy! It's a girl! And she's gonna give you complete hell, and I'm gonna help her slip out of the house to go fuck her boyfriend just to drive you crazy!"

"We bettin'?" He grinned up at me.

"I'm gonna kick your AAAAAAHHHH!"

Yeah. Not my finest moment.

Our son, Kurt, was born at three in the morning on Christmas Eve. Child was close to ten pounds of screaming, demanding, baby boy. I loved him from the moment I first held him. Hardest thing I ever had to do in my life was watch the man that baby had grown into disappear much the same way Pops and I had. He severed all ties with us. It wasn't until decades later we were reunited with a part of my son. Celeste Pleasant and her daughter -- our granddaughter and great granddaughter -- would come back into our lives. Thanks to some old friends.

And another devil.

Yeah. Life has funny ways of sneaking up on you.

So what did the future hold for us? We helped build a motorcycle club from a bunch of ragtag veterans to a force to be reckoned with.

But it wasn't just us.

Rylan "Ry" Gill would become president of Bones MC. He and his woman had one son, Joe Gill, who eventually took the name Cain and made a great MC president in his own right. He also started the company ExFil, a paramilitary organization that specialized in protection and extraction. That company, along with a bar called the Boneyard, kept the club financed well.

Ian "Mac" McGregor became vice president of Bones for a while. When drugs started moving steadily from Florida to Kentucky and Ohio, Mac took a few members of Bones to Palm Beach, Florida to start his own club. Mac was going to make it a second chapter of Bones MC but thought they'd be too far away to make that relationship work. So he started a new club and named it Salvation's Bane. Most members of Bane worked for ExFil, including Mac's son, Colin, who took the name Thorn. Thorn would go on to become president of Salvation's Bane.

Alex and Gracie's son, Abraham, had a son named Derrick. He took the name Shadow and became a patched member of Bones. Along the way, in Oklahoma, he would befriend a scruffy kid named Stunner. Stunner would catch the attention of a young El Diablo. Liam took over for his father as El Diablo,

The Devil, for the Brotherhood. I have no proof, but I'm pretty sure Liam intended for Stunner to replace him since he had no male children. At least, not at the time. Stunner married Cain's daughter, Suzie, and later became sergeant at arms of Bones after Bohannon left to start a sister chapter in Nashville.

Liam Rodrigues did indeed follow in his father's footsteps, becoming the most feared assassin in the world. He held the title of El Diablo longer than anyone in the history of the Brotherhood. Liam was also the man to put a crack in the mystique of the Brotherhood. As of the present day, the organization that once ruled the world from the shadows was splintering and warring with itself. Which suits El Diablo fine. They leave him and his city alone. They leave all those El Diablo claims as his alone.

Mitch Bohannon had a son, Gage Bohannon. Bohannon became sergeant at arms for Bones after Cain took over as president.

Gerald "Mo" Ferguson's son, Gavin "Torpedo" Ferguson, became vice president of Bones under Cain.

Mason Gray, or Gray, was a loyal member of Bones until his death. His son, Lars "Sword" Gray, became an enforcer in Bones.

Luca Romano eventually helped to found a company called Argent Tech with two of his closest friends and colleagues. They became some of the richest men in the world as well as vigilantes in their home city of Rockwell, Illinois. His son became one of the leading tech geniuses in the world. Giovanni Romano, along with Alexi Petrov and Azriel Ivanovich, would become known as the Shadow Demons.

Me and Pops? Well, we went home to Bones. We try to keep a close watch on all our children. They span over several clubs now. Iron Tzars MC might not have been able to recruit Pops back in the day, but they managed to work their way into our lives a few decades later. Shadow Demons, Salvation's Bane, Black Reign, and Grim Road round out our family, though Grim Road is one of those children who keeps to themselves for the most part. They're loners, every one of their members Black Ops. Some of them were buried in their cover so deep the government forgot about them, making integrating back into society nearly impossible. Most of them would be killed for what they know. A few would get everyone they'd ever met killed if the wrong people found out who they were, that they were still alive, and what they'd done that classified them as Black Ops.

Pops and I are getting older. One day, we'll leave this earth. When that happens, I hope we're side by side on our bikes, speeding down a long, lonely stretch of interstate. I hope the wind will be forever in my hair and that Pops still looks at me with love in his eyes.

I hope our story inspires all our children to do what's right, no matter how much it hurts. I hope we've left our mark on each and every member of every club we nurtured.

I hope... we were loved as much as we loved.

Marteeka Karland

International bestselling author Marteeka Karland leads a double life as an action romance writer by evening and a semi-domesticated housewife by day. Known for her down-and-dirty MC romances, Marteeka takes pleasure in spinning tales of tenacious, protective heroes and spirited heroines. She staunchly advocates that every character deserves a blissful ending.

Marteeka finds joy in baking and gardening with her husband. Make sure to visit her website to stay updated with her most recent projects. Don't forget to register for her newsletter which will pepper you with a potpourri of Teeka's beloved recipes, book suggestions, autograph events, and a plethora of interesting tidbits.

Marteeka at Changeling: changelingpress.com/marteeka-karland-a-39

Bones MC Multiverse

Contemporary MC and Crossovers
>Bones MC
>Shadow Demons
>Salvation's Bane MC
>Black Reign MC
>Iron Tzars MC
>Grim Road MC
>Bones MC Legends
>Kiss of Death MC

Print and Audio
>Bones MC Audio
>Salvation's Bane MC Audio
>Iron Tzars MC Audio
>Bones MC Print Duets
>Grim Road MC Audio

Changeling Press LLC

Contemporary Action Adventure, Sci-Fi, Steampunk, Dark Fantasy, Urban Fantasy, Paranormal, and BDSM Romance available in e-book, audio, and print format at ChangelingPress.com – MC Romance, Werewolves, Vampires, Dragons, Shapeshifters and Horror -- Tales from the edge of your imagination.

Where can I get Changeling Press Books?

Changeling Press e-books are available at ChangelingPress.com, Amazon, Apple Books, Barnes & Noble, Kobo, Smashwords, and other online retailers, including Everand Subscription and Kobo Subscription Services. Print books are available at Amazon, Barnes and Noble, and by ISBN special order through your local bookstores.

ChangelingPress.com